YUCATÁN DEAD

D.V. Berkom

YUCATÁN DEAD
Copyright © 2013, 2016 All rights reserved.
2nd Edition
By D.V. Berkom
Published by

ISBN: 0997970820
ISBN-13: 978-0-9979708-2-1

What people are saying about YUCATÁN DEAD:

"...an unrelenting thriller of a tension-filled novel... Yucatan Dead is the stuff of which blockbuster movies are made...very highly recommended..." ~ *Midwest Book Review*

"...Yucatan Dead ratchets up the tension from the start as Kate deals with hit women, warring Mexican drug cartels, and unofficial paramilitary organizations. Survival is never a given..." ~ *Big Al's Books 'n Pals*

"…The prevalence of drug cartels, kidnapping and human trafficking in Mexico is at a fevered pitch and this book presents it well. I highly recommend this book to readers who like fast moving, intriguing stories." ~ *Barbara Rauch, Reviewer*

"…a gripping thriller with a gutsy heroine and a tightly woven plot; it will no doubt please Berkom's current fans and gather more." ~ *Pacific Book Review*

"…Do yourself a favor: pour an ice-cold margarita, and curl up in the shade with Kate's latest adventure. Wait; make it a pitcher. You're gonna be there a while...this one is not letting go until the very end…" ~ *Ruth M. Ross, Reviewer*

"…Yucatan Dead will grab your interest from the very beginning and will not let you go. Fast-paced and full of action this installment of the Kate Jones series will keep you turning the pages…" ~ *Renee Swetlik, Reviewer*

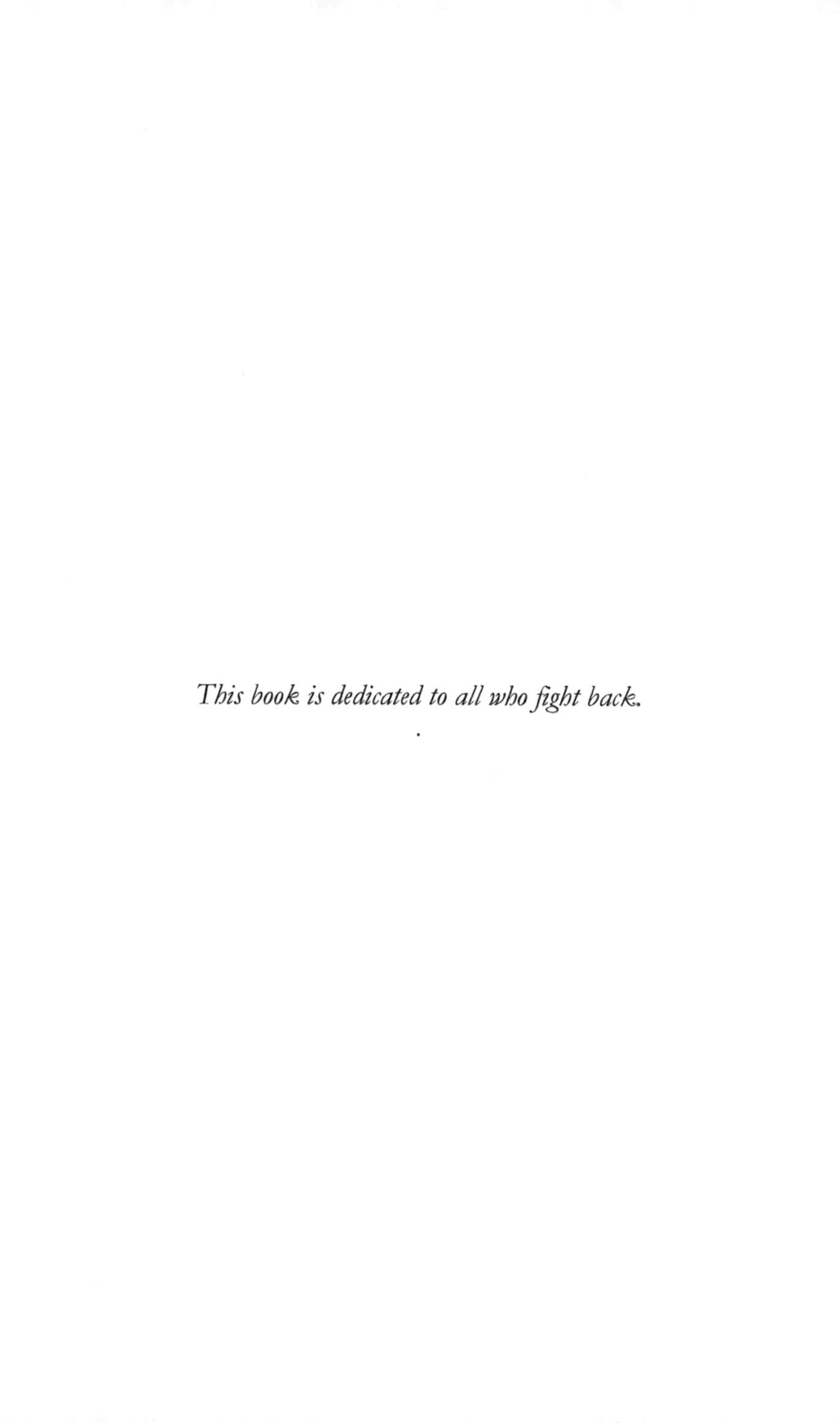

This book is dedicated to all who fight back.

1

THE STENCH OF DECAY ROSE from the unforgiving mattress as I shifted to a sitting position. My breath caught as sharp pain lanced through my body from the effort. I ran my hands over my torso, checking for injuries.

Good, no blood.

The watery gray light from a high window covered in metal bars illuminated the block walls that formed my prison. Musty air gave way to a whiff of mold and mildew, reminding me of an old flooded cellar. The thugs who brought me here had masks over their faces and smelled of stale *cerveza* and garlic, a familiar and unwelcome aroma.

Judging by what I saw in the short trip from the cargo van to the hulking concrete building, I was somewhere in the tropics. Dieffenbachia and philodendron grew in wild profusion while aggressive vines climbed stately royal palms, choking the life out of them. The air oozed damp.

How the hell did you wind up here, Kate? Abduction wasn't an entirely foreign event in my life, it's just that it hadn't happened in a while. Groggy from drugs and a vomit-inducing flight tied up in the back of a Cessna, pictures of a woman with short, blonde hair and familiar green eyes skated through my mind. Tired and disoriented, I couldn't catch and hold the images to remember her name.

That didn't stop the incipient panic sliding up my throat.

Footsteps broke through the fog in my brain and a curious cockroach I'd been watching disappeared through a hole in the bricks. I wished I could make myself that small and follow it, but it appeared my fairy godmother had taken the day off.

Not that she would have been much help. Hell, if changing my name, address, daily routines, and hair color didn't make me disappear, then nothing would.

The sound of a key springing the lock echoed through the room. The door's hinges creaked and I tensed, waiting to see who or what would emerge, working to combat the fear slithering up my spine. I tried to take a deep breath but couldn't.

Hyperventilating is annoying that way.

Sunlight blazed into the room as the silhouette of a man stepped through the doorway.

"*Vamanos.*"

The word came out as a deep grunt and matched the man who uttered it. Short and stocky with a deep scowl and no neck, his suave demeanor told me he probably wasn't the resort director.

Although, the AK-47 in his hands might have been the clincher.

I rolled off the bed and limped out the door in front of him. The rough handling I'd received on the way to wherever I now found myself hadn't exactly helped with my beauty regimen. It's not like there'd been padding in the cargo area of the plane, which I could have used about half-way into the trip when we hit heavy turbulence. I could've also used an airsick bag, but that's beside the point. Kidnappers R Us wasn't known for their customer service.

It was early morning, judging by the sound of the birds and the lack of mosquitoes. Even though the sodden air clung to my clothes, the day's heat hadn't yet bullied its way through the relative coolness. We crunched along a gravel path, neither of us speaking. Palm trees dotted the landscape, interspersed with out-of-control tropical plants. The shriek of a howler monkey serrated the air. A couple of low block buildings with red tile roofs peeked through the vegetation.

We rounded a bend in the path and came upon a concrete drive lined with palms nestled in terracotta pots leading to a huge Spanish-style hacienda. The kind where an old colonial family had decided to recycle the current occupant's building material for their own, whether a sacred temple or an ancient marketplace. The massive veranda spread across the entire front of the hacienda. Gleaming white marble steps climbed upward to meet an open doorway flanked by two wrought-iron chandeliers. Every few feet, a security camera dotted the roofline.

Evidently, this was the home of a wealthy and paranoid family. Judging by my guard's use of Spanish and the surrounding vegetation we were somewhere in Latin America. My heart did a half-gainer into my stomach, wiping out any semblance of denial from which I might have been working. January in Siberia would have been preferable.

"Move."

My talkative guard prodded me up the steps with his machine gun and I complied, hands cold and sweating, my heart racing past us, not waiting for me to catch up. I wondered how long I'd been unconscious from the drugs. By the taste in my mouth and the empty feeling in my stomach, I'd guess quite a while.

We reached the top of the stairs and continued through a breezeway to an ornately carved desk with matching chair. A computer monitor rested on its surface, alongside a telephone and radio. Several more security cameras rested atop the ancient bricks in strategic locations.

"Stop," he muttered as he keyed the mike. "We're here," he growled into the radio.

We waited in silence. His raspy breathing, too loud against the worn white bricks of the terrace walls, grated on my already frazzled nerves. A fly buzzed my face, trying to land; I slapped it away. My guard stiffened and repositioned his gun.

I decided to restrict sudden movements.

The radio crackled and a disembodied voice ordered us to proceed. The guard pushed me to the right, down another set of steps that opened onto a lush inner courtyard surrounded by a walkway. In one corner stood a three-tier fountain flanked by royal palms and verdant vegetation. Two peacocks strutted nearby, jabbing at the ground for insects. Parrots and cockatoos created a riot of sound that ricocheted through the courtyard and out into the dense jungle surrounding us.

We turned right along the walkway and continued until we came to another section of the sprawling home that jutted out like the short end of an 'L'. Framed by large windows and even larger foliage, the French doors reflected the two of us as we approached, making it difficult to see inside. An armed guard dressed in dull green military fatigues stood to one side. His eyes flicked over me once before he snapped back to attention. We stopped and waited.

Memories from a few days ago decided at that precise moment to come flooding back.

Cole.

2

One week earlier…

Y OU UP FOR SOME SUSHI?" Sheriff Cole Anderson asked as he opened the passenger door to his SUV and motioned for me to get in.

Cole's smile had a way of melting my heart. I loved how the dimples deepened in his cheeks and his blue eyes danced the mambo, enticing me into doing just about anything he asked.

"Sure. Can we stop by my place so I can change first?"

"By all means." Cole grabbed me around the waist and leaned in to nuzzle my neck. "As long as you wear those sexy panties I like so much…"

We stopped at my cabin and I changed into the underwear in question, a clean shirt and fresh pair of jeans along with my favorite boots. The nights were still chilly here in northern Arizona, even though spring had begun to explode in new growth from the longer days.

I'd moved to the cabin from my Airstream trailer next to the HoHoKam River after the incident with the psychotic banker the spring before. Cole and Art, my boss, were both adamant that I move closer to town where Cole could keep an eye on me. I agreed to move as long as I could stay near the river. Not that I didn't like the small town of Durm, I just preferred to live out of sight of civilization with a clear 360-degree view. Cole found me the solidly built cabin and was in the process of installing a security system. Not that the same guy would be coming after me again. It was more as insurance for my past transgressions.

There were still a couple of people who wanted me dead.

Durm had one sushi joint to its name and it was run by a master chef named Bob Yamaguchi. He had fish flown in daily and what he didn't use he donated to the local food bank to feed the homeless. We each grabbed a stool at the counter, preferring to watch the show.

"Welcome, sheriff," Bob said to Cole, shaking his hand. Then he turned to me and bowed. "Miss Kate. You are most radiant this evening. I am honored to have you both here."

Bob always had a smile on his face and a wry joke to share with his customers. He loved it when Cole stopped in because he'd try anything Bob suggested at least once. One time, he persuaded Cole to eat puffer fish, normally poisonous, with a side of *uni*, or sea urchin roe. The puffer fish hadn't been too bad, according to Cole, but the *uni* didn't do anything for him. I usually stuck to yellow fin tuna and *unagi*, with maybe a couple of orders of flying fish roe. I'd never felt the need to ingest poison. Let's just say I had bad memories I didn't want to duplicate.

I handed my order across the glass counter to Bob. Cole was still deciding when my cell phone went off. I excused myself and walked over near the bathrooms to answer.

"Kate? Luis Gonzales. How you doing?"

Luis Gonzales was my contact in the Drug Enforcement Administration. He'd become my lifeline after I'd testified at the trials of two powerful drug lords a decade before. Any news from Luis probably wouldn't be good. I took a deep breath and squared my shoulders before I replied.

"Great, Luis. What can I do for you?"

"A friend of yours from Alaska is trying to get in touch with you. He contacted me through the Anchorage DEA office. A Sam Akiaq?"

My face grew warm as my heartbeat banged in my ears. I bent over, put my hands on my knees, and tried to breathe.

Sam.

"Kate? Kate, are you there?"

Luis' far away voice barely cut through the memories spinning like a Tilt-a-Whirl through my brain. I recovered enough to lean against the wall and answer.

"Yeah. Sorry. I'm here."

"I take it you know him?"

"He was assigned to protect me after that PI was murdered in Quilete."

"I thought his name sounded familiar. He's the guy who took the bullet during the shootout and ended up in ICU, right?"

"Right." Yet another reason I should never let myself get close to anyone. I glanced over at Cole chatting amiably with Bob and felt my heart constrict.

"Anyway, Sam asked for your contact info. I told him I needed to check with you, first."

It had been well over five years since I'd been to Alaska. I ran to the small town of Quilete after all the shit went down in Mexico, hoping to get lost in that vast state. Needless to say, my plan had been flawed. Despite its size, Alaska was essentially a small town. An assassin had tracked me down using a private investigator. He'd lost his life for his trouble.

Sam and I developed an intense attraction to each other during our short time together, and that's what I told myself was still the case. An attraction. He almost died in the shootout and I vowed to never again become involved with anyone, knowing that the people who were after me remained alive and would kill anyone in their way.

And then I met Cole.

When I didn't reply right away, Luis continued.

"You don't have to agree. He told me you might be hesitant. He said if you were, that I should give you a message." Luis paused. "It's not good, Kate."

My stomach contracted as though anticipating a hit. "Tell me."

Luis sighed. "Angie's out and word is she's coming to finish the job."

Angie McKenna, better known as The Red Fox, happened to be the assassin hired by my ex-, Roberto Salazar, to kill me.

"How the hell did she get out?" I didn't think Alaska would release a known killer that quickly. "Did she get time off for good behavior or something?" I didn't try to mask the sarcasm.

"Evidently, her reputation has grown as the go-to killer for underworld organizations since her incarceration. Looks like someone linked to *El Castillo* broke her out of prison. Somebody started a riot and she disappeared in the confusion."

"Must have had a good publicist," I said, not quite as fearless as my remark would have Luis think.

There's no worse feeling than to realize all you've tried to do to get on with a normal life has failed, and would continue to fail, as long as the head remained attached to the snake. In this case, there were two heads: Salazar and his old boss, Vincent Anaya, with whom I'd had the unpleasant opportunity to cross paths while on a Caribbean cruise a few months back. Cole and I had been lucky to escape with our lives.

Unfortunately, so had Anaya.

The futility of running forever slammed into my gut, clawing at the relative safety I'd felt living in the little town of Durm, Arizona. I had to fight to quash the hopelessness threatening to overwhelm me.

I was damned tired.

Tired of looking over my shoulder, trying to fly low so I didn't endanger anyone I cared about. Tired of trying to distance myself and not form attachments.

That went out the window with Cole.

They're going to win, my mind whispered.

Now, it had become personal. I'd slipped from their grasp one too many times. Especially Salazar. His reputation for ruthlessness and brutality was legend, and he Didn't. Ever. Lose.

Besides, I doubted the remainder of the drug money I'd stolen and buried in Mexico at a stranger's house so many years ago was even there anymore, and I assumed drug cartels didn't take payments.

I sucked in a deep breath and let it go, trying to think of a plan. I'd taken a few self-defense courses and was studying Krav Maga at a local gym, but that and my 9mm Glock would be like an armed mosquito going after a pterodactyl with a machine gun.

Then it hit me.

"Isn't *El Castillo* the cartel that absorbed Salazar's operation?"

"One and the same."

"Jesus, Luis. I'm going to have to call you back." I punched the end call button and burst through the door into the women's restroom, barely making it to the waste basket before everything I'd ingested earlier that day made a second appearance. When the wave of nausea passed, I leaned against the wall with my eyes closed and tried to take deep, cleansing breaths.

Funny how it sounded more like sobbing.

The door opened and a woman walked in. The smile on her face died when she saw me.

"Is everything all right, hon?" she asked as she leaned in and put her hand on my shoulder, a look of concern on her face.

I shook my head and wiped at the tears running down my cheeks. "It's about as all wrong as you can get."

3

Y FIRST REACTION HAD BEEN to pack my things and leave. Cole talked me off of that ledge and insisted I stay at his place. I refused. I wasn't about to put Cole or his girls in danger. Not only had I fallen hard for him, but I'd become hopelessly attached to his daughters: Lauren, now ten, and Abby, six. They were sweet girls, very different from their cold-ass, uncompromising mother, Lorna, Cole's ex-wife. Thank God she lived miles away in Scottsdale and didn't come to Durm often.

I opted to stay at the cabin, although by Wednesday nervous wreck would have been a mild description of the way I felt. Waiting for someone to show up and kill you is not an amusing way to spend your time.

The waiting brought back memories of Salazar. My mood plummeted as I remembered how happy, and how stupid, I'd been in the beginning. He'd kept his cartel dealings separate from our life together at first, and I'd remained blissfully ignorant, enjoying the life that came

12

with being the girlfriend of a powerful man. Eventually, the ugly truth became too blatant to deny. By then, I had become his prisoner.

One stupid mistake and a girl's gotta pay for it the rest of her life.

When I wasn't tripping over memories of Mexico, thoughts of Sam played like a loop in my mind. I kept telling myself I didn't have feelings for him, but it was a lie. Good thing I hadn't told Luis to give him my contact information. I didn't trust myself. It took me five long years to move past the events that happened in Alaska, and Sam's and my relationship turned out to be one of the hardest to overcome.

Scratch that. I hadn't exactly overcome it now, had I?

My last contact with him had been a late night phone call after I'd found out he'd asked a friend of his to watch over me in Oahu; yet another place I'd run after Mexico, not knowing where else to go. Someone I knew and trusted had tried to end my life and Sam's guy had shot and killed him before he succeeded. I called Sam to say thanks and we'd spoken long into the night. As we hung up, I knew I could never see or talk to him again. It would be too dangerous—physically for him, emotionally for me. Unless and until I ditched the bad spirits the old shaman in Mexico had said were following me through life, no one I loved was safe.

Which brought me to Cole. Whenever I mentioned my past, Cole argued he'd be fine, that he could take care of himself. He was the county sheriff and knew his way around a firearm so I should quit worrying. But I did worry.

It hadn't helped Sam.

To keep them out of harm's way, Cole sent his girls to their mother's, and stayed with me at night. One evening after dinner, he joined me on the couch in front of the fire. I relaxed into his arms as we sipped our wine and talked. One thing led to another and soon we were on the rug in front of the fire, his lips burning a path from the sensitive area of my neck to my breasts and back again. At first I matched his passion kiss for kiss, but tangled thoughts of Angie and Sam and the bloody scene on an Alaskan highway six years before doused the flames that had ignited between us. Unable to sustain my desire, I broke away, sliding across the floor to lean back against the couch. Cole's eyes clouded with concern.

"Talk to me, Kate."

"It's happening again."

"What is?"

"I swore I'd never put another person I cared about in danger." I held his gaze. "And now you're in danger."

Cole began to protest, but I raised my hand and he grew quiet.

"You sent Abby and Lauren to their mother, Cole. Are you going to tell me you don't believe you're in danger? You know it and I know it, and as long as Salazar and Anaya are alive, it's never going to change."

Cole drew in a deep breath and exhaled. "I knew the risks once you told me about your past and I'm still here."

"An intellectual understanding of the risks is far different from the reality of them. You know that."

He glanced away and sighed. "Nothing I can say is going to make you understand that I'm willing to risk my life for you to keep you safe. Yes, I sent the girls away, but I'd do that no matter what kind of threat I faced. I'm in law enforcement. I encounter risks every day."

"I realize that. But this threat is because of me. I can make it go away simply by leaving."

He closed his eyes for a moment and then opened them. Pain arced across their depths. "Don't my feelings factor into this at all?"

I went to him and cupped his face with my hand. "Your feelings mean everything to me, Cole." My heart squeezed tight at the misery on his face. Maybe he had a point. I'd grown out my hair and dyed it a different color. That, along with changing my name and address might confuse Angie long enough for me to escape before anything bad happened.

I hoped.

"Let's play it by ear, okay? If things get too dicey, I leave. Deal?"

"Deal."

Two days later, my restlessness and paranoia got the better of me and pushed me out the door of the cabin and over to the local tavern. I called Cole to tell him where I was headed and asked him to meet me there for lunch. I figured since it was a public place, it would be safe. Besides, I'd been going bat-shit crazy sitting in my little cabin, trying to entertain myself between shifts as a guide for Hard Rock Country Jeep Tours.

I walked into the Blue Iguana and was assaulted by a cranked up YouTube video of Van Halen's *Finish What You Started* on the big screen TV in the corner. Crisco, the owner, greeted me with a wave, his 1980s-era spiral-permed, hair-band tresses a retro match to his faded, ripped, leg-hugging jeans and open-to-the-navel Members Only jacket. I ordered a beer and watched Sammy Hagar's glowing white teeth and Eddie Van Halen's sleek bare chest as they mugged for the camera with a couple of Madonna-wannabe's vying for attention in the background. Not that I didn't like the song. Eddie's guitar riffs and Sammy's vocals were enough to forgive the band their silly rock star exhibitionism. Besides, it was the eighties.

At least it was at the Blue Iguana.

I'd finished half my beer when Cole walked in, his expression tight.

"What's wrong?"

A slight tic pulsed in his cheek.

"Grab your purse—we have to leave." He took his wallet out of his pocket.

"I've got it." My hand shook as I tossed money on the bar for the beer and followed him out. Shrugging on my coat, I hurried to keep up with his long strides.

"What's happening? Where are we going?"

Cole stopped at his truck and opened the door, waiting as I climbed inside. "Luis called me when he couldn't reach you."

I grabbed my purse off the floor and searched for my phone, but couldn't find it. "It must have fallen out of my pocket on the way here. What did he say?"

"A contact of his in Flagstaff said they arrested some guy for possession and he offered information in exchange for a deal. He told them he knew a woman who'd been putting out the word for contract killers. She fit Angie's description: Southern accent, tall, slender build, green eyes. Except she was a blonde, not a redhead."

"Shit."

"Yeah." Cole shut my door, walked to the driver's side and got in. "I'll take you to the cabin and you can get your things."

We pulled out of the parking lot and headed back toward my place.

"What should I do? I can't go to your house, and I sure as hell can't stay at some hotel around here." Angie was well-versed in finding folks hiding under an assumed name. Besides, if Vincent Anaya knew which town I lived in, and he alluded to that fact when I'd seen him last, then it wouldn't be a stretch for someone in *El Castillo* to get the information, for a price.

Especially Roberto Salazar.

"I'm going to bring you to a safe house Luis set up. You'll stay there until—"

"Oh, no I'm not."

"Kate, there's no other—"

"You know what happened the last time I stayed in a so-called safe house? Somebody blew it up. People died. Luis knows that." I shook my head and crossed my arms. "No, I am not going anywhere near a safe house. You might as well paint a big red bull's eye on the door."

I tried to slow my breathing, but hyperventilating seemed more appropriate. I was going to have to leave—again. I could never stop moving. Cole was in danger, not to mention everyone who knew me in town. My heart stuttered in my chest and I realized I was headed for a full-on panic attack. A technique Sam had shown me in Alaska to quiet the voices in my head popped into my mind. Calming down seemed next to impossible, but I was willing to give it a try.

"Kate—" Cole started to say something, but I cut him off.

"Give me a second." I closed my eyes and silently recited exactly what Sam had taught me, in exactly the same order, breathing in through my nose and exhaling through my mouth. Within a couple of minutes my heart rate slowed and the annoying spots in front of my eyes had disappeared.

"Okay. Now I can think straight." I took another deep breath and let it out. "I have to leave town, draw Angie away from Durm and no one else will get hurt. I'll call you as soon as I get settled somewhere."

Cole took a left toward the sheriff's office. He continued the conversation as though I hadn't spoken. "Since the safe house idea obviously isn't going to work, I can either give you twenty-four hour armed protection at a hotel room of your choice, or I can put you up at the jail. You'll be safe there, at least until we find her."

Extreme claustrophobia would have been a more welcome feeling than what I felt at the thought of being locked up in a cell.

"Sorry, Cole. I know you're trying to help. I've had armed protection and the armed folks always ended up dead or critically injured." I placed my hand on his arm, hoping he'd see the truth of what I was saying. "These people don't fool around. I'm not going to be responsible for any more casualties. You've got to let me do this my way."

We'd pulled over next to the sheriff's station, the car still idling. Cole let out a frustrated sigh and stared out the windshield, drumming his fingers. Then he turned toward me.

"I love you, Kate. I need to protect you. Trust me. I'm highly trained. You've seen what I can do." He shook his head, his intense gaze softening. "You're a hard-headed woman, you know that?"

"So I've been told."

"Fine," Cole said, his exasperation palpable. "Go. But leave your jeep. She probably already knows what you drive. Take the Subaru."

The Subaru was Cole's second vehicle, one he was saving for when Lauren grew old enough to get her license. It would be perfect. All-wheel-drive and low profile.

"Deal."

Several hours later, I pulled into a hotel on the outskirts of San Diego. After I dumped my stuff in my room, I walked over to the Mexican restaurant next door and ordered the special. Somebody's kid was having a birthday party and the attendees were all screaming and laughing and wearing sombreros. My thoughts turned to Lauren and Abby and I allowed myself a few moments of fond memories. Lauren riding her favorite horse. Abby learning how to swim. Cole kissing me goodbye and telling me to call when I stopped somewhere. I took out my phone and hit speed dial. It had been on the table by the couch in the cabin.

"Kate?" Cole's voice sounded close. Comforting.

"Yep. I'm stopped for the night. Everything is fine."

"Have you figured out where you're going yet?"

"Not really. I think I'll stay mobile for a while. We'll see how things go."

"We're going to find her, Kate. You'll be able to come home soon."

I cleared my throat and tried to sound confident. "I'm counting on it. I miss you already."

"Me too. G'night, babe."

"G'night."

I signed off and angrily wiped at the tears trying to ruin my dinner. Self-pity wouldn't do me any good. I had to think clearly, keep the emotion out of my decision. One thing was for sure—I couldn't go back. Even if they managed to stop Angie, Salazar and Anaya would just hire someone else to finish the job. I squeezed my eyes shut as the pain of leaving Cole and the life I'd built swept over me.

There had to be a way to get Salazar and Anaya off my back permanently, or I'd never be able to have any kind of normal life—people would continue to get hurt or killed unless something changed. There were two ways that could happen: either they died or I did.

Going after someone to kill them, especially a person who had the protection of one of the largest and most brutal cartels in Mexico, would be a fool's errand. No way could I get next to either Salazar or Anaya, and I didn't want to try.

Which left my death.

I hadn't quite gotten to the point that I'd want to off myself in order to find peace, and doubted I ever would. Cole had been right about one thing: I was as stubborn as they get. I wouldn't give up, if only to piss off the assholes who wanted me dead.

No, it would take my death, or, rather, news of my death, to get them off my trail.

But how?

A plan formed slowly in my mind. I grabbed a pen and notepad from my purse.

4

I WOKE BEFORE DAWN THE next morning and showered, exchanging my day-old clothes for a fresh t-shirt and clean pair of jeans.

Pulling my hair back in a ponytail, I sucked down a small pot of coffee provided by the good folks at the hotel. I'd chosen the place for the lack of outside corridors. Angie had found me easily at the Dew Drop Inn in Alaska: the motel had open breezeways leading to the rooms. A room with a door opening onto the parking lot would leave me too exposed. I didn't want to make it easy for her.

After checking the area near the Subaru from my third floor window and making sure it was clear, I grabbed my overnight bag and purse and rode the elevator to the lobby. I sucked down another cup of coffee and ate a banana from the not-yet-stocked breakfast bar, settled my bill and walked out to the car.

As I stowed my things in the back, I felt the hairs prickle on the back of my neck, like someone was watching. Warily, I checked each direction, but saw nothing suspicious. I shook it off, got inside and started the car, making sure to lock the doors. Before I pulled out of the parking lot and headed for the freeway, I slid the Glock under my purse on the seat within easy reach.

Thirty-four miles later, I left the highway and drove into a rest area, cursing the coffee and my tiny bladder. I locked the car and walked toward the restroom. Long shadows of pungent eucalyptus trees stained the ground black. The parking lot appeared deserted other than a sole big rig parked nearby. The rumble of the idling diesel engine cut through the early morning silence as I hurried inside the building.

When I came back out, another car had pulled in next to mine. I slowed my steps and absorbed the details of the black SUV, memorizing the Arizona license plate and wondering if I should turn and head the other direction. There didn't appear to be anyone in the front seat, but someone could have been sitting in the back behind the smoked windows.

I changed my trajectory and breezed past both vehicles, catching a glimpse of someone near the rear of the SUV. Eyes forward, I kept walking toward the big blue semi, hoping I looked like I belonged to it.

I heard a door slam shut behind me. Heart in my throat, I quickened my pace.

"Turn around Kate, honey."

The southern drawl stopped me in my tracks. *Angie.* I took a deep breath and pivoted slowly on one foot, hand reaching behind me for my Glock. My heart kicked up a notch when I remembered I'd left it on the front seat. She wouldn't gun me down in the middle of a rest area with potential witnesses, would she?

Of course she would.

Wearing a Cheshire-cat smile, she stood near the now-closed back door of the SUV, a semi-auto with a suppressor pointed at me. Big, tortoise-shell sunglasses perched on top of her head, corralling her short blonde hair like a headband. Her feline-green eyes were in direct opposition to her poison apple-red lipstick, but she made up for it with a leopard print shirt belted at the waist with black leather leggings. A pair of flat, sensible shoes marred the ensemble.

She noticed my gaze lingering at her feet and her expression hardened. "Thanks to you, darlin', I'll never be able to wear heels again. You have no idea what being shot in the foot does to a person as fashion forward as I am." She nodded her head toward the Subaru next to her.

"It didn't look like you had a gun on you. Leave it in the car?"

My expression must have given her the answer, because she shook her head.

"Honey, you've gotten soft. Easy to trace, easy to catch…" Her voice trailed off. "You should never, ever leave your phone unattended. It's way too easy for someone untrustworthy to install tracking software that way…"

I should have known. My phone had only been out of my possession once. "You've changed your hair." Engaging her in conversation was a delay tactic we both knew wouldn't buy me much time, but I had to try something.

She patted her coif. "Why, yes, thank you for noticin'."

"It makes you look so much more…mature."

The air stilled. Her lips thinned to a red slash across her face and her eyes narrowed. She rapped on the window beside her.

The side door of the SUV opened and a dark-haired man the size of a lineman for the Chicago Bears got out. I got a brief glimpse of a gun in a shoulder holster underneath his jacket. His belly protruded over his belt by several inches and his tie was askew.

I half-turned, hoping to signal somebody, anybody, in the semi so they'd call the cops. Although the way Angie stood with her body angled just so, I doubted anyone would be able to see the gun.

"Come on, hon. Times a wastin'," Angie said. The big guy walked toward me and I took a few steps back. Why hadn't she shot me yet? It's not like the trucker would hear anything, even if he was awake. Not with the engine idling.

Startled, Angie raised her head, as if sniffing the air. The big guy paused in his beeline toward me and they both looked left. A dark blue Tahoe with its cherries flashing roared into the parking lot and skidded to a stop between me and the killers. Angie and the gunman dove behind the SUV as the driver's side door of the Tahoe burst open and Cole vaulted out. He aimed his gun over the hood and squeezed off a few rounds, then dropped down when one of them returned fire.

"Move!" he yelled over his shoulder. I dove under the semi and scuttled for the rear wheel well, heart hammering in my chest.

The scene blurred as if in slow motion as memories of the shootout with Sam flooded back, paralyzing me. More gunfire erupted between the two trucks. Bullets pinged off metal and asphalt. Willing my legs to move, I slid to the side of the truck closer to Cole. My stomach churned, the acid rolling like a slow boil toward my throat. It could've been from the greasy smell of diesel or my fear for Cole. Probably both.

I estimated the distance between where I now crouched and the SUV to be too far for me to safely cross. I didn't want to distract him. My mind raced for a way to get my hands on the gun in the Subaru or move across the parking lot to the Tahoe without Cole noticing. I had to stop myself from running to him as I watched him fend off Angie and the big guy without my help. He must have been following me, keeping the Subaru in sight in case anything went wrong.

The door to the semi opened and a pair of jean-clad legs and scuffed cowboy boots appeared on the step at the other end of the truck. The driver climbed down and squatted beside the front wheels of the semi, shotgun in his right hand. Too absorbed in the action, he didn't notice me when I waved at him and yelled, trying to get his attention. The rattle of the diesel engine drowned out my attempts.

I dropped to all fours and worked my way toward him. Just as I got close enough for him to hear me, he took off running toward Cole's truck in a crouch, shotgun in hand. Bullets chipped the asphalt near his feet.

He'd almost made it to the Tahoe when he staggered back, gripping his right shoulder. He stumbled the last few steps to the SUV and collapsed against the rear tire. Blood soaked his white t-shirt and ran down his arm. Cole glanced behind him at the commotion, leaving himself open for a micro-second. I screamed as he lurched sideways, hand to his head. His gun fell to the ground and he grabbed onto the front seat of the SUV with his free hand. He wavered for a second, then dropped to one knee. The two shooters split up; Angie angled around the front of the Tahoe, the big guy came around the back, guns drawn.

"No!" I scrambled from underneath the semi and pushed myself to my feet. Hands in the air, I walked toward them.

Angie turned, a triumphant smile spreading across her face. She skirted the open door and walked up behind Cole, kicking his gun away and aiming hers at the back of his head, all the while watching me. At the same time the trucker raised his shotgun with his good arm, but he was too late—the big guy came around the rear of the truck and shoved his gun in his face. The trucker dropped the shotgun and raised his good hand.

"It's about damned time." Angie turned and considered Cole. "My, my. You certainly do collect some fine lookin' men, don't you?" She motioned me forward with an impatient wave of her hand. "Hurry up. I'm on a deadline."

"Let them go. You wanted to kill me. Do it already." I shot a glance at Cole. The skin on his face had turned the color of ash. His profile was to me so I couldn't assess the extent of his injuries, as he'd been shot on the opposite side. He wasn't doing well; his breathing was labored. My chest squeezed tight in panic at the thought of him dying and the voice in my head screamed at me to go to him.

If I did, we'd both be dead.

A slight breeze scuffed up a plastic bag lying on the ground. I barely registered the tears streaming down my cheeks. I took slow steps toward her, expecting the agony of a bullet with each one. "Please—" I couldn't control the anguish in my voice. I saw Cole's shoulders stiffen.

Angie scoffed. "Oh, I'm not going to kill you, darlin'. There's much better money in deliverin' you alive. As for your man, I'm just not sure he's gonna make it." She raised an eyebrow. "Funny how this keeps happenin', isn't it?"

The big guy came up behind me and grabbed my wrists, corralled them with a zip tie and cinched it tight.

"Get in the truck."

We stopped at a private airfield outside of Bakersfield. Big Guy had thrown me in the back of the SUV and they'd taken off without so much as a backward glance. Cole and the trucker were left there to die. I forced myself to stop crying and shoved my fear for Cole's survival deep. I'd be no good to anyone if I allowed myself to fall apart. I welcomed the white-hot loathing I felt for my captors, imagining myself ripping them apart the first chance I got.

It's amazing how hatred focuses the brain.

The cinch ties cut into my wrists as I tried to wriggle my hands free. Big Guy had done a good job. My fingers were going numb from lack of blood flow.

He came around the back and pulled me out of the SUV, shoving me toward a red and white Cessna parked a few yards away. By the looks of it, we were flying somewhere. I'd lay five-to-one I hadn't won a trip to Vegas.

Angie walked over to a corrugated steel hangar to talk to a tall man standing in the shade who I assumed was the pilot. While Big Guy and I walked, I took stock of my surroundings: one small airstrip, one twin-engine Cessna, one hangar, and one large, open space. A stand of trees grew about two football fields from where we now stood. If I could make it to the tree line, I'd have a good chance of escape.

Maybe.

As we neared the Cessna, I pretended to stumble. Big Guy grabbed my arm. At the same time, I shifted my weight to my forward leg and twisted as hard as I could to the right, sweeping my other leg around, trying to build momentum for a kick. I got lucky and connected. Big Guy doubled over with a groan, clutching his privates. I threw myself forward and slammed into him shoulder first, but it was like trying to knock over a refrigerator. Still bent over, he staggered back a step. Turning, I pushed into a back kick that clocked him square in the face. His head snapped up and his hand flew to his nose. Score one for self-defense training.

I sprinted past the Cessna and out to the field beyond, keeping the small plane between me and the line of sight of the hangar. Running with your arms bound behind you isn't easy.

I'd made it halfway to the tree line when I heard shouting behind me. I gathered every last shred of energy and sprinted for the finish. The pop of gunfire spurred me on. I had no idea how close they were to catching me.

Only twenty more yards to go…ten…nine…it was my own private football game and I was the quarterback. My breath came in short bursts as my eyes zeroed in on a break in the trees ahead of me. Eight…seven…

The force of the tackle threw me face first to the ground and knocked the wind out of me. I struggled for breath, but the weight on my back prevented me from taking in air. I fought through the panic, spitting bits of dirt and grass on the ground.

"Get off me." My voice came out weaker than I intended.

The weight finally lifted and I sucked in a greedy breath. A hand grabbed me by the elbow and jerked me to my feet. Something hard rammed into my side.

A gun. Anger roiled inside me and quickly replaced any sense I had. I turned my head and leaned back to look into his face. My jaw dropped and I caught what breath I had left. My anger morphed into disbelief, then skidded downhill into dread.

John Sterling's smile could only be described as merciless. He hadn't changed much for a man I swear had been buried alive in a mine shaft.

The last time I'd seen Sterling, we'd both been trapped inside a collapsed mine. I thought he'd been killed. At least, I'd hoped he had.

I remembered to breathe, but my throat contracted, making it difficult.

"What's the matter, Kate? Looks like you've seen a ghost." He grinned, but his eyes had a calculating gleam.

"I thought you were dead."

He dragged me toward the airplane, his grip hurting my arm.

"Ever find my car? No?" He increased the pressure on my elbow until I cried out. "Didn't it occur to you I might have made it out when you didn't find a body?"

I had to admit, Cole did raise that possibility, but I hadn't been ready to hear it. I'm nothing if not good at denial.

"Lady Luck was with me that day. Evidently, she doesn't have very high standards, since you made it out, too." He shook his head. "I've never met a woman with so many fucking lives."

His legs were longer than mine and I struggled to keep up, stumbling several times. My calves had become one solid cramp by the time we reached the Cessna.

Angie walked around the back of the plane to meet us and slapped me hard across the face. I tasted blood on my lip.

"Don't try that again. The contract said alive. It didn't specify what shape you had to be in."

"Fuck you, Angie." I spit the words through my teeth, hoping to mask the shock and anxiety working its way up my shoulders.

Angie smiled. "Honey, if anyone's fucked, it's you."

5

Two days later, at the Hacienda…

THE FRENCH DOORS SWEPT OPEN and my guard shoved me forward into the well-appointed, old-world room dominated by leather and dark wood. A second guard took up space in the corner closest to me. Angie stood at one end in front of a tall bookcase, arms crossed, her expression unreadable. Sterling held court in a comfy chair near a heavy wooden desk which boasted a MacBook Air, a rosewood humidor and—Salazar. My shoulders went rigid at seeing my worst nightmare: the coldblooded reptile of an ex-lover who wanted me dead.

"See? She's fine. I told you she hadn't been banged up too badly," Angie said.

Salazar rose from his chair and walked over to stand in front of me. His dark brown eyes looked black in the early morning shadow. The set of his mouth indicated strain, though I couldn't be sure if it was because of me or something else. When you're a cog in the wheel of a drug cartel, your life is defined by stress.

"You look different." He took a step back and his gaze flickered over my body, assessing me. He lifted my chin and looked into my eyes. "Older."

I resisted the urge to spit in his face. It would have been tough, with a mouth dry as sand. I tried to swallow, but only ended up making a smacking sound. Salazar smirked. Dread mixed with anger plowed through me like a potent cocktail, and I realized for the first time I could kill him.

"It's been over ten years, Roberto. We've both changed." I looked pointedly at his now graying hair, let my eyes travel down his impeccably tailored suit to his expanding waistline, then back to his face. By the looks of it, my attempt at a pitying expression worked. His eyes grew cold and he stiffened.

"When Anaya conceived of this plan, he'd assured me you hadn't changed. He must have been speaking of your insubordinate attitude."

I ignored the bait and asked, "What plan would that be?" The mention of Vincent Anaya's name didn't help lessen my fear factor. I should have known he'd try to get to me, should have left Durm when I had the chance. I mentally shook myself. That kind of thinking would do me no good.

"It's actually a pretty good one." Salazar moved in so that his face was inches from mine, his breath hot against my skin. I stared back, not wanting to give him the satisfaction of seeing me squirm. "It gives us both the pleasure of making you suffer, while recouping the money you stole. Although," he looked me up and down again, his lips forming a moue, "it could take a little longer than we originally envisioned."

Sterling guffawed. Smiling, Salazar stepped back and pulled a nearby chair closer, indicating I should sit. My guard pushed me to comply. I balanced on the edge of the seat, tension thrumming through my body.

They were going to make me work off the money, but how? Becoming a mule and transporting drugs? Doubtful. I'd be too much of a flight risk. I knew Salazar wasn't expecting me to clean anything, since I was the world's worst domestic. Although, that could have been the reason for his jab about it taking longer to recoup the money and making me suffer. What else? The acid forming in the pit of my stomach told me I hadn't gone low enough on the humiliation scale.

Angie stayed where she was, speaking in a low voice into her cell phone. I couldn't catch what she was saying, so I turned my attention back to Salazar and Sterling.

"I'm afraid there's not a lot of room for creativity in your new position, although there is a heavy travel element. And, you'll be coming into contact with a lot of people. Mainly men." Salazar leaned next to my ear and said in a low voice, "I'm sending you to one of my brothels in Playa del Carmen for training." He lifted the hair off my neck. "Once we brand you, the whole of Mexico will know whose *puta* you are."

Sterling watched us with a sneer on his face, chair tipped back with his arms crossed. I would have given anything for a gun.

Salazar continued. "As a gesture of my great esteem and concern for your well-being, I'll make sure it's the filthiest whorehouse we operate with the most debased clientele. Once you've proven your worth, Anaya and I have worked out an agreement to shuttle you between the worst of the ones we now own." He gazed off in the distance. "There's huge money in sex and far less risk. Its potential makes the drug trade look like an underperforming stock." He smiled and spread his hands wide. "Be happy, Kate. You'll be able to do what you do best." He narrowed his eyes and his smile vaporized. "Fuck and travel."

Now off the phone, Angie came forward and slid onto the desk, crossing her legs at the knee. "And don't think your sweet sheriff is going to come and save you. I was just speaking with the guy who helped me the morning we picked you up. He sent me a link to Channel 7 News in San Diego. " She turned her phone to face me so I could see the screen. "Looks like your boy didn't make it."

I leaned forward and squinted, trying to read the headline.

Arizona Sheriff Found Shot to Death at Rest Area.

As what I read registered, my initial shock turned to rage. Coiled like a snake, I threw myself out of my chair toward her, a snarl forming on my lips, yearning to wipe the smug look off her face. "You BITCH."

Angie's expression turned from smug to alarmed as I closed the distance between us. She scrambled behind the desk as Salazar's guy lunged forward and grabbed me by the hair. I was beyond the point of feeling pain. My chest heaved from the force of my anger and the adrenaline spike, and I struggled to break free. I didn't care what they did to me as long as I could feel Angie's scrawny little neck snap between my fingers. Sterling was on his feet, gun drawn, but Salazar shook his head.

"We can make this easy or not, Kate." Salazar's voice carved through my fury, bringing me back to my senses. Using any strength I had left to fight would be counterproductive. I needed to encapsulate the anger I felt toward Angie and the rest of them, save it for when it would make a difference. I stopped fighting. Salazar's goon slammed me back in the chair.

Salazar looked at his watch and frowned. "I originally had your welcome party set for eighteen hundred hours, but I can tell by your actions that you're eager to start. John, could you reschedule everyone for earlier? Say, right after siesta?" He reached over and patted my cheek. "You're going to need your beauty sleep."

I jerked my head away from his touch. He laughed.

"My pleasure, boss," Sterling answered.

The urge to include John Sterling in my vendetta almost overwhelmed me. Salazar must have noticed my reaction. He leaned over and whispered in my ear. "The men like it when you fight them. You'll be one popular *puta.*"

"Take her," he ordered with a wave of his hand. Both guards grabbed me by the arms and heaved me off the chair and out the door, back toward my prison.

We'd barely made it halfway when the ground shook as a loud explosion erupted behind us. The two guards wheeled around, their mouths slack, with me sandwiched between them. Black smoke poured into the sky from the other side of the hacienda.

"*¡Mierda!*" my guard swore as he dragged me toward a nearby outbuilding and shoved me inside. Shouting and sporadic gunfire could be heard in the distance. Salazar's bodyguard raced back toward the chaos. With a curse my guard slammed the door shut.

I waited for the scrape of a key in the lock but heard only the guard's footsteps hurrying away, the sound fading as he ran toward the action.

I crept to the door and leaned against it, listening for movement. Not hearing anything but the distant *rat-tat-tat* of a machine gun, I leaned my shoulder against the paint-flaked wood and pushed.

Nothing happened. There was no handle on my side of the door. I estimated where the latch would be on the outside, took a step back and kicked. The old wood held.

After a couple more tries, I gave up and turned my attention to the room itself. The damp, moldy smell told me the building wasn't on Salazar's regular maintenance schedule. In a tropical environment maintenance is key to the integrity of a structure. I worked my way around the room, kicking and poking at the wall in several places, hoping to find rotted wood or maybe an insect infestation.

A third of the way around the perimeter, I felt the wall give. I kicked again and a section of plaster fell away. I turned around and surveyed the room, looking for something harder than my boot. A three-foot piece of steel about a quarter-inch thick lay on the floor amidst a roll of rusted, coiled fencing. I slid the metal stake free and returned to the wall. Using the end, I scraped and stabbed at the soft spot, enlarging the hole until I could see daylight.

Another explosion rocked the compound. Dust and pieces of plaster rained down and I covered my head with my arms expecting the roof to fall in. When it didn't, I continued pushing through the damaged section. Soon I'd enlarged the hole to a couple of feet across. I set the metal stake aside and ripped out sections by hand. A short time later, the hole looked big enough for me to wiggle through. I lay on my stomach to look through the opening. The outside wall faced the back of the building, leading to an overgrown section of the compound.

As I slid through, the remaining plaster scraped the skin on my arms and sides. Ignoring the pain, I turned onto my back and pushed at the wall, trying to force my hips through.

Finally free, I stood up and scanned the immediate area. The grounds surrounding the building weren't as manicured as those near the hacienda. In fact, the jungle loomed steps away. I had no idea what was going on behind me, but I figured the explosions had something to do with a rival cartel. This kind of attack had become the norm in my last days with Salazar and had been a large part of what prompted me to leave.

That, and the fact that he slit the throat of his closest confidant for a small infraction. You tend to get a little paranoid after something like that.

More gunfire accompanied by another explosion further inside the grounds prodded me to move. I broke into a run, sprinting away from the sound of the war erupting behind me.

6

SOON THE JUNGLE BECAME TOO dense to run through and I had to pick my way past the vines and trees, slowing my progress. Undaunted, I continued to fight through the dense underbrush, determined to put distance between me and Salazar before I stopped to rest, even though I had no idea which direction to take.

My emotions were off the charts and I found myself not being able to stem the flood of tears. I swung wildly between out-of-control fury, the likes of which I'd never experienced, to despondency over Cole's death. The only coping mechanism of any use was to believe I would be able to someday avenge his murder. The thought of wiping Angie and Salazar off the face of the earth made me feel better. Taking out Sterling and Anaya would be icing on the cake.

A myth, certainly, but it was my myth and I decided to stick with it for the time being.

Drained from the surge of adrenaline I'd experienced back at the hacienda, I paused in my single-minded march and allowed myself to rest for a moment. I had to fight the strong pull of stopping altogether. Why not let nature take its course? I wouldn't be able to form any kind of attachment with a person for fear of them becoming a target. That made for one long, lonely existence. I was not a hermit, hard though I tried. A life lived with no one to talk to, or be with, or love, was a desolate life indeed. More tears welled in my eyes and spilled over at the soul-deep pain of losing Cole. The force of my grief hit me hard and I sank to my knees to sob out my agony.

I knelt like that until I couldn't feel my legs. When the tears subsided, I inhaled a ragged breath—and realized I had to keep going.

The reality of my predicament slammed into me like a crowbar to the solar plexus, knocking me off guard. The fact that I needed to get help or I'd die alone in the jungle had me focused and alert, and I immediately turned my attention from revenge to what I needed to survive. The abrasions on my arms and sides from squeezing out through the hole in the wall had turned red and angry-looking. Threat of infection was a serious concern in the tropics. I needed to find a way to clean and cover the cuts. I didn't relish the idea of visiting insects homing in on the infected area to lay eggs.

Though the morning remained cool, I knew it wouldn't last long. I stood and brushed the dirt off my jeans. Salazar had mentioned Playa del Carmen, so it made sense that I was somewhere in the Mexican state of Yucatán, or possibly Quintana Roo. I glanced at the sun, now rising, and headed east.

Springtime on the Yucatán Peninsula could be pleasant in the mornings, not so much in the afternoons.

The mosquitoes weren't bad around the hacienda—but that didn't mean they wouldn't be ferocious away from the areas where pesticides had been sprayed. I had no idea where I stood in relation to the coast, or even where the closest town might be. The best I could do was to keep heading east until I found a road, a home, a village, something.

As I fought my way through the thick jungle, I searched my memory for what I remembered about the area. Having visited many of the Maya ruins both as Salazar's girlfriend and as a college student, I had some knowledge of the ancient legends of the Maya and Toltec. Their history was rich with amazing stories and myths, and when I wasn't trying to bust through dense vegetation, I tried to remember the ones specific to the jungle in the hopes that they'd trigger memories with useful information.

Not that legends would help me survive long without finding food and water. As I recalled, the Yucatán plains were comprised of limestone and boasted no rivers or streams. There were, however, hundreds of sinkholes carved out of the terrain by underground waterways, which often created *cenotes*, or wells.

I just had to find one.

The Maya were a fiercely proud people and had survived in this area for centuries. Their history was drenched in violence and the blood of human sacrifice, but as a Maya man once told me, they were originally a peace-loving, agricultural civilization conquered by other violent and blood-thirsty tribes. Before competing groups arrived on the scene, sacrifices had been limited to animals, not humans, and the ball games hadn't yet become a blood sport where the captain of the winning team was sacrificed. They also lived in sync with the natural world, believing in nature spirits similar to many indigenous cultures, assigning names and special powers to the plants and animals that called the Yucatán home.

Jaguar sightings, though rare, still occurred. I'd always been fascinated by the big cats: they had a mesmerizing combination of lethal grace and ferociousness and were such beautiful animals. The Maya revered them and equated their presence with strong power and protection.

Snakes were another matter. Several poisonous species called this area home.

I hated snakes.

I remembered reading about poisonous spiders and fresh water crocodiles, as well. Still, I'd take my chances. Critters, dangerous or not, were way more predictable than enraged drug lords.

Glad to be wearing leather boots in case I ran across an unfriendly pit viper or coral snake, I continued east. The temperature rose steadily and I knew I'd need to find water, soon. There were healing plants available throughout the jungle but I didn't trust my ability to identify the right ones.

I angled my path in the hope that I'd come across the road leading to the hacienda and follow it, hidden by the jungle until I happened on a settlement or town.

The grass ahead of me rustled and I stopped, spooked by the thought of jaguars and snakes. I scanned the area for the source of the sound. A leathery gray iguana peered at me through a mat of dried leaves. I exhaled and the reptile continued on its way, long, scaly tail sweeping the ground behind it.

The sun scorched my uncovered head and flies buzzed around my sweaty face, pissing me off when they wouldn't leave me alone. Frustrated by my slow progress and hot as hell, the familiar feeling of panic burned low in my gut and traveled upward toward my chest. I'd walked for hours, but hadn't found anything resembling food, water, a road or a home. I squashed my doubts flat. Indulging in fear would not get me closer to safety. *Don't look a gift horse in the mouth, Kate. You got away from Salazar. You'll be fine.* My resolve returned in tiny, jagged increments and I continued.

Not having had a meal in recent memory, I was running out of fuel and losing strength, fast. After the tenth time I tripped and almost did a face-plant into the ground, I realized I was exhibiting signs of heat exhaustion, as well. Dizziness and a low-grade, annoying headache accompanied my rapidly beating heart.

I doubled my efforts to find a place to rest for the night. About the time I'd decided I needed to stop before I collapsed, I stumbled into an open area with a large stone covered in vines, rising from the ground. I walked over to it and sank gratefully to my knees, taking advantage of the cool shade.

I'd been thirsty for hours now, and knew I'd lost a lot of fluid from sweating during my hike through the jungle. Nausea had become a constant companion and my legs were beginning to cramp. I needed to find water, soon. Severe dehydration ain't pretty.

After a few minutes of being in the blessed shade, I looked around and realized the rock I'd been sitting next to had a twin. Curious, I climbed to my feet and headed toward it, stopping when I tripped over a raised mound. I pulled aside the grass and vines to reveal a block the size of a notebook with something carved into its surface.

From what I could see, the carving depicted a relief of an animal's head. The section surrounding the face and neck was covered in concentric circles. *Jaguar.* A trill of excitement swept through me. Forgetting my thirst for a brief moment, I allowed myself the possibility that I might be the first person to see this particular carving in hundreds of years. A faint red stain outlined the big cat's profile, and I could see bits of blue next to that. Fascinated, I picked it up and turned it over in my hands.

You might be the first person to see it, Kate, but what good will that do if you're dead?

Feeling foolish, I replaced the stone and studied my surroundings. The shadows had grown longer, meaning I'd better find somewhere safe to stay for the night. The thought of using the large-leaved plants surrounding the stones to collect dew occurred to me. That wouldn't happen until morning, though. It looked like I'd have to go to bed thirsty.

I skirted the second stone, hoping to find an enclosure or some sort of shelter. I assumed I had stumbled on an ancient Maya settlement. There were said to be hundreds of undiscovered sites situated throughout Mexico and Central America.

Before me stood a massive mound which I estimated to be at least fifty feet high covered in trees and thick vegetation. I'd read about archaeologists coming across ancient sites in the middle of nowhere in the Yucatán; the pyramids the Maya built centuries ago were essentially overtaken by the encroaching jungle and many of them remained undiscovered because of the natural camouflage.

I went over to the larger mound and walked around its base as far as the closely growing vines and trees would let me. The undergrowth had completely covered it and I couldn't make out anything resembling ruins, much less a wall. There appeared to be a faint trail away from the mound through the trees to my left so I headed that way, pushing back vines and treading carefully in case I surprised an unhappy snake.

The trail descended at a gentle slope and the ground beneath my feet transformed from matted grass to small pebbles, then to smooth rock as the path became more defined.

The temperature dipped as I continued several feet further in. The dense vegetation thinned, revealing massive boulders surrounding the mouth of a dark cave. Afternoon sun streamed through gaps in the nearby tree branches and glinted off the clear turquoise water pooling at the cave's base. Relief swept through me and I covered the remaining section of trail in two strides. I kicked off my boots and socks, stripped off my clothes and waded into the ice cold water. After drinking as much as possible, I cleaned the cuts and scrapes on my arms and torso.

Surrounded by lush trees and vines, birds chattered in the deep shade of what I'd decided to call the grotto. Smooth stones of varying sizes lay beneath me in the water, clearly visible in the pristine pool. I swam into the shallow cave, hoping to find a secure place to spend the night. Jagged stalactites descended into the depths, disappearing beneath the surface. The bowl-shaped cavity amplified the smallest sound; a drip became a loud splash. Vines cascaded over the smooth rock walls, dampened by the odd trickle of moisture.

Not finding anywhere to make camp for the evening, I swam back through the entrance of the cave. A large Ceiba tree grew nearby, its branches and massive roots stretching toward the water. The Maya considered the Ceiba the 'tree of life' and believed it represented the main link between earth and sky. As such, all Ceibas were protected by powerful forest spirits.

I sincerely hoped they weren't related to the bad spirits that followed me.

The light had faded to dusk. Bats flitted past as they silently hunted their meal. I waded to my clothes and got dressed, flushing a bird from the branches of the Ceiba. My heart skipped a beat and I froze, memories flooding back of Alaska when a murder of crows took flight after Angie's gunmen shot and killed the unwitting PI who led them to me.

Another person dead because of me. The repercussions of one stupid decision made years ago were breathtaking in their reach. *Stop it, Kate. What's done is done. You only have today.*

An image of Cole's face swam to the surface and I put my hand out to steady myself. Rock-steady Cole; the man I hoped would help me break whatever curse I carried. A decent man who did everything right—upstanding father to his kids, patient and kind to his awful ex-wife, a fair and impartial sheriff—one of the good guys. I should never have dragged him into my messed up, sorry-assed excuse of a life.

But I'd thought things had turned around. That maybe, just maybe, I'd get a reprieve from all the shit, all the bad things happening because of that one fateful decision to run.

It had all been a lie. I'd lost everything that meant anything to me, except for Sam. I would never make the same mistake by seeing him again.

In effect, I'd lost him, too.

That's enough of a pity-party, Kate. If you want to survive, you have to come back to the present. But what did surviving really mean? Sure, I might make it out of the jungle in one piece, but what then? Did I really want to go on? Alone?

I shoved the debilitating thoughts to the back of my mind and busied myself looking for a place to bed down for the night. The grotto would work as well as anywhere. With water nearby and the small enclosure, the place felt safer than being out among the ruins. I had no way to make a fire, so I set about collecting leaves to use for cover. I wanted as much protection from the cold night and the biting insects as I could get.

The Ceiba's trunk split in a deep Y, its center large enough for me to use as a sleeping platform. Being off the ground seemed like a good idea, not knowing which local fauna used this pool as a water source. I didn't know if the fresh-water crocodiles frequented *cenotes,* or if they kept strictly to inland lakes. Snakes, on the other hand, knew no such boundaries. I'd just have to take my chances.

On my way back to the tree with an armful of leaves, I kicked up a rock with my boot. I bent down to grab it, cradling the smooth, black stone in my hand. Once I'd cleaned off the dirt, I realized I held a carved statue of a jaguar, jaws open, its sharp canines giving it a lethal expression. The stone looked like obsidian, although I couldn't remember whether it was common in the area.

My fingers closed around the figurine. She'd be staying with me for the night.

The big cat crept closer to the sleeping figure, its curiosity aroused. The jaguar stretched upward, front paws against the tree and sniffed, then wrinkled its nose and drew its lips back. Unable to identify the unfamiliar smell, it dropped to all fours and circled the base, looking for the easiest route up the Ceiba's trunk. The figure above it shifted position, still asleep, showering the big cat with leaves from its nest. The feline shook them off and sat back on its haunches, considering this new intrusion into its realm.

After a few minutes, the jaguar rose to all fours and shook. Tail twitching, she padded toward the pool for a drink. Discerning no threat at this time, she was content to let things be. She finished drinking and, with a backward glance, silently loped off in search of prey.

7

WAKE UP."

My eyes popped open. Frozen in place I stared up at the Ceiba's leafy green canopy. Someone stood below me on the ground, his tone anything but conversational. Although he spoke Spanish, I detected an American accent.

It can't be Salazar, and it doesn't sound like Sterling.
Shit.

Slowly, I rose to a sitting position and looked down.

A man I'd never seen before stood below me. A large German Shepherd watched me, ears pricked forward in curiosity, its tongue lolling out to the side. The man had short, dark hair flecked with gray. His tanned and weathered face had been covered in camouflage paint, giving his hazel eyes a fierce quality. The material of his clothing and backpack matched the paint on his face and showed signs of heavy use. He had broad, muscular shoulders and long, lean legs. The machine gun he pointed at me looked at home in his arms.

I swung my legs over the edge of the tree and raised my hands.

"Can I climb down, or are you going to shoot me?" I asked in English.

He lowered the barrel of the gun with a scowl. His stance reminded me of an angry Rottweiler: legs apart, chest forward, hyper-alert, ready to attack.

"What about the dog?" The shepherd had made its way over to the tree, and was now sniffing around the base, particularly interested in the area directly below my feet.

"Aries, come!"

The dog lifted its head and immediately trotted back to join Rottweiler.

I rotated onto my stomach and lowered myself down, sliding the last couple of feet on the massive roots. Brushing leaves off my shirt and out of my hair, I squared my shoulders and looked him in the eye. The scowl deepened as the gun barrel returned to its original position. The German Shepherd cocked its head at the man as if to say, *What's up? I don't see any threat.*

Animals always were good judges of character.

"Who are you? And what the hell are you doing out here?" Rottweiler demanded.

"I'm unarmed." I lifted my hands again and turned around to show him I didn't have any weapons on me. I faced front and bent to raise first one pant leg, then the other, looking up to see if he was satisfied. The gun didn't waver. Sighing, I rolled my pant leg back down and smiled at the dog.

"You didn't answer the question."

"My name is Beyoncé Smith. And you are?"

He narrowed his eyes at the made-up name. "That's not important. You need to tell me why you're here." His gaze shot through mine like a laser. I tried to match his stare, but broke contact first. Who the hell was this guy?

"I—" I began, but stopped when two more men in camouflage carrying backpacks burst through the trees with automatic weapons.

"What have we here?" the taller one said, with the hint of a New Zealand accent. He had a blond buzz-cut and grinned as he walked toward us, his teeth ultra-white against his green-and-tan painted face. The other guy looked younger and had long, black hair pulled back in a ponytail, reminding me of Sam. Shorter than both his compatriots by at least six inches, what he lacked in height he made up for in composition. All three of them were in phenomenal shape, as though working out was their only quest in life.

"This is *Beyoncé*. She doesn't want to cooperate," Rottweiler replied.

"Really?" The blond came over and looked me up and down, circling behind me. I noticed he wore a pair of expensive sunglasses around his neck. Jungle fighting must pay more than I thought.

Finished with his perusal, he walked back to where Rottweiler stood and slipped his gun over his shoulder. "She looks cooperative to me. Have you asked her to sing?" he quipped, and flashed me a dazzling smile. I smiled back at him, relaxing for the first time that morning. Rottweiler scowled even deeper.

"She's an American woman, sleeping in the middle of the jungle. Doesn't that raise any red flags to you?"

The man with the ponytail joined his colleagues and gave me the once-over, as well. "She's not armed and she's probably not more than a hundred and thirty-five pounds soaking wet. What kind of a threat do you think she'd be?" Ponytail spoke with a Mexican accent, but used perfect English.

Rottweiler narrowed his gaze at me. "She's within a day's walk of Area Five, so I'm guessing she's one of the cartel's playthings who didn't get enough attention."

"I am *not* anyone's plaything." My anger came bubbling back to the surface and I glared at the man in front of me. "Who the hell are you?" I glowered at him with what I hoped passed for a contemptuous stare. "And what are you? Some kind of paramilitary bullshit group, out to play soldier in the jungle?" Anger always did give me false courage. The German Shepherd growled low in its throat. I took a deep breath and tried to calm down.

Rottweiler's expression hardened and he turned away, emitting a disgusted sigh. "I got no time for this shit," he said. "You guys do what you want with her. She's now *your* responsibility. Let's go, Aries." He walked up the path toward the clearing, the dog following him. "Don't forget the water," he growled over his shoulder.

From the frying pan into the fire.

Blondie shook his head. "Come on, then. Looks like you managed to get on *El Jefe's* bad side already." He turned to look at his friend. "That's a record, right?"

Ponytail shrugged. "Doesn't take much."

I stayed where I was. "You haven't answered me, and I'm not leaving until you do."

"You don't have to worry about us," Blondie said. "Think about it—we'd have already either killed you or bound, gagged and dragged you somewhere if we intended harm. You're a lot safer with us than alone."

Where have I heard that before?

He paused. "We have food."

At that moment, my stomach decided to make its presence known, growling loudly. Ponytail chuckled.

"Look," Blondie said, "you can take your chances out here by yourself. By the sound of it, you don't have much food with you, if any. And," he nodded at the ground next to me, "looks like you had a visitor."

I glanced where he indicated and noticed some fresh-looking feline scat that hadn't been there the night before. It was a hell of a lot bigger than any kitty turds I'd ever seen.

"Or," he continued, "you can come with us and have a meal, some protection from the elements, and our sterling companionship." He flashed a smile as he squatted beside the pool and filled his canteen. Ponytail did the same, then produced a plastic bladder and filled that, too.

"Then what?" It's not like they were going to keep me around long. Not in the jungle. I'd just be another mouth to feed. I still didn't have a read on these guys and what they were all about. DEA? CIA? Some kind of paramilitary group I hadn't heard of?

"We'll drop you off in Tabai. It won't be for a few days, though."

"Why is that?"

"Let's just say we can't sacrifice a vehicle or the manpower to be your escort service at the moment."

Ponytail added, "We're your best bet. Don't be afraid."

I wasn't afraid. Suspicious was more like it, but I let it slide. These guys weren't cartel members. Like the blond guy said, I'd be dead or on my way to Salazar by now. My gut told me to go along for the ride, but to stay alert and keep to myself.

"Fine," I said. "The sooner you can get me to Tabai, the better."

I took one last look at the grotto and followed them out through the vine-covered pathway, hoping my instincts were right this time.

8

WE TREKKED THROUGH THE JUNGLE, rarely stopping to rest. My lack of food became apparent—my energy level had plunged and I lagged behind. In stark contrast, the three men and the dog were hiking machines. I marveled at their ability to make time through the visually impenetrable jungle.

The ultra-sharp machetes might have helped.

No one said a word, except once when Ponytail offered me his hat with a, "Here." I accepted after he stripped off his t-shirt and wrapped it around his head, leaving him in a lightweight, long-sleeved tunic. Bare skin in the tropics was never a good idea, especially this time of year, with heatstroke a serious possibility. Grateful for the sun protection, I doubled my efforts at keeping up. I especially didn't want to give Rottweiler a reason to ditch me.

I pushed thoughts of Cole away by turning my attention to my surroundings, though if I wasn't careful my mind would slide back to the scene at the rest area where he'd been shot.

A couple of hours later, Rottweiler's left hand went up and we stopped. He cupped his hand to his ear and Aries sat back on his haunches.

I waited in silence, wondering what he was listening for. Evidently not hearing anything except for an occasional growl from my stomach, he raised his hand and motioned to move forward. Ponytail walked to my side, a black bandana in his hand.

"Sorry about this, but I'm going to have to blindfold you from here on out." He stepped behind me and looped the cloth over my eyes.

"Great. How am I supposed to walk?"

"I'll be right next to you." He finished tying the blindfold and I felt his hand on my elbow. "Just take it slow. It's pretty level terrain."

Ponytail tugged on my arm and I stumbled forward, hands out in case I tripped and took a header into the ground. Blindfolded in the middle of the jungle with a trio of commandos of unknown origins and a big German Shepherd didn't foster a serene frame of mind, to say the least. Definitely preferable to being Salazar's welcome mat, but still not what I'd call safe.

With my concentration focused for so long on remaining upright, I was surprised when Ponytail tightened his hold on my arm and stopped. He tugged on the bandana's knot at the back of my head and the blindfold dropped away. I blinked against the light.

We'd stopped just above a clearing bordered on all sides by thick jungle. Eight or ten tents with camouflaged netting over them had been constructed around a central area, along with a few traditional Maya structures similar to the ones dotting the landscape everywhere in the

Yucatán: vertical wooden stakes bound together with twine, topped by a thatched palm roof. Three groups of men dressed in fatigues sparred with each other on a cleared, level field several yards to our left. Three separate groups of rifles each formed a teepee. Another German Shepherd raced back and forth with the men, barking in excitement. Aries gave a short yelp and wagged his tail. The other dog stopped and turned its head toward us with an answering bark and wag. Aries glanced up at his owner, tongue out.

"Go ahead," Rottweiler said and waved him on. Aries bounded down the embankment toward the other dog.

It was midmorning, judging by the sun. Rottweiler continued down toward the camp and the three of us followed. The growling from my stomach had grown incessant and annoying as hell. Once inside the perimeter, Ponytail motioned for me to follow him to a screened-in tent near the center of the encampment. He swept the mesh door aside and I walked in with him close behind.

Six men sat eating together at a long metal table flanked by folding chairs in the center of the room. Situated at one end was a make-shift cooking area that consisted of a folding table with a couple of gas burners hooked to propane tanks. The burners supported the same number of stock pots. Activity ceased as I entered, forks suspended in mid-air. Ponytail emerged from behind me and the tension eased as they collectively went back to their meal.

"Looks like there's still some food left," Ponytail said, lifting a lid off one of the stock pots. The savory smell almost did me in and I leaned against the table to steady myself. He handed me a metal bowl and a spoon and then picked up a ladle and filled the dish with what looked like ranchero beans. Then he grabbed a handful of tortillas and lay them on top of my bowl, directing me to an unoccupied section of the table. He poured two steaming cups of coffee into canteen cups before sitting down to join me.

I dove headlong into my first real meal since the mini-breakfast at the hotel outside of San Diego, filling first one tortilla, then another with the most delicious beans I'd ever tasted. At least they were at that moment. I could have been eating cardboard covered in gravy and I'd have been ecstatic. Ponytail watched me with a bemused expression. I ignored him, shoveling it in as fast as I could swallow.

After cleaning the last drop of gravy from my bowl, I sat back and took in my surroundings. Now that my body didn't have to worry about starvation, my mind cleared and I realized I still had no idea where I was.

"Thank you for breakfast…I'm sorry, what's your name?" I asked Ponytail.

"Call me Pascal," he answered. "You're welcome."

"Is this some kind of pseudo-military enclave or something?"

Pascal remained quiet for a moment. "The only thing you need to know is that we're the good guys. Although—" He shifted in his chair. "We are not what you would call sanctioned."

"You mean no government oversight, right?"

Pascal watched me without answering.

I leaned closer, meeting his gaze. "So what is it that you so-called good guys do? That is, besides rescuing American women from the deep, dark jungle?"

He frowned. "Quinn will decide whether to tell you more."

"Quinn's the Rottweiler from earlier?"

"Good comparison." He sipped his coffee. "Yes, the Rottweiler."

"I assume that he's the head honcho, am I right?"

Pascal nodded. "He is our CO." He worked his jaw and his frown deepened. "This isn't a game, Beyoncè, or whoever you are. You need to stay out of sight until one of us can take you to Tabai."

"And when will that be?"

"I can't say. You must be patient."

"Sure." Patient. Yeah, that'd happen.

"Have you had enough?" he asked.

"Yes, thanks. I feel like a human being again."

"Good. I'll show you to your quarters."

Pascal rose to his feet and I followed suit. I put my bowl and spoon where he showed me, and refilled my coffee. We walked out of the mess tent and through the camp to one of the huts on the perimeter. He opened the door for me and we walked inside.

The structure had a dirt floor with a high, beamed ceiling that supported a thatched palm roof. A faded green hammock hung from a large beam at one end, with an area for cooking at the other. Three large stones sat on the floor with a kettle on top. A large plastic container stood in the corner with a plastic drinking cup on top of it. Despite the rising temperature outside, inside the structure remained cool and dark.

"This will be your hooch—sorry—your quarters until we can bring you to town. Water is over there," he indicated the plastic container in the corner. "And there's a latrine two rows that way," he said, pointing. His cheeks colored. "I'm sorry, there is only the one. There are no women here."

"This is more than enough, Pascal. Thank you. I should be fine."

He smiled and offered his hand. I pulled mine from my front pocket to shake his. When I did, the jaguar figurine fell out onto the dirt floor.

"Oh, I'd forgotten about this," I said, and stooped to pick it up.

"May I?" Pascal asked.

"Of course." I handed it to him and he held it up to the light, the same as I'd done the day before.

"*B'alam*," he said, his attention riveted on the carved stone. "Where did you find this?"

"Near the *cenote*. I came across it by accident. It's beautiful, isn't it?"

Pascal nodded, studying the figurine. "Jaguars have much power. The fact that one visited you last night is significant."

"I'd say it was scary as hell and one of the main reasons I agreed to come with you."

He shook his head. "There's no need to be afraid," he said, more to himself than to me. I didn't understand what he meant, but thought it prudent not to press him for an explanation. As he handed the carving back to me, his face reverted to his closed look, as though a curtain dropped behind his eyes.

"You're welcome to move around, but stay in camp," he instructed. "Chow is at twelve and eighteen hundred. Quinn will probably stop by to speak to you before nightfall."

Oh, joy. I wasn't looking forward to having a conversation with Rottweiler. My feelings must have been obvious, because Pascal continued.

"He's not as bad as you think. If it wasn't for him—" He stopped. "If he chooses, he will tell you. Let me know if you need anything. My hooch is the next hut over."

"Thank you, Pascal. I appreciate your help."

With that, he walked out the door.

I tucked the jaguar back into my pocket and looked around the hut, trying to ignore the feelings that came flooding back now that I was alone with my thoughts. The place was cool and shady, and the hammock would keep me off the jungle floor and away from big, scary felines. And Salazar.

For now.

What more could I ask for?

9

THE MEETING WITH QUINN DIDN'T happen.

With nothing else to do I went for a walk around the compound, trying to get a handle on what these guys did. A few minutes into the walk some type of signal I didn't catch triggered a frenzied response in camp, ratcheting activity to just shy of Def-Con One. Men in jungle fatigues with weapons across their backs raced past me toward the center of the encampment. I followed them to where a small gathering had formed. Pent-up adrenaline and excitement surged through the crowd. Different languages vied for dominance, with English and Spanish in the majority. I remained in back at the edges of the group, trying to catch snippets of conversation without being noticed.

Quinn stood at the front consulting a document, both shepherds at his side. The men joining the group slowed to a trickle and conversation quieted. I found myself riveted like everyone else. Blondie leaned in to say something to Quinn who glanced up and surveyed the crowd.

Evidently satisfied, Quinn folded the paper and stuck it in his front pocket, then faced the group.

"Listen up. We've just received confirmation on the whereabouts of a certain high-ranking member of Area Seven." The murmurs increased and Quinn held his hand up. The talking abruptly ceased. "We'll head out at zero-three."

More murmuring broke out as the men turned to each other to discuss the new development. Blondie put his fingers to his lips and blew, the shrill whistle slicing through the compound. Everyone quieted. Quinn continued.

"We've been handed an opportunity we can't miss." He scanned the crowd, his gaze flickering over each member. He appeared to look straight through me, then moved on. "This is what we've been training for. All the blood and sweat, the sacrifices, come together tonight. We pull this off and we'll have taken a big, bloody bite out of the beast."

Murmurs of anticipation rippled through the crowd. I spotted Pascal standing in the back a few feet from me, and I walked over to him.

"Area Seven? Bloody beasts? Seriously, Pascal, you need to let me in on this. What the hell are you guys up to?"

"I take it you didn't meet with Quinn." he said. When I shook my head no, he took me aside, out of earshot of the other men. "We're here to help make the area safe. That's all I can tell you."

"This have anything to do with a drug cartel?"

Pascal shrugged and looked away, the curtain closing over his eyes again.

"Are you affiliated with the Mexican army?" I assumed not, since I hadn't been handed back to Salazar.

Pascal looked at me like I was crazy. "No."

"DEA?"

Pascal squinted into the lowering sun. "Not officially, no."

"Unofficially, then?"

"Sort of." He turned to me, his expression serious. "Look. I've told you all I can. More than I should have. If he thinks it's necessary, Quinn will brief you on the rest." He started to leave and I grabbed him by the elbow.

"Wait a minute. Remember how pissed off I got when Quinn said he thought I was one of the cartel's unhappy playthings?"

"Yes, of course."

"Well, I used to be." I exhaled and steeled my courage, unaccustomed to copping to my past so quickly. Least of all to a complete stranger. "I testified against Roberto Salazar ten years ago. My testimony helped put him in prison."

Pascal frowned. "Then why are you in Mexico? I'd think you'd want to be as far away from them as you could get."

"Salazar had other plans." An idea occurred to me and I asked, "Was it your group who attacked Salazar's compound yesterday?"

He cocked his head to the side. "Salazar? Don't you mean Morales?"

"I don't know who Morales is, but I was being held captive at Salazar's hacienda. At least, I thought it was his. I escaped when they came under attack."

"*Salazar's* hacienda—" Pascal grabbed my arm and pulled me behind him through the crowd. "You need to talk to Quinn."

We reached him just as he was handing out what looked like topography maps to a group of fatigue-clad men.

"Quinn. You need to hear this."

When he looked up and realized I was with Pascal, his expression morphed from alert to guarded. He folded his arms across his chest and leaned back, clearly unhappy with the interruption.

"This better be good, Pascal. What does Miss *Beyoncé* have to tell us?"

"She says she was a prisoner at *Salazar's* hacienda yesterday."

Quinn's demeanor changed from annoyance to cautious interest. "Roberto Salazar?"

Pascal nodded.

He scoffed and turned away. "Salazar's out of Sonora. I've got no intel on his being anywhere near here," he said over his shoulder.

I walked in front of him, matching his crossed arms with my own. "Well, you'd best believe it, because he's here."

Quinn frowned and glanced at Pascal. "You believe her?"

"Ask her some questions. She says the place where he held her came under attack yesterday. Thought it might have been us." Pascal and Quinn exchanged a look I couldn't read.

Quinn turned to me. "All right. How do you know Salazar?"

"Like I told Pascal, I testified against him over ten years ago and helped send him to prison. He's been trying to kill me ever since." I didn't think I needed to get into the fact that I stole his money. Not my most shining moment.

"The timeline works," Pascal said. "Didn't the DEA mention an American woman helped convict him?"

Quinn nodded, his eyes boring into mine. "Yeah. According to them, she's living somewhere in the States."

"I live in the States," I said.

"It's a big place. How'd they find you?"

"I don't know. I changed my location several times. I went as far north as Alaska, then south to Hawaii, and have been living the past five years in a tiny town in Northern Arizona. I changed my name, my hair, and I distanced myself from my family. Somehow they tracked me."

Quinn's expression said he didn't believe me. "You changed your name to Beyoncé?"

I rolled my eyes in frustration. "My name doesn't matter. Although, if you must know, most folks call me Kate. Look. I already told you something you didn't know. Salazar's here in the Yucatán, and he's obviously involved in some kind of conflict with what I can only assume is a local cartel who's pissed off at his being here. That alone should be helpful to you, right? I mean, why is he here, other than doing the legwork for *El Castillo*?"

"There have been no reports of *El Castillo* operating in this region." Quinn checked his watch. "We've got time to check her story before we head out," he said to Pascal. Then he nodded my way. "You, come with me and I'll decide if what you're saying changes the plan. One of our guys is ex-*El Castillo* who knows Salazar very well. He'll be able to verify if you're the real deal."

10

I FOLLOWED QUINN TO HIS quarters. The place looked like it had been decorated by Spartans R Us: a rusty metal bunk squatted against the right side of the tent, its sheet stretched tight across the top and tucked under the mattress with precision. Try bouncing a quarter off of that and it'd end up embedded in the roof.

A lantern sat on top of a plastic soft-drink rack that had been tipped on end and used as a bedside table. A rip-stop duffel bag with a red circle and the numbers 1-7 stenciled on the bottom lay near the foot of the bed. The only other objects in the room were an old plastic card table and three chairs.

And a wooden crate filled with guns.

Blondie sat on one of the chairs next to the table, cleaning machine gun parts. The two dogs lay on the floor next to him. He looked up when we entered and flashed a smile.

"Well, if it isn't *Beyoncé*." He laughed when I grimaced. "Well, then what's your real name so I can give you a proper moniker?" He set the piece he was cleaning on the table and picked up another. "Everyone here gets one."

"Kate."

Blondie thought for a moment, then said, "Yucatán Kate it is."

It had a ring to it. "What's yours?" I asked.

"One Shot."

"I'm not going to ask you why."

He chuckled. "That's probably wise."

Quinn moved over to the table and pulled out a chair, motioning for me to sit, which I did. The tent flap opened and a dark-haired man I estimated to be in his early thirties walked in.

"Have a seat, Lalo."

Lalo nodded and sat in the remaining chair, his eyes steady on me. He wore the requisite camouflage cargo pants, but sported a black t-shirt with a picture of Bob Marley on the front instead of jungle green. Uneasy under his intense scrutiny, I stared back at him, hoping he'd turn his attention elsewhere. He did.

"Lalo, I asked you here to listen to this woman's story and tell me if what she describes is true." Quinn turned to me. "Lalo was a trusted member of *El Castillo*, the cartel formed in Sonora and run by Leonardo Diaz. That is, until he sided with us." Quinn gave him a nod. Lalo lifted his chin in acknowledgement and turned his gaze to me. The machismo oozed from his pores, and I caught myself wondering what happened to make him switch teams in the middle of the game.

Quinn continued. "You already know that *El Castillo* absorbed Roberto Salazar's operation while he did time in prison."

I nodded.

"What you may not know is that Diaz made a play for two of the smaller cartels operating in Sonora and succeeded. He's consolidating his power base and has become a major player in northern Mexico." He watched me intently. "If what you've told me about Salazar being here is true, that means Diaz is branching out and we can expect a lot more activity."

Lalo's gaze barely wavered but I noticed a flicker of something resembling fear cross his face. It was quickly replaced by a confident stare. His reaction was a familiar one, and I could only guess why he left *El Castillo*. Cartels didn't think twice about eliminating weak links. For whatever reason, Lalo had most likely been branded as such and decided his best bet for survival was to join up with the pseudo-militia group Quinn had created.

Whatever that might be.

Quinn waved his hand toward me. "You have the floor, Kate."

I cleared my throat and looked Lalo in the eye. He returned the favor. "I lived with Roberto Salazar for three long years." Surprise rode his face, but only for a moment before the blank stare returned. "Without going into too much detail, I escaped. To get out of Mexico safely, I cooperated with the DEA and your government, testifying against both Salazar and another man. Many people died before that happened."

I took a deep breath. The memories weren't easy, even after this long.

"Salazar's been trying to kill me since then. In fact, I was his guest yesterday morning at a hacienda a little less than two days' walk from here."

"How is it that you are here now?" Lalo asked, the disinterested look gone.

"Someone attacked with firearms and explosives and I escaped in the resulting chaos." I glanced at Blondie and Quinn. "Evidently, it wasn't your operation. I have to conclude a rival cartel attacked, trying to stop them."

"So the rumors are true." Lalo shook his head. "I never believed a woman would be able to do what they say you did. Your betrayal made Salazar look weak. He is not one to forgive easily." He looked at me with renewed interest. "Tell me about Salazar's mother. She is someone he listens to, yes?"

"As I'm sure you already know, Roberto Salazar's mother is long dead. He wouldn't listen to anyone, especially not a mere woman—another reason I left." A minor infraction in my long list of reasons for having escaped. In any normal relationship it would have been enough for me to bail.

Lalo nodded, apparently satisfied. "What is the name of his family's yacht?"

"*El Beso de la Vida*," I answered. During my time with Salazar, the infrequent vacations on the ninety-foot cruiser were some of the happiest. Probably because I was still blind to his true nature and hadn't tumbled to the fact that he was a psychotic asshole.

Naiveté had its good points.

"She's got everything right," Lalo said to Quinn. "Should I ask more?"

"Something personal," Quinn prompted.

Lalo sat for a moment, frowning in concentration. Then he said, "What is his favorite meal?"

Without hesitation I answered, "Kraft Macaroni and Cheese with habañero sauce."

Blondie grinned. "Seriously? The stuff in the box?"

"This is *verdad*," Lalo said, nodding at Quinn.

"I always knew when he had a bad day. He'd have the cook make a huge pot and it would be gone by morning." We all had learned to lay low on those evenings. He usually finished a bottle of tequila along with the mac and cheese and then took out his favorite weapon and shot anything that moved.

"Thanks Lalo. You've been a big help." Quinn walked him out of the tent, murmuring something I couldn't make out. Blondie stopped cleaning and cocked his head to the side.

"So you spent a lot of time with Roberto Salazar."

"Yes. An unfortunate life choice."

"I'll bet. Well, it's good information you've given us today, Kate. It could've been a real shit storm out there not knowing what we were walking into." He picked up the barrel assembly for the gun on the table in front of him and inspected it. "Looks like we'll have to pull back and regroup."

Quinn walked back inside the tent, carrying a rolled-up paper under his arm. "I'm postponing the operation until we get a handle on this."

Blondie nodded, screwing the last component of the gun together. "Right you are, chief." He rose from his chair and headed for the door. "You want me to give them an explanation, or just tell 'em it's been canked due to unforeseen circumstances?"

"Unforeseen circumstances. I'll brief everybody when I have more information." He turned to me. "Think you can find that hacienda on a one-over-fifty map?"

"I'll try." I watched Blondie leave. "If everyone here has a nickname, what's yours?" I asked.

"The men call me Q."

Surprised, I resisted the urge to ask him why not Duke or Killer or some other butch dog name. It was probably best to try and stay on his good side, if he had one. "So what's Lalo's story? How do you know you can trust him?" I asked.

"I just do." Quinn moved over to the table and unrolled the paper, which turned out to be a topographical map of the surrounding jungle. He pointed to a section marked with a small green dot. "We're here." He moved his finger to the left and stopped. "We found you at the *cenote*, here."

I glanced at the map and traced a path with my finger, heading west with a bit of an angle, hoping I came close to the direction I'd traveled. "I can't be sure how far I walked, but I started out early in the morning and didn't stop until late afternoon. Say, eight to ten hours. I also can't be sure I moved in a straight line. I moved east and angled toward where I thought there might be a road, but had to detour around a few obstacles."

"Did you come across any lakes?"

"No."

"Good thing. A lot of the lakes around here are home to *Crocodylus moreletii*—Morelet's crocodile. They're not partial to humans. Although, it would give us a better idea which hacienda you're talking about. There are three within that distance."

"Do you have an aerial photograph of the area? I might be able to recognize more that way."

Quinn walked over to his bunk and squatted next to it, pulling out a hard black plastic case from underneath. He brought it over to the table and flipped open the two latches, revealing what looked like a laptop on steroids. I waited as he opened the cover and booted up.

"Satellite?"

Quinn nodded, watching the screen come to life. He entered a password, then clicked on an icon and punched in some coordinates. The picture zoomed into focus and we were looking at an aerial view of the camp.

"Can you zoom out in increments?"

He depressed a key and the picture expanded to the surrounding area. He repositioned the area of focus and pointed to a heavily-treed area with small pockets of open space.

"That's where we found you."

I leaned in and looked closely at the terrain, taking in the obvious shape of the ruins. "May I?" I asked, reaching for the keyboard. He pushed it toward me and I expanded the view further. Finally, things began to look familiar. I moved west a little further and came across a fuzzy area. Everything around it was in sharp focus. I pointed at the screen. "That's where it should be."

Quinn took over the keyboard and changed the view, zooming in and out, trying to find something tangible, but it didn't work.

"I'm sure that's it. I wouldn't have been able to cover more ground than that."

"I know the ranch, but was under the impression the place has been run for generations by a family with roots in Spain. Whoever owns the place paid to have it scrubbed from the satellite photos."

"Wouldn't that take a lot of money?"

Quinn nodded. "Or influence."

He jotted down the coordinates and pushed a piece of graph paper toward me.

"Draw an aerial view of the hacienda. Include everything you can remember. Tell me what you know of the terrain and buildings."

I took the pencil he held out and did a rough sketch from memory.

"They kept me in a locked cement building here." I pointed at my rendition of the concrete bunker where Salazar's thugs had put me. "It had been used as some kind of living quarters, although not for a long time. The main drive leads to the entrance, fronted by several stairs. My guard used a radio to call Salazar and let him know we were there."

"What did the radio look like?"

"Pretty serious. Not a hand-held, if that's what you're asking. Similar to a police radio."

Quinn nodded his head. "Did you see a computer?"

"Yes, although I'm not sure what brand. The entry opened on both sides and led to a landscaped inner courtyard."

"Go on."

"Once the guard received the go ahead, we walked down the stairs and turned right. We then followed a sidewalk several yards to what I assumed was his office." I indicated my drawing of the attached building where I'd met with Salazar and the others.

"Salazar's guard let us inside. A desk with a laptop and phone sat in front of a wall of books." I felt the anger boil to the surface as memories of Salazar, Angie, and Sterling replayed in my head. Too bad the other cartel hadn't gotten the right building when they attacked the place.

"When the guards took me back to the first building, all hell broke loose and they locked me inside a run-down shed before running back to assist." I tapped my finger on the drawing. "Luckily, the place had been built out of wood and part of the wall had rotted. I broke through and escaped."

"Did you notice any cameras or other surveillance equipment?"

"Pretty much everywhere."

"Show me on the map. What did they look like?"

I drew little Xs where I'd seen cameras, describing them as I did. "Are you planning to hit the hacienda?"

Silence.

"Are you going after Morales, too?"

Silence. Again. He sat in his chair and fixed me with a stare.

Frustrated, I stood up from the table. "When can I get a ride into town?" I asked.

"I'll have my guys check into your information, ASAP. In the meantime, you'll have to stay here. I can't allow anyone to leave now that it's possible *El Castillo* is making a play for the area. I need everyone here."

I started to protest, but then thought better of it. The look on my face must have given something away because his expression hardened, summoning the Rottweiler.

"Looks like you're going to have to suck it up and wait until we've dealt with this new development. Sorry."

He wasn't sorry in the least. My anger spiked. I fought to keep my mouth shut.

I lost.

"Would you just tell me what you guys do? Look, I've been cooperative with you. Don't you think the least you could do is let me in on what you're all about? I deserve to know what I'm dealing with."

Quinn put the computer back in the case and closed the latches with a grunt. "I'll tell you one thing: all of these men are committed to eliminating the cartels operating in this country and freeing the oppressed."

"Isn't the Mexican government also committed to that?"

He snorted. "Some are, some aren't. We're the next line of defense. Where the government's hands are tied or, shall we say, *ineffective*, we come in and do the job."

"Does the government know about your group?"

"We try to keep a low profile. Corruption is the norm. Officially, they've sanctioned the groups they have some control over. We operate outside of that control. The DEA, ICE, CIA and the rest of the alphabet soup guys are the same. They tend to disagree with our tactics."

I wasn't about to ask him which ones they used. I'd had far too much experience with unofficial tactics. Enough to last a lifetime.

"How long have you—"

"Q&A is over." Quinn rested his hand on the back of my chair, indicating an end to our conversation.

As fast as the fuse of my anger had lit, it sputtered out. I got up and walked toward the door. When I was about to step outside, I turned back.

"I'd like to help you."

Quinn squinted at me, frowning. "You what?"

"I said I'd like to help you."

Quinn's laugh sounded like a bark. Rottweiler strikes again.

"What would I do with a woman who has no combat experience? Let you tuck my guys in at night? Or maybe read them a story?" He shook his head in disbelief as he walked over to the bed and slid the computer back in place.

"I lived with Salazar for three years. I can identify several of his current associates. I know things I don't even know I know. Ask me questions. Pick my brain."

Quinn continued to ignore me and I continued to press my case.

"Come on, Quinn. I can be of use to you. I know it."

He stopped and looked at me. "Assuming that you have more than what you just gave me and I can use what you know, what's in it for you?"

"He's responsible for a lot of bad things, and not only in my life." I hesitated, not sure I could trust my voice. "I want to stop running, to stop being afraid. But more than that, I want him and his people to pay."

11

THE NEXT DAY, QUINN CALLED several of his men together and began to formulate a plan of attack on the rival cartel's compound. While discussing the operation, a guy I hadn't noticed before walked to the front of the group and leaned over to talk to him privately. Quinn's eyes flicked to me and then back to the new guy. He nodded and the new guy joined the other men. Quinn cleared his throat, getting everyone's attention.

"Ramirez just informed me that a local hacienda, most recently host to a certain Roberto Salazar and several of his soldiers, has been hit. We think it was most likely the Morales crew."

Nice to know my story had been verified. Quinn gave me a quick, almost imperceptible nod.

"In addition," he continued, "Salazar and company are believed to have repelled the attack." Several groans broke out among the men, but Quinn held his hand up and everyone fell silent.

"They're regrouping, probably to counterattack. We're not sure if he's called in Diaz for reinforcements. My guess is he hasn't yet. That would be the same as saying he wasn't up to the task and Diaz would cut him loose without a thought now that he's got Salazar's men under his thumb." Quinn paced, his expression taut. "Shit's heating up, gentlemen. We're going to have to push our timeline to the right or this could turn into an all-out bloodbath the proportions of which will be difficult to contain."

"Why not let the bastards kill each other off?" a tall guy with a tattoo on his arm of a skull with flames shooting through its eyes said. "I mean, hell, let 'em at each other, right?"

"Yes, and that has worked so well throughout Mexico," Pascal answered, his eyebrow raised. A couple of the men chuckled.

Quinn shook his head. "We can't sit back and do nothing. Once word gets out, other cartels will head this way like vultures and try to pick off the weaker players. We've got to hit 'em now and smoke these ass wipes, then keep picking off any new ones that show up."

"How do you want to do this?" Blondie asked.

"First, we monitor Salazar's movements. When an attack on Morales' compound appears imminent, we go in, out-flank both groups, and waste as many as we can."

"Isn't that what I said?" Skull Boy asked.

"No, it isn't. You suggested they kill each other without interference from us. That could take longer than necessary, not to mention the possibility of opening up a merger between them. What I'm suggesting is we give them a little help. Hasten the process, if you will." Quinn leaned back. "The floor is open."

"What happens when they figure out there's another group helping the process along?" a dark-haired man to Quinn's left asked. "Wouldn't that give them a reason to join forces, at least until the threat is neutralized?"

"That's why we leave a calling card pointing to Salazar and *El Castillo*," Quinn replied. "Assuming there are key survivors on Morales' side, as long as they believe the attack came from Salazar it shouldn't be a problem." Quinn looked around the group. "So put on your thinking caps, boys and girls, because we need something specific to Salazar that's immediately recognizable. Say, a tactic he's known for using, a type of weapon or explosives…a Salazar signature."

Ideas were thrown out and discussed, then either discarded or written down to come back to later. I remained silent, preferring to watch and listen. The group obviously harbored a lot of respect for Quinn and he appeared to return the sentiment. It was the closest thing I'd seen to a democracy; everyone had an equal voice, an equal opportunity to persuade the others that their idea had merit. Quinn was a natural leader and I found my respect for him growing.

After extensive back and forth discussion and having exhausted as many worst-case scenarios as everybody in the group could dream up, Quinn turned his attention to me. "Kate, you know Salazar as well as anyone here. Probably better. I want to hear from you. How can we make sure there's no question he's responsible for the hit?"

"Actually, I do have an idea." The group parted to give me room and I walked to the front. "Back in the day, when Salazar was the big dog and consolidating his power in Sonora, he made all of his soldiers get the same tattoo on the left side of their neck so that when they were in a fight or under attack, they'd be easily recognizable. He had a template designed to look the same on everyone: a coiled rattlesnake eating a scorpion."

Lalo's eyes lit up. "I have seen the tattoo. He still requires the men under his command to do this."

"That way, once they see the tattoos Morales' men will think your men are Salazar's, and Salazar's men will hesitate to shoot, giving your men a measure of safety."

The energy of the group changed palpably as Quinn nodded his approval. "Think you can replicate it?" All eyes were on me. I nodded.

"I'll do my best, although my graphic skills aren't great." I remembered thinking I'd seen that same tattoo years earlier when I ran to the North Shore of Oahu, and it shook me to the core. If seeing it could still affect me that much, I figured others who were familiar with the design would know it right away. I'd committed the drawing to memory back then, aware that someday I'd escape Salazar's hold and recognition might save my life. It wouldn't be hard to fake the pattern. As long as the snake was viewed from a distance or during the chaos of combat, no one would be able to tell the difference.

"What do you need from me?" Quinn asked.

"Practice paper and some markers."

Several hours later, the men who would be involved in the operation were sporting brand new rattlesnake/scorpion 'tattoos'. Skull Boy had experience with tattooing and suggested I combine dark blue and green to make the ink appear more realistic. I agreed and asked him to work on the men with me. The first two I did turned out a little shaky compared to his, but by the time I'd done a few more the realism had improved to the point that no one could tell the difference between it and an actual tattoo unless they were up close and personal.

As the evening drew to a close, the stress of dealing with everything that had happened over the course of the last few days, not to mention the long, hot march through the jungle, had me wiped out and needing sleep. Most everyone else had turned in. The next twenty-four hours would dictate when Operation Demolition Man would be a go.

As I walked through the camp, the faint glow from interior lamps shone through cracks in the walls of the men's quarters, exuding a deceptive calm. The way the place looked along with Quinn's apparent military background, I figured breaking down camp would take very little time. They'd be on the move before either of the cartels could get to them, if it came to that.

The route to my hut ran past Quinn's tent and I glanced inside the open flap, my curiosity about him piqued. What was his story? Why did he decide to fight here in the Yucatán on the outer banks of legitimacy, waging a probably endless war against an incredibly adaptable and amoral foe?

I understood Quinn's frustration at the ineffectiveness of the attempts at stopping the cartels. Experience told me working outside the parameters of sanctioned government entities was probably the only tactic left that held any chance of eliminating the cartels. Like the DEA, the Mexican military and other groups fighting them were hamstrung by public opinion and laws, not to mention having to deal with endemic corruption within the Mexican government. I wondered what had driven Quinn to adopt the life of a mercenary. I also wondered where his funding came from.

No one occupied the tent. I continued along the path, looking up at the velvety night sky sprinkled with sharply-lit stars.

His tongue hanging out, Aries came running toward me to give me the sniff test. The other one joined him and soon I was acting as the resident petting machine.

"Aries, Artemis. Come."

The dogs turned in unison at the voice. Startled, I glanced up to see Quinn watching me from a couple of yards away, arms crossed, partially obscured by shadow. With a soulful glance at me, the two shepherds bounded back to their master. Quinn reached down and scratched them behind their ears. Then he straightened and leveled his gaze at me.

"You did good, Kate."

I exhaled, relaxing my shoulders. "Glad I could contribute."

Even in the darkness, his eyes held an intensity that would make a lesser woman swoon. Swooning's not really my thing, but if it was, I'd definitely have done it. I stood my ground as he came to a stop inches from me. Not much taller than I was, his center of gravity and muscularity exuded a masculine electrical force that came close to sucking me into his orbit.

I shook off the effect and took a step back. Unbidden, memories of Cole flowed through my mind like a breached dam and I had to blink back the sudden well of emotion. I cleared my throat and tried to smile.

"Beautiful night, isn't it?" I said, leaning my head back to look at the stars.

He didn't reply for a moment. Lowering my gaze, I watched him, deciding to give as good as I got. We stood like that for a few beats before he broke the stare-down. I drew a quiet sigh of relief.

"How did you end up as Salazar's woman?" he asked, totally out of the blue. I'd been right in my assessment—Quinn was a what-you-see-is-what-you-get kind of guy. No small talk, no B.S. It was refreshing.

And unnerving.

I shrugged. "Stupid, naïve college girl meets dashing Latino man who knows how to show her a good time. Stupid Girl doesn't figure out Dashing Latino is the head of a drug cartel until it's much, much too late." No B.S. Just his kind of explanation.

Quinn appeared to think about that for a moment. Then he asked, "How did Stupid Girl escape from Dashing Latino?"

I thought back to the night my life changed forever, and not in a fairy-godmother-grants-a-wish kind of way. "I watched Salazar slit the throat of one of his best friends for a minor infraction and realized it could happen to me." I frowned, trying to remember the reason, but gave up. Salazar exhibited a lot of bizarre personality changes in those last few months, not the least of which included severe paranoia. If I hadn't known better at the time I'd have thought he'd been sampling too much of his own product, à la *Scarface*. "I think the pressure got to him."

A brief silence followed before Quinn guffawed. It took me a second to realize what I'd said that had been so funny.

"No shit, right?" I said, joining him.

"Talk about an understatement," he said, wiping his eyes.

The laughter broke through the tension I'd been holding onto all day and I finally felt myself relax. By the looks of it, it did the same for Quinn.

"You need to understand something about Salazar, and I don't think it's changed in the ten years since I was with him," I said.

Quinn looked at me expectantly.

"He may be working under the wing of *El Castillo,* but his true loyalties are with Vincent Anaya."

The smile left his face, replaced by a look of acute interest. "I heard Anaya got out of the business, sold off the assets and connections to some billionaire in the U.S. for big bucks. Why would Salazar want to align himself with someone who hasn't got a dog in the drug trafficking race?"

"Because Anaya continues to have his hands in massive amounts of illegal shit and is making a lot of money doing it. The reason Salazar ordered me brought to him and not immediately killed is because he and Anaya had cooked up a hellacious way for me to pay back—" I hesitated, not wanting to let on about the money. "To pay him back for testifying against them."

When Quinn gave me a look that said he needed more of an explanation, I added, "It sounds like they're concentrating on human trafficking." The reality of what I'd escaped slowly seeped back and settled in my brain. *Why the hell am I not a million miles away from here?*

I was just beginning to understand the answer to that question.

12

THE NEXT EVENING, QUINN, BLONDIE, Pascal and I sat in the mess tent, enjoying a cup of coffee and a few moments of peace before the men showed up for dinner. The conversation revolved around the most recent report on Salazar and Morales from one of Quinn's reconnaissance guys.

"Initial observation of Morales' compound showed no sign of Morales and his defense appeared light, especially for anticipating an attack from Salazar." Quinn shot a glance at Blondie. "You want to take care of locating him and finding out why?"

Blondie nodded. "Roger that, Q."

Quinn continued. "I've got eyes on Salazar at the hacienda. The evidence points to him making his move against Morales' compound soon. I'm betting in the morning, by the looks of it. I'd welcome anything you might remember about his tactics, Kate, how he thinks, what his weaknesses might be."

Blondie gave me a hearty slap on the back and I almost spewed my coffee onto the table.

"Good on ya, Yucatán Kate." He pulled on the neck of his shirt and pointed at the fake tattoo. "This'll give 'em something to think about, I guarantee."

"Absolutely. Well done," Quinn agreed. "I'm counting on the element of surprise along with the tats to provide just enough confusion at the outset of our attack to give us a tactical advantage with Salazar's men. Initially, they'll shy away from shooting soldiers with the same markings as they have."

Shy would not be a word I'd use to describe any of Salazar's men. I'd had time to think through Quinn's plan, and as the rest of the group discussed the finer points of mounting an assault on Morales' location, warning bells were going off in my head. On paper it looked good, but I knew Salazar. He wasn't one to blunder into a trap. During my last few months with him his paranoia had become severe enough that he'd had spies stationed everywhere. He wouldn't take a crap without someone checking the toilet to make sure it hadn't been wired with explosives. I doubted he'd changed much in the intervening years.

"I'm sure I don't have to tell you Salazar is hyper-paranoid," I said. "He'll have sent someone ahead to check out Morales' place before going in. He's anal retentive to the extreme and will perfect a plan before implementation. And when I say perfect a plan, I mean go over and over and over the thing until there's nothing to chance. I'd be extremely careful when dealing with him. He rarely makes mistakes with tactical operations." I didn't know if these guys understood what they'd be up against. A local cartel boss was one thing. Salazar was something else, entirely.

Quinn gave me a look that said I hadn't told him anything new and he was way ahead of me. "I'm aware Salazar's paranoid. I plan on using that to our advantage. His paranoia will give him a reason to bring more people to the party. That way we can take out a greater number of his men."

I decided to try a different tactic. "Okay. Let's say you succeed with this 'grand cleansing' of the two competing groups. What's to stop another, more powerful cartel from stepping in and making things even worse like you mentioned last night? It'll create a vacuum." I watched Quinn for a reaction. His face remained impassive. "Getting rid of Salazar and Morales' bases is a start, certainly. But once they're exterminated, a worse infestation will likely occur." The guys remained silent while I walked through my reasoning aloud. "I guess what I'm asking is, where does it all lead? To me it looks like a never-ending, blood-soaked conflict with casualties on both sides."

"And that's the same conclusion the Mexican government has come to. They take dollars and manpower away from fighting the cartels, allowing them to grow unchecked." Quinn leaned forward, his face a study in resolve. "The only way to eliminate the cartels is to continue to track them down and destroy their assets. That includes soldiers."

"But they'll multiply like termites and there are only so many of your guys. What happens when you lose?" I crossed my arms. "I guarantee you're going to sustain casualties if you haven't already, at least a percentage of the time. These guys aren't just ignorant thugs, although they certainly employ them. Organizations like *El Castillo* are becoming more and more sophisticated with each iteration because of the insane amount of money involved. They'll out-man you, out-gun you, and out-think you."

All three men watched me without saying anything. I shifted in my seat and looked away. Quinn cleared his throat.

"Are you finished?"

I nodded my head. "I think so."

"Good." He rose from his chair. "I understand your views on cartel violence in Mexico. I get it, Kate. You're playing devil's advocate and I can appreciate that. I also understand where you're coming from. For whatever reason, you feel a responsibility to my men and you want to make sure they don't go into this without looking at all the issues. For that, I'm grateful. But," he continued, "you have to realize we've been on the front lines for a while now and we've found that the only—I say again, only—way to eradicate this problem is to fight them on their level."

"I don't agree."

Quinn shrugged. "Then we'll have to agree to disagree. The minute you come to me with a detailed, logical plan of how to stop these guys without doing what we're doing and it passes the sniff test, then I'm all ears. Until then, you're welcome to offer ideas or solutions to what we're planning."

"Fine. Point taken." My fight mode kicked into flight and I was ready to get the hell out of this turkey shoot now, before I watched Quinn and his men get massacred. How could one group led by one man make any difference to the proliferation of cartels in this country? It seemed destined to fail. The more I thought about it, the more I realized Quinn's group would be damned lucky if they returned from this mission without casualties. I needed to leave, now. "When do I get my ride to Tabai?"

"I'll have one of my guys take you tomorrow evening."

"Thanks." I grabbed my coffee and got up to leave. Pascal and Quinn exchanged glances, which I ignored as I walked out. Pascal followed me.

"Wait." He matched my pace.

I kept walking, but slowed.

"Don't leave like that, Kate. This is his baby, his operation. Quinn came to the Yucatán three years ago and built this group into what it is today. He trained every one of us the way he thought counter-cartel operatives should be trained." He touched my arm and I stopped. "He's been effective. In the States, how often do you hear about cartel activity in this area of Mexico?"

"Less than Sonora or Sinaloa."

"It's because of him. Because of us."

I stood with my arms crossed and considered what he'd said. Like most of Quinn's men, Pascal appeared to be a straight-shooter without a hidden agenda. I could feel myself being pulled into wanting to support their cause, wanting to be a part of something larger than myself. To fight the bastards on my terms and not continue to run. But my usual response was to get far away from this kind of trouble. I didn't have the strength to fight it any more than I had the strength to fight my grief from losing Cole.

"Look, Pascal. I appreciate what he's trying to do and I wish you guys all the best. But I'm tired of being on the losing end of things. I'm going to disappear again, and hopefully this time I'll be able to cobble together some semblance of a life. Yes, I know I will always be on the run and looking over my shoulder. And yes, it's going to be lonely, but at least I'll be alive."

Pascal cocked his head to the side. "That's not living, Kate."

Where have I heard that before?

Time to change the subject. I took a sip of my coffee and studied his hawk-like nose, strong jaw and forehead, full lips. "Your face reminds me of the carvings I saw in Chichen Itza depicting great Maya warriors."

He smiled. "I am Maya."

We continued to walk through the compound, his soothing voice a balm to my anxiety.

"I serve as both medic and soldier here," he went on. "My ancestors settled this land many centuries ago. Some of them were shamans, handing down knowledge of the jungle spirits and medicine. Others were of the warrior class, even the women."

My face must have shown my surprise because he continued. "Historically, Maya revered women for all abilities. Some were warriors, some priestesses. Many were healers." He glanced inside one of the tents at a small group of men playing cards. "Many of the men in this country have a different view of women. Not as good, I think."

"But it's slowly changing, wouldn't you agree?"

He shrugged. "A little, I suppose."

"Do you know a lot about the old ways? A Maya man I met years ago told me that he was teaching his children and grandchildren the old beliefs in the hope that they would live on."

"Yes. My father was a shaman and he taught all of his children how to communicate with the spirit world."

Abruptly, I stopped and turned to face him. "Which means you know how to talk to them?" My heart beat faster. Maybe he'd be able to intercede with the ever-present bad spirits the old man had warned me about so many years ago. "I've been told I have a couple of bad ones who've decided to stick around."

Pascal studied me for a moment without answering. Then he closed his eyes and inhaled deeply, growing quiet. His nostrils flared and he grew deathly still. He opened his eyes and stared through me.

He remained like that for a few minutes. Alarmed, I touched his shoulder, wondering if he was having some kind of seizure.

"Pascal?" I said his name in a low voice, hoping he'd snap out of whatever state he was in before I enlisted the help of the men playing cards in the tent we'd just passed. I leaned closer to see if he was still breathing and waved my hand in front of his face. Nothing.

Finally, he drew in a breath and blinked. I stepped back, relieved. His gaze returned to normal and he shrugged his shoulders and cracked his neck from side to side.

"What the hell was that?" I asked.

"You wanted to know if I could communicate with the spirits, right?"

"Well, yeah, but not if you're going to go all comatose on my ass. Jesus, Pascal. Where did you go?"

"I am not allowed to tell this to curious *gringas*." He grinned at me, and my annoyance factor skyrocketed.

"Fine. Don't tell me. I'll deal with it without your help."

"I'm just messing with you, Kate." A serious expression erased his smile. "You've got some bad energy circling you. The kind that can hurt you and the people around you."

"Tell me about it. Will I ever be free of them?" Funny, I'd never thought of the spirits as a 'them' before. That made it way too personal.

"It's possible. I sensed something heavier, something more potent behind you."

Reflexively, I turned my head, half-expecting to see something.

Pascal ignored my foolish reaction. "I couldn't quite make out the form, but it looks like you've attracted a powerful ally since you've been in the Yucatán."

"An ally? You mean something that might actually help me with this mess of a freaking life?"

"Like I said, I couldn't quite make out what it was, but I got the impression it's plenty able to take on the others."

I took a deep breath, unaccustomed to the feeling of relief that flowed through my body. For some reason, I believed him. If what Pascal said was true, I finally had an opportunity to get rid of the spirits wreaking havoc on my life.

"Does this mean I'll be able to leave them behind?"

Pascal shook his head. "I didn't say that, exactly. These are strong spirits, Kate. They're not just something you can 'leave behind'."

The flame of hope that ignited inside me fizzled like a match in a rainstorm. Would I never be able to get off this rollercoaster ride of a fucked-up life?

"Thanks, Pascal. You just confirmed what I've thought all along. The bad spirits aren't ever going to leave." I shook my head and walked away. "I need to go somewhere and think."

The thing about a camp in the middle of the jungle, there's nowhere to go other than where you sleep. I walked into my hut, shut the door, and fell into the hammock, staring at the beams above my head.

What the hell was I doing? My knowledge of Salazar might be able to help these guys and their cause, but all I wanted to do was run. The idea of fighting Salazar, Morales, or any number of cartel vampires exhausted me. I just wanted to live my life in a quiet, peaceful manner. Didn't I deserve that?

Apparently not.

I liked Quinn's men. A lot. I wanted to help them wipe the drug cartels off the face of the earth, help Mexico's citizens live the peaceful lives they deserved. I could never understand Salazar's assertion that he loved his country. He was part of an insidious cancer spreading swiftly across Mexico, reaching its tentacles into a generous and kind nation, bleeding it dry with its horrific acts of violence and incessant thirst for power. No, the cartels didn't love their country. They loved money.

And power.

Sighing, I laid my arm over my eyes and tried to calm down. My anxiety intensified at the thought of Quinn and the others fighting against such a ruthless enemy. What if the tattoos ended up hurting rather than helping them? *It's not your call, Kate. They know what they're doing. They've got experience.*

To make matters worse, images of Angie with her gun to the back of Cole's head swam into my mind, seeking a foothold. I swatted the air, trying to physically brush away the sadness running deep in my soul. Tears sprang to the surface and my nose burned as I tried to dam them. No amount of crying would bring him back. Bleakness filled my heart at the thought of his two little girls without their father, having to live with a witch of a mother, uprooting their lives, starting school in a strange place, making new friends.

All of it my fault.

I shook my head and opened my eyes, willing away the unbearable emotions. My ability to go into complete and utter denial came in handy during times like these. If I allowed myself to collapse into the reality of my situation, I wouldn't be able to escape the endless memory loop of people I'd lost: Cole, Sam, Oggie, my sisters, my parents, my old friend Gabe.

Not being able to lie still, I sat up and swung my feet to the floor. The only way I could think of to stop the incessant memories from flooding my mind was to move.

I stepped outside and found myself walking toward the mess tent. Surely I could do something to keep busy and help at the same time.

Most of the camp had lined up for the evening meal. I walked over to one of the tables at the head of the line and smiled at the guy ladling food onto plates.

"Can I help? I ladle a mean stew."

The guy raised his eyebrows and glanced at the man standing next to him, who nodded. The ladle-guy grinned and untied his apron, handing it to me.

"Be my guest."

I put on the apron and skirted the table, grabbing the empty bowl from the first guy in line and filling it with stew.

By the time I'd served the last person I was down to the equivalent of two bowls left in the pot. Quinn walked in and headed for the table, surprise showing on his face when he caught sight of me. He grabbed a bowl off the pile and held it out.

"I don't have much left," I said, as I dipped the ladle into the pot and filled it.

He watched me, his gaze cutting like a laser into my soul.

"I know."

13

I SNAPPED AWAKE AT THE shouting. Both feet hit the floor. In seconds, I had my jeans and boots on and had raced out of the hut toward the voices.

Several lanterns hung from poles inside the mess tent. Silhouettes flickered as men dashed inside.

Heart in my throat, I hurried into the tent, stopping short at the scene before me.

The row of tables down the middle of the mess area, usually reserved for eating, now acted as ersatz gurneys with bloodied casualties lined up end to end. At the front of the tent, Quinn barked orders to the able-bodied men while he wrapped a tourniquet around the wounded leg of the man lying on the table in front of him. I could feel the blood drain from my face as the import of what happened slammed into me.

Like a zombie in a bad late night movie, I made my way through the throng and stopped at one of the tables to see if I could help. It was Skull Boy, the man who'd helped me draw the snake eating the scorpion on the others. His shoulder was a mess, the bullet wound a dark, ominous circle surrounded by a field of blood. He tried to smile, but it looked more like a grimace. Shaking off the disbelief clouding my mind, I grabbed two towels from a guy walking by with a stack in his hands and folded each of them over again to make them thick. Skull Boy winced as I gently lifted his shoulder and placed one of the towels at the back where I estimated the bullet exited, and pressed the other onto the entry wound.

Then I took his hand and placed it on top of the front towel. "You're going to be okay. Keep applying pressure to help stop the bleeding. I'll be back to check on you in a couple of minutes, okay?" He nodded that he understood, and I went to the next table.

Whenever I had a moment, I checked to see if I could catch sight of Pascal in the madness. Since he was the chief medic in camp I figured he'd be in the middle of the chaos, calmly tending to the wounded. He was nowhere to be seen.

Everyone with anything to contribute worked past the point of fatigue, trying to stanch the bleeding on some, bandaging the others, and treating signs of shock in still others. I tried to do a quick count of the men, but there was no way of knowing if everybody had made it back.

A couple of hours later, when the survivors had been attended to, I walked outside for some fresh air. Two of the men had died. The rest would live unless infection got a foothold. Not horrible, considering what it looked like in the beginning.

A few yards away, Quinn and Blondie stood in the moonlight, heads bent together in what appeared to be an intense conversation. I waited for a few minutes but then couldn't stop myself and walked over to them.

"Have you seen Pascal?" I asked. Blondie glanced at Quinn who shook his head.

"Salazar got him."

"What? How? I thought you had it all planned out."

"We did, but Morales called up a hell of a lot more soldiers than we predicted. Salazar's men were getting slaughtered by the time we showed up and fell back sooner than anticipated, surprising our front line."

"I had Salazar in my sights but he pulled Pascal in front of him. I couldn't get a clear shot, not without shooting Pascal." Blondie's jaw flexed as his eyes narrowed. "Salazar's a dead man. We'll see who uses my friend as a fucking human shield."

"We need to think this through," Quinn said. "Morales was more than ready for Salazar. Too ready. It was like he knew somebody else was coming to dinner." He looked at me. "If I ask around, you never left camp, right?"

Seriously? He wanted to go there? I could feel my face flush as the anger rose in my chest. *Relax, Kate. Everybody's had a hard night. He didn't mean anything by it.*

"Obviously. I'd never even heard of Morales until I met you guys. As for Salazar, why would I go to the trouble of making sure your guys had a realistic tat in the first place?" I was tempted to remind Quinn of my earlier soliloquy about how fighting the cartels with violence would backfire, but decided he had enough to deal with at this point.

"Could be that you suggested it so it would be an identifier *for* Salazar, to let him know who wasn't batting for his team."

"Flawed logic, Quinn. Lalo told you he'd seen the tats on Salazar's men, that he still made his guys get them. It's not like Lalo and I were in on this together."

"Yeah." Quinn rubbed his hand over his face. "You're right. I don't know what to think." He looked exhausted. Blondie didn't look much better. "We've got to get to Pascal before they…" He stopped.

"Before they torture him?" I finished the sentence for him. "Believe me, Quinn, I know all about Salazar's enhanced interrogation techniques."

"Right." He turned to Blondie. "Tell the men to stand to in case we don't get to him in time. If there's some kind of leak I'm not going to risk the lives of everyone in camp if our location's been compromised. We need to be packed and ready to go."

Before I could stop myself, I blurted, "Why don't you make a trade?" Quinn and Blondie both looked at me like I had two heads.

"For?" Quinn asked.

"Pascal for me."

Quinn shook his head, his face like stone. "I'm not putting a civilian in danger. Especially not an untrained one. We'll figure it out."

I took a deep breath and continued before I lost my nerve. "Listen. Salazar expended a lot of personal capital to settle an old score. He talked Diaz into breaking a well-known assassin out of prison to track me down, smuggle me into Mexico and deliver me to him, just so he could have the satisfaction of watching me suffer. His hatred, as well as his pride, runs deep. We can use that against him. Trust me."

Blondie nodded at me. "Let's hear her out, Q."

Quinn folded his arms, silent.

"I'm not suggesting that you actually hand me over to him. I'd rather you didn't. I'm sure you guys can figure out how to make it look like you're willing to trade. Then, when they bring Pascal to the meet, you ambush his men, rescue Pascal and leave."

"And you'll be where during all of this?" Quinn asked.

"Somewhere they can see me, of course, or it won't work. It's dangerous. I get that. I can handle dangerous." The sane part of me was wondering why the hell I just offered to use myself as bait. The not-so-sane part held its ground.

Quinn scowled, evidently not sold on the idea.

"It could fly, Q." Blondie said.

"No. I'm leaning toward extraction. We've got the hacienda's layout. I say we go in dark, find Pascal and slip away. Take out anyone who looks at us wrong. Live to fight another day."

"He knows we're coming. Don't you think he'll be ready for that? This, he might not expect," Blondie argued.

Good to know Blondie was on my side, although I'd been half-hoping Quinn would reject my offer. We watched as he thought through the idea.

After a few minutes, Quinn said, "Okay, here's how we handle it." He looked at Blondie. "You figure out how to let Salazar know we're willing to trade. It's gotta be in daylight, somewhere open. You choose the location. I'll do reconnaissance." He turned to me. "You know how to handle a gun?" I nodded. "Good. I'll get Lalo to give you a loaner. This could get ugly."

"I know. I'm still willing to try."

"What if he doesn't bite?" Quinn asked.

"Don't worry. He will. Salazar doesn't need Pascal. He'll figure he can break me easier than him, find out everything he needs to know about your operation. At the same time he gets to torture me. I'm pretty sure that'd be his dream come true."

"All right. Let's do it. Blondie, get word to your contacts in town that we're willing to trade. It shouldn't be long before we know whether it's a go or not." Quinn gave me a curt nod and walked away. Blondie watched him leave.

"That guy's been through it today," he said.

I shuddered at the thought of Salazar interrogating Pascal. "He's not the only one."

Salazar didn't waste any time taking the bait. The handoff was scheduled for two days later in the afternoon, a few miles from the hacienda in an agave field. The morning of the op, Quinn grabbed a handful of guys to scout the area. Lalo and I walked to the back of the camp to practice with the Glock he'd found for me. I wasn't as rusty as I thought I was going to be, and hit every target he set up.

"Now we find out how good you really are," Lalo said. He walked out a few yards and threw a soda can into the air. I squeezed off two rounds and hit it once. On the next attempt, I hit the target on the first try.

"Pretty good," Lalo said, as he showed me the bullet hole.

"So, if you don't mind my asking, why are you working with Quinn? I mean, the money can't be all that great, if you guys are even getting paid, right? Working for Diaz had to be a lot more lucrative."

"Yes, of course, but money isn't everything."

"No, but leaving the cartels is risky. Not what you'd call a light decision. I'm just wondering what happened to make you choose to do something that dangerous."

Silent, Lalo picked up the used targets and placed them in a plastic shopping bag. I was about to move on to another subject when he stopped and cleared his throat.

"Why did you leave Salazar?" he asked.

"Because I saw him cut the throat of his close friend over nothing and knew I'd be next."

Lalo nodded, a solemn look on his face. "They killed my family." The words were small and quiet, the implication insurmountable. My heart squeezed tight at how senseless and tragic it was.

"I'm sorry."

His eyes grew dark with anger. "I only returned home for my youngest sister's wedding. I did not have permission from Diaz." He spit out the cartel boss' name. "He ordered them all killed. Even Lidia. She was only seven." Horror and grief were etched across his face. He wiped his eyes, took a deep breath. "I knew then I had to work against him. I found Quinn and this group by accident. Quinn saved me from destruction."

"But Diaz and *El Castillo* hadn't been seen in this area. As I understand it, only Morales' cartel operated here."

"That is true. Because of Quinn, I decided to dedicate my life to ridding Mexico of all the cartels. In time, I knew God would give me the chance to avenge my family." His eyes shone in the early morning sunlight. "And now he has." He tilted his head to the side and squinted at me. "I think that God has brought you here for the same reason."

Unable to answer him, I slid the gun into my waistband. What could I say to that? He could be right.

But he could also be dead wrong.

14

THE SUV kicked up a cloud of dust on our way to the meet. The temperature had spiked to an uncomfortably humid ninety-six degrees. Trying to stay dry in that kind of heat was pointless, especially while sporting a Kevlar vest which Quinn insisted I wear. I didn't argue. The air conditioning helped, but only temporarily. I shrugged my shoulders to relieve the tension and checked the gun's chamber for the tenth time.

Quinn drove while Blondie rode shotgun. I sat in the backseat. Several of Quinn's men left earlier to get into position. Although flat and open, thick jungle surrounded the agave field, providing good cover for the snipers. Both Quinn and Blondie had assured me the shooters were the best and that I'd be in good hands. Their assurances helped—a little. The possibility that one or more of us wouldn't make it back alive hadn't been lost on me.

"Hey, Blondie," I said to the back of his headrest. "What the heck is your name, anyway?"

He took off his sunglasses, turned and smiled, showing off his impossibly white teeth. "My given name is Frederick."'

"Why does everybody call you One Shot? Does that relate to booze or targets?"

He laughed. "Both. Except I tend to like a bit more than just one when it comes to tequila."

"You mean one bottle, don't you?" Quinn joked.

Blondie cradled his head in his hands. "Oh man, remember the night in Merida?"

Quinn laughed, nodding. "Yeah. Epic." He gave Blondie the stink eye. "Just shoot me if I ever go drinking with you again."

Blondie punched him on the arm. "Shit, you had a great time that night, who are you kidding? What was her name, Rita? Lita? Mamacita?"

Quinn didn't answer him, but I could see the ghost of a smile on his face in the rear view mirror. He glanced up and caught me looking. I smiled and shrugged, and turned my attention to outside the window.

"If it's all right with you, I'm going to stick to calling you Blondie."

"That works," Blondie said. "As long as you call me."

We raced past rocky fields of spiky, blue-green agave plants, or *agave azul,* the kind used for tequila production. It was only recently that someone local had realized the agave plant responsible for tequila would grow well in the Yucatán. Hundreds of hectares were now in cultivation. That and tourism had revived this section of Mexico.

I sighed and leaned my head against the glass. I used to love coming to this part of the world; the jungles, the ruins, the beaches. Cole and I had been in the middle of planning a vacation a little further south in Belize and—I closed my eyes as the sharp pain of Cole's death swept through me. When I opened them I had to blink back tears. I drew in a deep breath and reminded myself why I had volunteered to be used as bait. Rage slowly replaced sadness at his senseless death. Getting Pascal back was priority one, certainly, but anything I could do to help bring Salazar and Angie down would be all right by me.

The SUV slowed and Quinn glanced in the rear view mirror. "Ready?" he asked.

I nodded as I slid the gun into a modified holster in the front of my jeans, pulling my shirt down over the exposed grip.

I was not reassured by its presence.

The SUV rolled to a stop next to a large field. Salazar's men hadn't arrived yet, at least not that I could see, although they could have been watching from a distance, like I hoped Quinn's sniper teams were.

The energy in the vehicle changed as Blondie and Quinn launched into business-mode and checked their weapons, discussing the plan between themselves. My role was simple; show up and be seen, hopefully drawing Pascal and the others out of their vehicle, and be ready to take cover when the shooting started.

My heart hammered in my chest and I tried to take a deep breath to calm down. It didn't work.

"There they are," Blondie said.

I looked out the windshield at the approaching SUV. Painted a dark gold with metallic flake, it sported the requisite blacked-out windows. "A bold color choice," I commented. No one laughed.

They pulled up several yards away and parked. We sat inside our vehicle, waiting to see what their next move would be. As the dust settled, the front passenger door opened and a dark-haired man of medium height wearing a black t-shirt, black pants and dark sunglasses got out.

Carrying the requisite machine gun, he kept the door between him and us. He pivoted, checking the surrounding area. Evidently satisfied, he skirted the door and walked to the front of the vehicle near the fender to stand point. I couldn't see the driver or if someone sat in the back seat.

"Do you see Pascal? I don't see Pascal yet." Blondie's demeanor had switched from laid back, party-ready Kiwi to strung tight and ready to rock and roll. I could feel my own adrenaline ratcheting up, along with a healthy dose of fear. I glanced at Quinn. He appeared calm, focused and quiet.

The driver's side door opened and another man dressed in black got out. Mirroring the other gunman, he held an Uzi in his hands as he stepped from the car, swiveling his head to take in everything around them. I didn't see Pascal.

Quinn and Blondie both opened their doors at the same time. Blondie got out first. He too remained behind the open door.

"Come out when I tell you," Quinn muttered under his breath before exiting the vehicle.

I watched through the windshield as the four men stood rooted to their respective spots, staring each other down. After a few moments, Quinn broke the silence.

"I haven't seen Pascal yet."

"And we haven't seen the *puta* yet," the guy on the left shot back. The other one snickered. My stomach dropped to my feet. If this went sideways I had no doubt these guys would be the first of Salazar's thugs to break me in. Not a pleasant thought.

Petrifying, actually.

"Pascal first. I want to make sure he's all right," Quinn called out. "Then you can have her."

The driver shrugged and tapped on the back window. The door opened and Pascal tumbled out with his hands tied behind his back. He tucked a shoulder and rolled, ending up on his knees.

"Stay down," the driver snarled at him.

Pascal sat back on his heels, watching the driver closely. His face was a bruised and battered mess. One eye had swollen shut, but he was alive.

"Come on out, Kate." Quinn's voice sounded calm, but I detected a hint of Rottweiler. It gave me the courage I needed to open my door and step outside the relative safety of the vehicle.

The driver's grin spread from ear to ear. "Come on over here, *puta*. We've been waiting all day for you." He grabbed his crotch and leered.

Quinn shook his head. "Pascal first."

The grin disappeared as the driver turned to look at the other gunman. "It seems we have a problem, friend." He frowned as he peeled off his sunglasses, his expression grave. Then his face split into another grin. "I guess we'll just have to do the handoff at the same time." He stepped over to where Pascal was still on his knees and kicked him in the side. Pascal grimaced but didn't cry out.

"Get up, *pendejo*."

Pascal struggled to his feet. Apparently disgusted with how long he was taking, the driver waved him toward us. "Hurry up. *Vamonos.*"

"Walk toward them. Slowly," Quinn instructed under his breath.

My mouth dry, I didn't even try to swallow as I took one baby step followed by another toward the other SUV. Pascal had limped a couple of yards to my paltry few feet when the driver raised his gun and peppered the ground near Pascal with bullets. He stopped, his chest rising and falling with his breathing, eyes trained on Quinn. Quinn's head moved imperceptibly.

"Hurry the fuck up, woman." The driver aimed his gun at me.

I took another step, my hand hovering near the gun hidden at my waist. Pascal and I were abreast of each other when a gunshot cracked through the silence. The gunman on the passenger side of the SUV stiffened and dropped his weapon to the ground before crumpling to his knees. Another shot put him on his side, mouth open, staring at nothing.

"Move!" Quinn's voice echoed in my ears as I spun and sprinted toward the truck, expecting a bullet in my back at any moment.

A loud thunk followed by a swooshing sound screamed past me on my left. The world exploded in a howl of sound and white heat and compression, knocking me off my feet and catapulting my body through the air like a ragdoll. I landed hard on my side a few feet away next to a drainage ditch and watched as huge chunks of Quinn's truck launched into the sky, arced gracefully and then slammed to the ground. Flames erupted and black, billowing smoke filled the sky.

Then, nothing. Eerie silence enveloped the surreal scene before me. Three bodies lay on the ground; the driver of the SUV along with the man Quinn's sniper killed. Pascal lay near the charred remains of our truck.

Disoriented, I searched the ground in front of me, trying to locate the Glock. It had landed a few feet away in a copse of long grass, and I crawled toward it, wincing with pain. Quinn ran to Pascal and bent down, yelling something I couldn't hear, since my ears were ringing. He draped his arm over Pascal's shoulder and lifted him to his feet. Clumps of dirt exploded behind them as bullets hit the ground, tracking them as they ran for cover in the jungle. My fingers had closed over my gun when I glimpsed movement inside the cartel's SUV. I picked up the semi-automatic, elbows on the ground for support with both hands on the grip, waiting for a clear shot. A figure climbed between the front seats and sat behind the steering wheel.

Salazar.

Heart racing, I froze. I willed my hand to obey, but my trigger finger remained locked in place. I couldn't move, couldn't breathe, couldn't act.

A muted popping sound came from the left of the SUV. The bullets pinged off the metal and barely chipped the window glass. I should've known Salazar would bring an armored vehicle to the meet.

The back tires spitting rocks, Salazar slammed the truck into gear and screamed past me without a backward glance.

Blondie appeared in my periphery and pulled me to my feet. Red in the face with a vein bulging on his forehead, he shouted at me but the words sounded like we were underwater. I stared at his lips. He was screaming at me to *fucking run.*

I fucking ran.

We followed Quinn and Pascal, stumbling the last several yards into the jungle, and didn't stop there. Only when we'd worked our way in and found cover did we stop to catch our breath. At that point, a portion of my hearing had returned and their voices were muted, but decipherable.

"What the fuck was that?" Blondie asked, anger clouding his face, his chest heaving from the run.

Quinn shook his head as he tended to Pascal, whose complexion had turned a sickly shade of gray beneath the bruises. "RPG."

"I *know* it was a fucking RPG, Q. What I meant was, where the fuck were *our* guys?"

"They're what kept us alive long enough to get the hell out of there. Where do you think they were?" The intensity of Quinn's expression combined with his coiled, taut body practically begged Blondie to argue with him.

"Yeah, well, they could have—"

"Enough!" Quinn bit the words out through gritted teeth. "Until we get back to base, no one's going to speculate on what did or didn't happen. Are we clear?"

Blondie clamped his mouth shut, his lips a thin, colorless line. "Clear."

I shifted my legs, trying to find a comfortable position.

Quinn glanced at me. "You all right?"

"Yeah," was all I could say.

Blondie scrutinized my face as he checked me over and nodded his agreement. "Cuts and scrapes, significant bruising. It's a fucking miracle she's not dead."

My stomach rumbled as my abdominal muscles contracted, pushing bile into my throat. I rolled onto my side and heaved into a nearby clump of grass.

"She'd probably like to be about now," Quinn said.

15

W E MADE IT TO THE predetermined rendezvous point on another dirt road a couple of kilometers from the original meet, next to an abandoned agave field. Two of Quinn's men were parked nearby in a four-wheel-drive van, and ran to take Pascal from Quinn and Blondie, who had teamed up to get him there in one piece. The tension between the two had dissipated, owing as much to their ingrained sense of duty to the mission as to the difficulty of traveling quickly in high temperatures and over difficult terrain.

My body had recovered sufficiently enough from the blast that I had been able to walk on my own, although I was still pretty wigged out. My familiarity with explosions notwithstanding, being that close to the detonation of a rocket-propelled grenade gives a whole new meaning to the term 'blown away'.

We got in the van and headed for camp. One of Quinn's guys went to work on Pascal, hooking him up to fluids and stabilizing the injuries he sustained from the explosion. I curled up in the corner and closed my eyes, and tried to block out everything around me.

An hour later, we pulled into base. I worked alongside Blondie to empty the van, ignoring the sharp pain in my back. Quinn stopped by later to see how I was doing as one of his men swabbed a cut above my eye.

"You're looking…better," he said, giving me the once-over.

"He says I'm lucky," I replied, indicating the guy tending to me. "Apparently I have a bruised rib. I could have sworn it was broken."

Quinn turned to him and said, "Can you give us a minute?" The guy nodded, picked up his first aid kit and walked back toward the mess tent.

"How's Pascal?" I asked.

"He's doing well, considering."

"Did they—" I stopped, not wanting to ask about his interrogation.

"No. He said they didn't get anything. They tried damned hard, though."

"I imagine. I'm glad he's going to be okay." I waited a moment before continuing. "Not trying to be a pain in your ass, but now that it's over, when can I get a ride into town?" I was more than ready to be out of the war zone, whatever fate threw my way. It had to be better than this.

"I'll get one of my guys to take you in after dinner. I'd have them take you sooner, but I want to give them all a little down time before asking one of them to do anything else."

"Of course. Any time is fine."

"I suggest you stay at the Hotel Maya. It's owned by a guy named Ernesto. I've worked with him before. You'll be relatively safe there."

"Thanks for the reference."

Quinn squinted at me, the waning afternoon light casting a shadow across his face. "You did good today."

"I don't know if you noticed, but we almost got our heads blown off."

"Almost."

"That was a little too close for me."

"We got Pascal back alive. That was the object of the exercise."

"True." I studied him for a moment and realized what happened earlier was indeed a victory, explosion or not. When the sole purpose of an organization was to fight evil—and to be sure, Salazar and the drug cartels fit squarely into the evil category—any time you could rescue one of your own from the grip of that evil was to be considered a triumph.

"I'd better go," Quinn said, the conversation obviously over. He turned to leave, but then stopped and reached into his pocket, pulling out a wad of pesos. "You're going to need this—for the room and a couple meals."

Grateful, I accepted the money. "Thanks. If I knew where to send it, I could pay you back as soon as I got back on my feet."

"No need. It's the least we can do. Take care of yourself, Kate."

"You too, Quinn." As I watched him go, melancholy swept through me. I'd become attached to him and his men, this place.

Time to leave, Kate. You know what almost happened today. The longer you stick around, the worse it's going to get. More people will die. Bad spirits, remember?

Sometimes I hated listening to myself.

Quinn and his men were fighting a difficult battle and sooner or later more would be lost. Whether that would include him and his soldiers or the cartel thugs remained to be seen. Probably both. I didn't want to stick around and watch these men die or die with them. I was all about running and hiding and living another day. Besides, the reality of dealing with Salazar and his thugs had me seriously rethinking my need to engage the enemy. The fact that I choked when I had a shot at Salazar and didn't take it scared the hell out of me.

I drifted toward my hut, wincing with each step. Not having ever been hit by a truck, I wasn't sure if the pain I was experiencing qualified as such, but I figured it was close. I refused to think about what could have happened if things had gone even further south at the meet, and concentrated on formulating a plan to follow after I reached Tabai. Once I got to town I could email Luis, my contact in the DEA, and hopefully get some help—but to where? And doing what?

Mentally frazzled and physically beat, I limped in the door and carefully stretched out on the hammock, mindful of the cuts and bruises, craving solitude. I hoped a nap in the hours before dinner would give me the space I needed to figure out what to do next.

Despite the pain and my chaotic thoughts, I fell asleep in seconds.

Dinner turned out to be another round of beans and tortillas but tasted as good as any five-star meal at the Ritz. Pascal didn't show, having opted to remain in his hut and rest. I volunteered to bring him a meal and was plating up when Quinn walked into the tent. I grabbed a handful of the fresh tortillas and threaded my way through the diners and tables to where he stood in the doorway.

"I'm going to have Charlie take you into town." He nodded toward a sandy-haired guy talking to a group of men seated at one of the tables. "He'll drop you at the hotel."

"Thank you, Quinn. If it's okay, I'd like to have a couple of minutes before we head out. I want to bring this to Pascal," I said, indicating the plate of food.

"Sure. I'll tell Charlie to meet you by the vehicles in half an hour."

"Great. Thanks again."

"No problem," he said, his attention already somewhere else. He walked over to talk to Blondie waiting in line for food and I headed for Pascal's hut.

Now that I was going to finally get back to civilization, I had to figure out where I'd be the safest. I'd have to choose carefully. Too many times I made the decision to move somewhere based on fear, not reason. I'd thought Alaska was remote enough and cold enough to keep Salazar at bay. I'd been wrong. After Angie shot Sam and almost killed him, I ran to Hawaii, hoping to lose myself in what I remembered as a happier life. The bad spirits followed me there instead of Salazar, but still I had to leave.

Which brought me to Arizona and Cole. For a few years things had been relatively calm, giving me a false sense of security. But here I was, on the run again, looking over my shoulder, hoping Salazar or Anaya wouldn't find me.

There had to be another way.

I stopped outside Pascal's hut and knocked.

"Come in." Pascal sounded as though he'd been sleeping. I opened the door and walked inside. His good eye lit up when he saw me. The other had puffed up to the size of a golf ball and was swollen shut. "Hey," he said.

"I thought I should bring you something to eat. Help keep up your strength."

Pascal breathed in the aroma and smiled. It looked like it hurt. I walked over to his cot and set the dinner on a box nearby.

"I would have brought you a margarita, but the blender's busted."

Pascal laughed but then caught himself, a pain-filled grimace crossing his face. He winced as he tried to sit up.

"Here, let me." I reached for his pillow and doubled it over, pushing it into position so he could sit partially upright. The look on his face told me even a small movement was difficult for him. I filled a tortilla with beans and cheese, rolled it up and handed it to him to eat.

"Thanks," he said, and took a bite. "Delicious."

"There's another reason I wanted to bring you dinner."

Pascal polished off the tortilla, watching me with his good eye.

"I'm leaving tonight. Charlie's giving me a ride into town." I picked up another tortilla and filled it, then handed it to him. He accepted it, but didn't take a bite right away.

"Can I make a suggestion?"

"Sure."

"Think about staying."

I nearly choked at his words. "And do what, exactly? I'm done being bait for the cartels, and I'm really done putting myself in the path of a psychotic and paranoid ex-lover."

His steady gaze was unsettling. "Give me a minute before you make up your mind." He leaned forward.

"We're doing a good thing here, Kate. I see something in you, something deep that compels you to fight. Whatever that is, this group can help you harness it, make it work for you instead of against you."

"I don't know what to say." My first reaction was to run far, far away from everything Quinn's group of commandos represented. Why would I continue to put myself in the way of the very danger I'd been trying to outrun all these years? Not only that, but what if it didn't 'work out'? What then? *So long, Kate, don't let the door hit you on the way out?*

"Thank you, Pascal, but I—"

Blondie's voice bellowed from outside the hut.

"What the hell's going on in there? I smell food." The door opened and he ducked under the header. He looked from Pascal to me and back to Pascal. "Did I interrupt something?"

"I was just trying to convince Kate to stay on with us."

Blondie cocked his head my direction and winked. "You want to give her a gun and shove her into battle like cannon fodder?"

"Not exactly. There are other things she could do."

"What'd Q say?"

"Haven't talked to him about it yet."

"You think he'd go for it?"

"Maybe. If I suggest it."

Blondie nodded, looking at me. "Pascal's very persuasive. Unlike myself."

"I never said I'd do it, though, did I?" I didn't like that they were discussing my life without me.

"Why not?" Blondie asked.

"She doesn't want to put herself in the path of a quote, 'psychotic and paranoid ex-lover', end quote."

Pascal finished his tortilla and glanced at the plate. I prepared another one for him and handed it over.

"Can't really blame her, can you?"

Pascal shrugged. "It was worth a try. With preparation I think she could turn out to be good as well as effective, as long as Quinn agreed."

"Thanks, guys. I appreciate your encouragement. Both of you." I made up the last tortilla and handed it to Pascal. "But I'm done. I can't do this anymore." I picked up the now empty plate and turned to leave. "Take care of yourself, Pascal. You too, Blondie. I wish you the best of luck. I hope you take them all down."

"Thanks for everything, Kate. I don't think I'd be around if it weren't for what you did. I owe you." Pascal attempted a lopsided smile.

"You don't owe me a thing. Be well."

Blondie followed me out and waited next to my hut as I gathered together what little I had. I slid the gun into the front of my jeans, the grip accessible at the top of my waistband. I may be going somewhere Quinn deemed 'safe', but in my experience safe was usually a misnomer. Then I threw a couple of boxes of ammo into an old backpack I'd found next to the wall of the hut, along with a bottle of water. That was the extent of my belongings.

We continued walking toward the mess tent.

"Pascal has a point. We're not so bad, you know. It'd liven things up having a woman around."

"Sorry to disappoint you."

"Worth a shot," he said with a grin.

Quinn spotted us walking toward him and disappeared into the mess tent, reappearing with Charlie at his side.

"I'd like you to make sure she's settled in a room at the Hotel Maya before you leave," he said to Charlie. "Take the Dodge, just in case."

"No problem, Q." Charlie glanced at me. "Leaving so soon? Accommodations not to your liking?" His grin told me he was joking. I smiled.

"Not exactly the vacation I signed up for, no."

"It ain't for everyone, that's for sure."

I said my goodbyes and Charlie and I walked to where two of the vehicles were parked. We both climbed in and he started the truck. Then he hacked a U-turn and sped out toward the road.

"What did Quinn mean when he said to 'take the Dodge, just in case'?"

Charlie patted the dash. "She's one of three armored trucks we have."

"In case of an RPG?"

"Nah. If that happens, it's been nice knowing you. This one's rated for assault rifles."

"Comforting."

"Don't worry. Q's just being cautious."

"Good to know."

"You're going to have to wear this. Sorry," he said, his voice apologetic as he handed me a blindfold.

"Way to make a girl feel special, Charlie."

Before I put it on, I glanced out the side mirror as darkness swallowed the compound behind us, and wondered if I'd made the right choice.

16

WE HIT BLACKTOP AND DROVE for about half an hour before Charlie said I could take off the blindfold. I did and squinted into the night, the lack of streetlights accentuating the inky darkness. The only light came from the brilliant stars peppering the night sky.

The warm, humid air flowing in the window reminded me of the last night Cole and I spent on the cruise ship several months prior, before Anaya's men climbed aboard and kidnapped three of the passengers, including me. My heart sank at the thought and I took a deep breath as I fought back the now-familiar rage threatening to overwhelm me.

Charlie wasn't much of a talker, which was fine by me. I doubted I'd be a scintillating conversationalist. A chorus of frogs punctuated the stillness as I watched the road rush past in the truck's headlights. This part of the Yucatán didn't boast much of anything but agave fields, a few scattered haciendas, and jungle.

I leaned my head back and thought about what I needed to do. Just because I would soon be in town didn't mean I could consider myself safe. I'd use the pesos Quinn had given me to pay for a night at the Hotel Maya, and then visit an internet café in the morning to contact Luis. Other than that, I had no plan. The thought of returning to Durm after Cole's murder wasn't an option. I couldn't face the lives I'd destroyed, especially not Abby and Lauren's. I'd never be able to look either of those kids in the eye, not after being responsible for their father's death.

My old friend despair returned with a vengeance and I squeezed my eyes shut, my attempt at blocking the pain futile. The view of life from where I was sitting had changed to a dull, listless gray without the possibility of joy or love. It had taken such a long time to find Cole, losing him to the monsters that stalked my life added unbearable agony to my list of constant emotional companions.

And guilt. I was already well-versed in that emotion.

Charlie glanced at me and cleared his throat. I returned his gaze, waiting for him to say something.

"If it's any consolation, I know Q was impressed with how you handled yourself at the meet."

"Thanks." Much as I appreciated hearing Charlie say that, it was a small comfort. We'd been lucky to get out of there with our lives.

Charlie cleared his throat again. "No one expected it to turn out the way it did. Q was adamant that you be our first priority if things went to shit. I know I speak for myself and the others when I say we all felt…protective, for lack of a better word."

"Thanks, Charlie, I appreciate that. I feel the same way about you guys."

We lapsed back into silence and watched the road, each alone with our thoughts.

A few miles later, we rounded a bend in the highway and Charlie stiffened. "Somebody's behind us." His clipped tone told me it wasn't good.

I glanced in the side mirror at the approaching headlights. It looked like they were coming up fast. Charlie stepped on the gas and the Dodge shot forward. I eased the gun out of my waistband and waited, eyes glued to the mirror.

We cleared the bend in the road and Charlie hit the brakes.

"Shit," he muttered under his breath.

Startled, I glanced at Charlie and then out through the windshield.

Bright flares glowed on the road ahead of us, illuminating a local police cruiser parked in the middle of the highway blocking the way forward. Typically, in the U.S. you could assume the roadblock was there to catch a criminal. One could never be absolutely certain whose side the local law enforcement were on in Mexico. The cartels paid many times more than what the *policia* earned, and the threat of violence to the families of those who balked ensured compliance.

As the truck slowed, Charlie reached under his seat and pulled out an MP5K. Quinn mentioned in one of the pre-op briefings that the submachine gun had become the weapon of choice for the cartels, although Kalashnikovs were easier to get. Some in the old guard still preferred AK-47s, but their popularity was waning. MP5s were more accurate.

We stopped several yards in front of the roadblock. Charlie let the engine idle while a burly uniformed officer emerged from the shadows.

"Stay in the truck. I'll see what he wants," Charlie said, as he released his grip on the pistol and set it on the floor. He opened the console between us and took out a smaller 9mm, which he slid into his waistband, pulling his shirt over to conceal it.

I glanced nervously in the side mirror at the headlights of the SUV skulking a few yards behind us. Though unable to see through their window to get a good idea of what we were up against, the growing unease in my chest told me it wasn't coincidence they were there.

Charlie plastered a smile on his face as he opened his door and stepped out with his hands where the officer could see them. The cop's eyes were partially encased in shadow from the brim of his hat, and he walked with the confident swagger of someone who knew he had plenty of backup.

They met in the middle, stopping to talk in the glow of the headlights. The cop said something to Charlie, who swiveled his head as he replied and waved his hand toward the truck, then turned back to the now-smiling cop. The two of them exchanged a few more words before Charlie turned and headed back toward the truck. He looked at me through the glass and nodded, and I relaxed my grip on the trigger, releasing my breath with a sigh.

The cop didn't move as he watched Charlie walk toward the Dodge. A heartbeat later, he went for his holster and drew his gun. Time slowed and I screamed at Charlie to move. He pivoted and reached for the 9mm hidden under his shirt. I dove to the floor for the MP5 as the back window fissured in a hail of bullets.

I remained on my back on the floor, the barrel of the gun angled upward and waited, pulse racing.

A rapid *pop-pop-pop* burst from the front end of the Dodge, followed by a groan from behind the truck.

One down. *Charlie must be okay.*

Automatic weapon fire ruptured the air in answer. Then, silence.

Seconds ticked by and nothing happened. *Stay here.* My instincts shouted at me to lay low, that whoever wasn't dead would be coming soon enough to check to see if I'd survived.

I hoped it was Charlie.

Footfall on pavement echoed in the stillness, closing in on the driver's side door. I craned my neck, aiming the MP5 toward the partially open window and held my breath.

The footsteps stopped near the door and hesitated. Sweat trickled down my face and I resisted the urge to wipe it away, concentrating instead on the feel of the pistol in my hands and my finger on the trigger. I cast a quick glance at the passenger side, but saw no one.

There was a soft click and the driver's side door inched open, telling me Charlie was down. He wouldn't be quiet opening the door of the truck. I squeezed the trigger and the gun went off, scaring the shit out of me, the bullets streaming through the narrow opening.

The door swung wide as the gunman groaned and fell to the pavement. I turned onto my side, my breath catching from the throbbing of my bruised rib as I inched closer to the open door, listening.

An eerie silence permeated the air. I waited a few more moments and then rolled out of the driver's side and onto the road, ignoring the pain shooting through my back.

Knees shaking and adrenaline careening through me, I scrambled to my feet and spun around, searching for more shooters. The cop lay face down on the road, his gun a few feet from his hand, the side of his head a gory mess. The man I'd shot lay on his back not far from the truck, staring blindly up at the night sky. I glanced at the SUV behind the Dodge. A second gunman lay on the ground. The man Charlie killed.

Charlie lay on his back next to the front tire, his chest rising and falling with shallow breaths. I rushed over and knelt beside him. His eyes were closed and a dark stain spread across his shirt. With light fingers I explored his chest, searching for the bullet's entry point. There were several. The skin on his face had drained of color. His lips moved and I bent my head to listen.

"Q…" He grimaced, his breathing coming in short bursts.

"What about Quinn, Charlie?" I said, cradling his head as I tried to distract him. He sucked in a ragged breath and tried again.

"Help you…he's…best bet…" The rest came out garbled, accompanied by a wet cough.

"Shhh. It's okay. Don't try to talk."

Charlie grew quiet. I couldn't leave him on the side of the road to die alone, but with each second my anxiety spiraled higher. When the cop failed to report, there'd be too much trouble headed this way.

Charlie stiffened and his eyes grew wide as he fought for breath. I held him gently, hoping for a quick release to his pain. The gurgling in his throat grew more pronounced and when he opened his mouth to take a breath, red-tinged saliva bubbled out. Moments later, his body went limp and his breath released with the ghost of a sigh. Gently, I lowered his head to the pavement and climbed to my feet, anguish at another senseless death washing over me.

Numb, I stumbled back to the truck and picked through the broken glass for anything I could use. The console held a box of ammo for the 9mm and some Chiclets, both of which I placed in my pack. I didn't see a phone. Except for the cartel's private network, reception wouldn't be great out in the middle of nowhere. I picked up the radio's mike and keyed it, but nothing happened.

The MP5 was almost empty and I didn't want the extra weight, so I ran to the side of the road and heaved it into the jungle. When I returned to the truck, I realized both back tires were flat.

The crush of time had me in panic mode and I sprinted to the gunman's SUV. Keys dangled from the ignition. I thought about using it to get back to camp, but I had no idea where to turn and didn't trust myself to find Quinn and the others, especially in the dark. Driving into town would be too risky. One of the cops could come along to investigate and recognize the truck. I couldn't count on getting off the road quickly enough to hide from oncoming traffic.

It looked like I would have to go on foot, although ditching the SUV made sense since anyone coming back to the scene would realize I couldn't have made it very far walking. I needed to make it appear that I left with the vehicle. Once I made it to the hotel, I'd be able to get word to Quinn about the ambush through his contact there. After that, I'd find a computer and send an email to Luis, and hope he'd be willing to help me get the hell out of Mexico.

Again.

I climbed into the truck and turned the key. The engine roared to life and I shifted into gear, hacked a U-turn, and headed back the way Charlie and I had come.

Once I'd made it around the curve in the road, I looked for a good place to abandon the SUV. Light from the headlights illuminated a dirt track to my left. I pulled in, relieved to see that the trail led to another road running along a field. I drove several yards further, shut off the lights and turned off the engine. I doubted anyone would find the vehicle until the next morning, giving me plenty of time. I exited the truck and threw the keys into the bushes, then grabbed the backpack and shut the door.

With one last glance behind me, I shrugged on the pack and headed for Tabai.

17

IT TOOK ME SEVERAL HOURS to walk to town and find the hotel, keeping to the shadows with an eye out for anything resembling trouble. I'd made it past the scene of the ambush before three police cars screamed by, lights blazing. Thankfully, I'd been well hidden and they hadn't stopped.

The Hotel Maya perched on a dark side street a few blocks from the main plaza. A sleepy woman answered the door and checked me in, taking my money for the night. Well-known on the travel circuit, tourists were generally welcome in Tabai. An American woman alone wouldn't send up any red flags.

Unsure if I could trust the night clerk, I asked if the owner was available. She said he was out of town but would be back later that morning. She gave me a stern look when I asked if she would try to contact him for me, and told me this was no time to bother him and that whatever I had to tell him would have to wait until morning. With no strength left to argue, I took the key and went to my room, telling myself I'd be able to get word to Quinn in the morning, only a few hours away.

Unremarkable on the outside, the room was clean inside and cheery, the walls painted white with bright yellow and green accents. A soft chenille bedspread covered a wrought-iron bed flanked by two nightstands. After a shower, I shrugged out of my clothes and slipped beneath the covers, weariness settling deep in my bones. The memories flooded back almost immediately. Rather than be sidelined every time they made an appearance, I now let them crowd my mind, working through the pain and shock of the events of the past few days, trying to understand my life, not knowing where to go or who I should turn to, masochistically saving memories of Cole for last.

Sometime later, spent from crying and exhausted, I lay on my back and stared at the ceiling, the hollow emptiness a welcome relief from the overwhelming pain and rage I hadn't been able to work my way through until now.

The fact that the local police had set up a roadblock bothered me, a lot. I wondered how they knew Charlie and I were heading for town. Or were they casting a wide net, hoping to catch someone other than us and we were in the wrong place at the wrong time?

I doubted they would have opened fire if the target had been someone else.

That meant someone was after either me or Quinn's group.

And they were close.

Sunlight streamed through the windows into the room, waking me from a fitful few hours of sleep. At first, I'd slept like the dead, but then woke up at fifteen minute intervals for the rest of the night. In and out of consciousness, I dreamed of Cole and the girls, waking after each episode only to remember he was gone.

I slid into my jeans and pulled on my t-shirt. I checked the amount of money I had left over from what Quinn gave me and decided I had enough for two more nights and some food. Later, when I got back from the internet café, I'd take the time to wash my shirt and underwear, and let them air dry.

There was little activity on the street below my room. I slid the gun into my pack and headed down to the lobby. A man wearing glasses who I estimated to be in his early fifties stood behind the counter, focused on the paperwork in front of him. He glanced up at my approach.

"May I help you, Señora?" he asked, peering at me over his glasses.

"Are you the owner?"

"I am. My name is Ernesto. And you are—" He frowned as he typed something into the computer. "Señora Johnson?"

I nodded. "We have a mutual friend by the name of Quinn."

Ernesto's eyebrows shot up and he glanced behind me before replying.

"And how is our old friend?" A practiced smile replaced his initial surprise.

I leaned against the counter, keeping my voice low in case anyone was within earshot.

"Do you have a way to contact him?"

Wariness replaced the smile and he took a step back. "It's possible. What is the message?"

"Last night, the truck I was in was ambushed on the highway. One of his men was killed." If Ernesto was shocked, he didn't show it. I continued. "I don't know who's responsible, although the *policia* were involved."

"How do you know Quinn?"

"I've been his guest for the past few days."

"I will contact our mutual friend and give him this information. Will you be with us long?"

"Two, maybe three nights, depending on how things go here in town. I need to send an email to a friend of mine in the States." I eyed Ernesto's computer. "Would you be so kind as to direct me to a place where I'd be able to use a computer?"

He raised his hands, palms up. "I'm sorry, Señora, but my internet access is down at the moment. I'm not sure when service will be restored. There is an internet café not far from here." He reached underneath the counter for a sheet of paper with a map of the town printed on it, and showed me the café's location. He glanced up as the bells on the door jingled and a young couple entered the small lobby. "I will be with you both in a moment," he said with a smile, then turned back to me, his demeanor switching to that of a brisk professional.

"Once you have completed your business there, may I suggest a visit to the jewel of the Yucatán, Wild Cenote? The park is only a few kilometers from here and is not to be missed. There are changing rooms and a snack bar, and snorkel equipment rentals. The cenote itself leads to an underground network of caves, in which one could be lost for days." His eyes held mine for a moment. Then he slid the map toward me. "Will there be anything else?"

"No, thank you. You've been most helpful, Señor. *Buenos dias.*"

"*Buenos dias,* Señora."

I folded the map and slid it into my front pocket, returning the couple's smile as I walked out the door and headed into the early morning sun. After a discreet scan of the area, I turned down the street Ernesto indicated.

A woman had just set out a handmade sign advertising a local *panaderia*, or bakery, as I walked by. She smiled when I told her how good her store smelled and offered me a sample. I shook my head but promised I'd be back after I finished my errands. The normalcy of the interaction helped anchor me in the moment, keeping me from spiraling into the anxiety I felt from Ernesto's reaction. His suggestion to visit Wild Cenote was his way of telling me to get the hell out of town and hide, with the park being my best bet. As soon as I heard back from Luis, I'd take his advice.

The sign for the internet café came into view. The café itself was hard to miss: painted a bright fuchsia with sunny yellow trim, someone had added a bunch of colorful, showy flowers to the walls, giving it a cheery, if slightly manic appearance. I walked inside the darkened interior, blinking as my eyes adjusted.

A younger man, maybe in his early twenties, sat at the back counter working on a laptop. He looked up at my approach and smiled. I smiled back and asked how much it would be for a half hour of computer time.

"If you buy a coffee, Señora, it will be much less," he told me with a grin.

"Done. Can you leave room for cream?" I asked in Spanish.

"Of course." He scribbled the internet access code onto a small piece of paper and slid it over the counter, then walked into the back, presumably to get my coffee.

I took the paper over to one of two older desktop computers and entered the code. Service was slow, but I'd expected that. A few minutes later, he came out with my coffee and a little pitcher of cream. I handed him some pesos and told him to keep the change. He smiled and thanked me and returned to his laptop.

The email account I'd opened with an alias appeared on the screen and I entered my password. I composed an email to Luis explaining that I was back in Mexico, although I didn't go into specifics other than saying my ex- from ten years ago had been looking at new homes in the area, figuring he'd get the gist. I then asked him if there was anything he could do to help expedite my departure, explaining that things were similar to the last time he'd helped me and that I only had enough money to stay two more nights at my hotel. No reason to alert anyone who might be on Salazar's payroll how to find me. Luis or the DEA had never identified the mole from years before. They could still be operational, even now.

I hated asking Luis for anything after all he'd done for me, but I didn't know who else to turn to. Not sure I should even mention anything, I added a line about meeting Quinn and his men, but with no other identifying information. I figured if Quinn had worked with the DEA, Luis would know who he was and why he was here.

Satisfied, I hit send and sat back to finish my coffee. As I gazed out at the tree-lined avenue, a dark sedan slid past too slowly. Tense, I waited to see if it came back, my coffee forgotten on the table in front of me. Two minutes later, the same car returned, making a second circuit of the shaded street.

As soon as the sedan cleared the window I leapt to my feet and shrugged on the backpack. The guy behind the counter looked up from his laptop, the smile freezing on his face when he caught sight of the car gliding by through the screen door.

"Do you have a rear exit?" I asked, trying to keep the anxiety out of my voice.

He nodded, a guarded look in his eyes. "It leads to an alley. You can turn right or left. Please go now, okay?"

He didn't have to ask me twice.

I slipped past the counter and into the back room, threading my way through a warren of boxes and old furniture, past the kitchen area to the rear door. I'd barely stepped outside into the alley when I heard voices behind me at the front of the store. Heart pounding in my ears, I veered right and raced along the length of the alleyway. If they were looking for me, the sedan would have to turn around in the street in order to come this way.

The sound of a door banging open behind me as I slipped around the corner told me I'd better get the hell out of there, now.

In a flat-out sprint, I raced past shopkeepers setting out their wares for the day and dark, empty storefronts. I ventured a glance behind me to see if they were close and almost collided with a man sliding a garbage can across the sidewalk. I self-corrected and jumped over a mangy dog resting in the shade.

The sound of screeching tires behind me spurred me around the next corner, flashbacks of my run from Salazar's men years earlier fueling my fear. I turned down another side alley, searching for something to hide behind in order to catch my breath and think. A rusty Toyota Land Cruiser was parked next to a building a few feet away. I vaulted over crates and cardboard boxes and dove behind the tailgate.

Heart racing, with my back to the Land Cruiser, I stole a glance around the side of the Toyota just as the dark sedan cruised past. I snapped my head back and froze in fear, afraid they'd seen me. I waited a beat, then two. When I didn't hear their return, I remembered to exhale.

I tugged the map of the town from my front pocket. Two main roads fed into and out of Tabai. One was a major toll road, while the other served the local population and led straight to Wild Cenote. If I could manage to make it to the park without being tracked, then I could hide in the caves with a water source nearby until things calmed down. The snack bar was a bonus.

Unable to think of a better plan, I shrugged my backpack on and peeked at the street once more. No traffic. In a crouch, I hugged the walls of the alley, staying to the shadows. I made it to the end and scanned the street both ways for the dark sedan. If I was lucky, they'd be searching another street, far away.

With the minutes ticking by, I hooked a left and ran opposite the way I came, reaching the plaza in the center of town a short time later. The bustling pedestrian traffic around the square gave me a small feeling of safety, as did the several cars now on the road. Glued to the shadows, I slipped in and out of the shops with an eye to the street, vigilant for signs of the black sedan.

The road leading to the park appeared ahead and I quickened my pace. A wide open courtyard with no cover loomed between me and the next block, with an ancient Spanish church to my right. I took a deep breath and pivoted, checking one last time for the car before I darted across the intersection.

I'd made it halfway across when a sound like firecrackers went off behind me. Someone screamed. The people near me ducked as bullets pinged off the sidewalk, chunks of concrete exploding at our feet. A woman holding a bag of groceries dropped them to the ground as she ran for cover. Canned goods and vegetables rolled in the street. Somewhere a child wailed. I spun toward the sound of gunfire in time to see the black sedan parked in the middle of the boulevard with both doors open and two men in aviator sunglasses standing next to it. Both had guns aimed my direction. I dove across the sidewalk and rolled, coming to rest behind the low concrete wall of the church. Several other people had done the same, while a few brave souls ran inside the church itself.

I tore open my backpack and fumbled for the gun, thankful I'd loaded it back at camp, and noticed a bullet hole through the outer pocket. I'd gotten lucky. I glanced behind me, praying my luck would hold. A concrete path wove its way up to the front of the church and split off in a 'Y' along its sides. Shrubs obscured the view between the path and the plaza, but would leave me open in a couple of spots. I scanned the other direction, but with no real cover choosing that way would have been too much like open season on Kate.

The decision made for me I crouched, counted to three, and sprinted for the side of the church. Gunfire followed as I ran full-out toward the walkway.

Doors slammed and tires squealed behind me as I ran. Cars honked and people screamed. Out of breath, I pushed past the fear and desperation, knowing full well if I didn't make it to cover I'd be dead.

The eerie stillness of the church grounds stood in stark contrast to the chaos erupting behind me. The sidewalk curved and I followed it around a smaller building—straight into a dead end.

Alarmed, I spun in place, frantically searching the stone and brick enclosure. I stood in an inner courtyard of the church, in the middle of which was an empty fountain. The crumbling façade of the sixteenth century building held no outlets, at least none that I could see. Arches curved in front of walkways that led to closed doors. I ran from one entry to the next, trying each with no luck.

On my second circuit, I passed by a recessed window I hadn't noticed before. It was small, about two and a half feet square, but big enough for me to wiggle through if I could get it open. It was too high to kick in—the bottom of the frame came to my chin—and the stucco made it too smooth to climb. I dropped my pack and ran back to a pair of wrought iron chairs I'd passed in my earlier search. Using what was left of my strength I tried to drag one of them beneath the window but it wouldn't budge.

In full panic mode, I raced to the center of the courtyard to the empty fountain. Several long wooden boards and lengths of metal pipe that looked like scaffolding were stacked against one side. I picked up the end of a board and half-carried, half-dragged it back to the window, propping it against the wall like a skinny ramp, the end of it wedged just below the bottom of the sill.

The far end of the board had nothing to anchor it, so I went back for another piece. I laid the second board flat on the ground, matching the end of the first one against a short wall surrounding the courtyard, wedging in place my makeshift ramp.

I looped my pack over one shoulder and stepped onto the board, balancing myself. It bowed with my weight, but ultimately held. I eased along the wood, inching my way higher toward the window. When the angle became too acute, I dropped to all fours and crawled the rest of the way.

When I got close enough to the window, I pulled off my pack. With one hand I swung it back and forth to gain momentum. On the third pass, I aimed at the window. The glass shattered. I stopped to listen, but didn't hear anything behind me. That didn't mean much, since the location and shape of the courtyard would preclude any noise reaching it from the street.

I leaned against the wall for balance and broke off the remaining shards before dropping my pack inside. I climbed the rest of the way onto the ledge and pulled the board through, sliding it into the dark room. Then I squeezed through the opening and dropped to the other side.

18

THE COOL, DARK ROOM HAD a mustiness I'd always associated with old buildings. As my eyes adjusted to the light, the furnishings of a monk's living quarters came into view: a single cot rested against one end of the room, a crucifix on the wall above it. A small side table stood by the bed, holding a well-worn missal and lamp. An arched doorway stood on the other side of the room and I ran to it, praying it wasn't locked. Prayer seemed appropriate, considering.

As I reached for the handle excited voices from outside filtered through the broken window. The thumb latch gave with a click and I yanked the door open and raced through, closing it quickly behind me.

I found myself in a long hallway flanked by more arched doorways with all them closed. A larger one graced the far end of the hall and looked like my best bet. I sprinted to it and pushed it open, squinting at the sunlight flooding through a bank of clerestory windows. From the stained glass, it looked like I was in the transept of the cathedral. The cavernous nave stretched in front of me with the main entrance to my right. I peered around the corner to see several groups of frightened people sitting huddled together on benches, speaking in hushed tones. Most looked like tourists, although a few appeared to be local.

The massive front door to the church opened and several local police spilled through the entrance. I turned away so they wouldn't see my face and sat next to one of the groups on a bench near the middle. A large brimmed hat lay on the pew beside me. An older woman who I assumed to be the owner was fanning herself and speaking in a low voice to two other women, her back to me. I made sure she was turned away as I eased the hat onto my lap and moved to another pew.

"Everyone must leave the church immediately," one of the policemen commanded in both English and Spanish. "The gunmen have been apprehended. It is now safe to go."

Excited voices in several different languages echoed through the cavernous room as people rose from their seats and milled toward the front door. I used the resulting confusion to slip on the hat. One of the policemen had stationed himself at the door and was searching everyone's faces, obviously looking for someone. A pair of sunglasses peeked out from the pocket of a woman's purse near me. As I was about to close my fingers around them, she turned. I snapped my hand back and looked the other way. I could feel her eyes on me for a few tense moments before she turned to the front. I moved closer and kept my head down. This time the sunglasses ended up in my pocket.

I allowed a few more people in the crowd to fill the space behind her, then slid the glasses on as soon as she moved out of range.

The crowd continued toward the door and I inched further away from the view of the policeman at the entrance, while at the same time staying in the flow of people heading outside. I turned my face away as I passed.

I'd just made it through the door when a hand gripped my arm. The breath caught in my throat as I turned.

It was the owner of the hat.

"That looks familiar." The older woman's tone was accusatory.

I smiled, attempting to keep the interaction calm while still moving with the crowd.

"I'm sorry?" I said and tilted my head, acting like I couldn't hear her.

Keep walking, Kate.

"That's my hat," she said, her voice rising. Her fingers gripped my arm tightly, surprising me with their strength.

We cleared the front of the church and I stepped to the side, pulling her along with me. She frowned but followed, a protest forming on her lips. I slipped the hat off before she could say anything and pushed it into her arms, then turned and walked calmly away, attaching myself to another group.

The activity on the sidewalk had quieted down. Still walking, I scanned the street for the dark sedan, but it was gone. It looked like most of the population had decided to be somewhere else at the moment. Two police cars parked in front of the cathedral presented another obstacle, with officers standing next to their vehicles watching the plaza. I continued past the police, skirting behind them, making sure to keep at least one person between us.

So far, so good. I walked with the small group of tourists until we came to a cross street I recognized and then peeled off as soon as I was sure none of the police would notice my departure.

I hurried along the sunny boulevard, working my way back toward the road that led to the park. Ten minutes later, the sign came into view and I turned onto the street, walking past a mom and pop *carne asada* restaurant, a television repair shop, and another *panaderia*. The heat beat down mercilessly and I longed for the woman's hat, especially if one of the policemen or a cartel member happened to drive by. I was too exposed and hid at any sign of a vehicle coming down the road.

It didn't take long before I reached the outskirts of town which meant an end to any cover except for the occasional tree or rusted shack. Most of the jungle had been cleared for farming or some other development, or had been taken over by weeds.

I made sure my pace was consistent, not wanting to waste energy in the mid-morning heat. The pesos in my pocket would be enough to get me into the park surrounding the *cenote* and maybe grab something at the snack bar. Once I got there, I could figure out how long I needed to lie low now that the hunters had caught my scent.

19

Y BOOTS WEREN'T WHAT I'D call appropriate footwear for walking more than a couple of kilometers, and I found myself wishing I'd found a bicycle to ride. Along with the high temperature and humidity, the knowledge that I'd landed yet again on someone's kill list had me in a shitty mood. I hadn't realized I'd been speaking out loud to myself until I flushed a flock of grackles from a nearby tree.

Their flight scared the crap out of me and I stopped, hand to my racing heart. At the same time, a car approached behind me and I slid into the ditch to crouch in the long grass. If not for the birds, I might not have heard the car. As soon as the light-colored van drove by me, I exhaled with a sigh, climbed out, and resumed walking. I'd gotten used to the dull, throbbing pain in my back. Shallow breaths were my friend.

After a couple of similar incidents, and with my jeans now wet to the knees from ditch water, a sign advertising the park came into view. I followed the arrows to the huge parking lot filled with tour buses. Perfect. I'd grown to love crowds. A few minutes later I was standing in line to buy a ticket.

The man at the window smiled as I approached and looked behind me.

"Only one ticket, Señora?"

"Please." I reached in my jeans for the money, reading the prices on the board. "With snorkel gear. I'd also like to hire a guide."

"It's a good idea, a guide, especially since you are alone." He handed my ticket through the window. "You can pick up your equipment over there." He pointed toward a kiosk with brightly colored flotation devices, snorkel masks and fins. "Your guide's name is Juan. He will meet you at the entrance. Give him this ticket. There is also a place to change there."

I thanked him and pocketed my ticket, heading for the kiosk. After I picked out my snorkel gear, life vest and a wide-brimmed hat, I walked to the changing room, occasionally looking over my shoulder as I did. The men who were after me had no idea where I might hide. I assumed the park would be one of the last places they'd look, if they even bothered. Still, I didn't want to take any chances. All I needed now was a layout of the caves which I'd get from my guide, Juan.

The empty changing room smelled of flowery soap and shampoo. Several pairs of shoes poked out from under parallel benches in front of a wall of metal lockers. The bussed-in tourists were already in the caves. I stripped to my underwear, confident the matching black bra and panties resembled a two-piece swimming suit. Although the bruises I'd sustained from the exploding RPG weren't pretty, there wasn't much I could do about them. I searched each locker that didn't have a lock on it until I found a nondescript white beach towel and another shirt, which I stuffed into my backpack along with my jeans, boots, and t-shirt.

As I neared the entrance to the caves, I noticed a younger-looking man in plaid swim trunks and a t-shirt with the park's insignia standing next to a sign with the park rules in both Spanish and English.

"Are you Juan?" I asked, smiling. He nodded and asked me my name, which I told him was Ava. He then asked to see my ticket, which I dug out of the front pocket of my pack.

After I explained I didn't have a lock and would like to take my stuff with me, Juan disappeared for a moment, reappearing a few minutes later with a dive float and a large plastic bag. I piled everything I didn't want to get wet inside the bag and he tied it closed.

"Follow me, please," he said, and walked down the steps toward the cave. He glanced at my 'bikini' with a frown. "Would you like a wetsuit? Depending how long you are in the *cenote,* the water can become quite cold. It is approximately seventy-eight degrees."

"No, thanks. I'll be fine." I didn't want to rent one, knowing that at the end of the day they might be able to overlook some run-of-the-mill snorkel gear, but never something as valuable as a wetsuit. I noticed a bright yellow, open-hull kayak resting near the sign and asked him if there were any boats available for rent.

"Unfortunately no, Señora. These kayaks are for employee use only."

I assumed it was for emergencies, like when one of the tourists didn't wear their life vest and got into trouble in the deep water.

We continued down the stairs to the water's edge. Several people floated on inner tubes wearing snorkels, and many had life vests. The pool was a brilliant, deep turquoise, and crystal clear. A few brave souls jumped from the viewing platform into the deep water at one end, screaming with delight. Young children laughed and played near the stairway, watched after by mothers and fathers, while older kids and adults floated farther into the cave, following behind their guides.

Juan waded into the water and placed the plastic bag containing my clothes and pack in the middle of the float, along with a large light.

"Keep this float in sight at all times," Juan instructed. I nodded and slipped on my gear. He did the same and we swam past the crowds, heading toward the back of the cave. The cool water felt refreshing after my long, hot walk. Once we swam clear of the other groups, Juan stopped and pushed his mask onto his forehead, keeping one hand on the float. I did the same.

"Cenotes are fresh water sink holes that the Maya considered to be sacred. The Maya also believed cenotes were the entrance to the underworld." Juan pointed to the limestone formations over our heads. "For thousands of years, the porous surface of the Yucatán Peninsula has filtered rainwater which in turn created a system of underground rivers and caves. This phenomenon is unique to this part of Mexico and makes up the largest network of caves in the world. Currently, an estimated six thousand cenotes have been found in both Yucatán State and Quintana Roo."

"Impressive," I said, noting the places where I'd be able to hide for the night. "Can we go further into the cave? I'd love to see more of the underground river system I've heard so much about."

"Of course." Juan pulled his mask down as did I, and we continued on.

The further into the cave we went, the darker it became. We paused several times as Juan explained the cave's features. About thirty minutes later we arrived at what Juan indicated would be our last stop and turned on the light, pointing it toward the ceiling. The beam picked up a massive rock formation above our heads, with dozens of stalactites reaching toward the water. I noted two distinct channels further inside the cave and asked Juan about them.

"They each flow to a different destination. As I said before, the underground system is extensive."

"I read somewhere that often these rivers terminate at other cenotes farther in the jungle."

Juan nodded. "That is true. Some are less developed than others." He swung the beam of the light to illuminate the channel to our right. "For instance, explorers have followed this one to an ancient Maya site never before discovered."

"Is it open to the public?"

"Not yet. Archaeologists are still exploring the ruins and cataloguing artifacts. It won't be available for viewing for several years."

I felt a slight tug and I tightened my grip on the float.

"Is there a current here?" It hadn't occurred to me that might be the case, although it was a river and rivers usually had currents.

"There is. Though negligible at the entrance of the cave, it becomes quite strong the farther you travel inside." He shined the light at me. "You look like you're getting cold. Shall we go back to the main cavern?"

"Sure," I said. "This is such a fascinating tour, I don't want it to end. Could we take our time going back and use the light?"

Juan agreed and kept it on as we made our way back toward the entrance with a running narrative at various places along the way. Sometime later, we reached the main cavern.

"Would you like to keep the snorkeling gear and explore a bit on your own?" Juan asked.

"I would. Thank you, Juan."

"Certainly. Just return them to the kiosk before the park closes for the evening."

He helped me carry my stuff up to a viewing platform in the sun where I could warm up. We then shook hands and I tipped him before he left for his next tour.

The sun had dipped lower in the sky and I estimated the time to be three or three-thirty in the afternoon. The park closed at five-thirty, which meant I had some time on my hands. I put on the sunglasses and hat and lay on the borrowed towel, hoping to relax before closing.

I woke a short time later and noticed the park had thinned out. Only a few swimmers remained. My stomach growling, I threw on my t-shirt and grabbed my backpack, asking a young family sitting nearby if they'd watch my gear for me while I went to buy some food. They agreed and I headed for the snack bar.

As I waited in line for my order of nachos two fully dressed men making their way through the crowd caught my eye. Everyone else wore either shorts or bathing suits and the men stood out. I sank down behind the guy in front of me, keeping him between me and the two men's sight line. They both wore sunglasses, but by the grim set of their mouths and the way they carried themselves they appeared to be looking for someone, and not in a good way.

The two stopped and conferred, with the taller one doing most of the talking. The shorter man nodded and they split up. He disappeared behind the bathrooms, while the taller one headed straight for the snack bar.

Heart in my throat, I ducked and peeled off the line, pushing through the small group of tourists. I turned the corner of the building and did a quick check of the perimeter for signs of the other guy. He stood near the ladies room as a group of women walked out the door, laughing. As soon as they disappeared, he slipped inside.

The entrance to the cave stood several yards to my left. I shed my t-shirt and stuffed it into the pack, and pushed the wide-brimmed hat down low over my face. Then I slid the sunglasses on and walked back to the cenote, glad no one could notice my rapid heartbeat and dry mouth. I showed my ticket to the man at the entrance and proceeded down the stairs to the viewing platform. As I approached my things I smiled at the family and thanked them as I picked up my gear. Still working at appearing relaxed and in no hurry, I continued down the stairs to the edge of the pool and slid into the water.

Stay calm, Kate. Don't draw attention to yourself. I placed my pack and the big flashlight on the diving float and then put on the snorkel gear, saving the fins for last.

"Hey! Watch it, will you?" someone above me said. I sank deeper into the water behind the float, keeping my pack between me and the people on shore, and allowed myself a quick glance up the stairs.

The taller man had stopped halfway down and looked out over the remaining swimmers. People nearby gave him dirty looks until he removed his sunglasses and glared at them. The people in his direct line of vision drew back, and the steps in front of him emptied. He turned his head my way, but before his gaze found me I side-stroked away, putting distance between us. Once I'd traveled a few yards I turned onto my stomach and put my face down in the water, the snorkel mask a welcome disguise.

A shrill whistle echoed behind me but I kept swimming, one hand on the float, as though I hadn't heard anything. I rounded the first section of the cave and checked to make sure no one could see me from the platform. They couldn't and I hauled ass, working the fins hard, and passed a small group of snorkelers returning.

The light faded as I continued to swim one-handed, dragging the float along, until I'd gone far enough into the cave to be enveloped in darkness. I stopped and turned on the light to get my bearings. I estimated I'd gone about halfway to where the two channels split, so I turned off the light to save the batteries. Water dripping from above echoed in the pitch black as it landed on the surface of the river. A chill raced up my arms and along my scalp. My earlier trip with Juan had lowered my body temperature. Evidently I hadn't been out of the water long enough to regain sufficient internal heat. With an involuntary shudder I clamped my mouth shut to stop my teeth from chattering. If I didn't keep moving and moving fast, the gunman behind me would be the least of my problems.

Pushing through the cold I continued to swim, stopping at intervals to listen behind me. My instincts told me to keep going, but my body had the final say in the matter. Once more I flicked on the flashlight, searching for something to climb onto in order to get out of the bone-chilling water.

In the middle of the channel sat a large limestone formation with several divots and holes marking the surface. I floated over to it and shoved the dive float onto the rock so it wouldn't float way, then hoisted myself up and out of the water.

With numb fingers, I untied the plastic bag and unzipped my pack to pull out the towel and wrap it around my shoulders. I rubbed my arms and legs to get some feeling back. Then I performed several crunches and swung my arms in a wide arc.

I thought I heard a noise and froze. A faint light wavered in the distance. The rhythmic sound of splashing, like oars cutting through water, floated toward me.

Shit. I thought back to what equipment had been available to rent, but I didn't remember seeing any kind of boats listed. *They must have taken the kayak from the entrance.*

Which meant they'd taken it by force.

As the steady sound grew louder, I stuffed the towel inside the pack and zipped it closed, pushing the float back into the water. Then I climbed off the rock and swam for my life.

20

UNABLE TO USE THE LIGHT in case the men following me could see it, I stayed to the right of the cave so I wouldn't miss the channel once I'd gotten that far. I wouldn't know when I reached it, not in the inky darkness surrounding me.

Memories of being buried alive in an abandoned mine in Arizona popped into my brain and a shudder spiked through me. At least I didn't have to contend with snakes this time. The water was too cold for vipers or Cantils. At least, I hoped so. With any luck, I'd last long enough to get to the channel and beyond, and then find a place to hide.

My teeth chattered and I found it hard to swim. The splashing behind me sounded a lot closer and I switched to sidestroke to minimize noise. My breath came in bursts and echoed like a bomb going off in my ears, although realistically I knew they wouldn't be able to distinguish my breathing from the other cave sounds. Not unless they were close.

My arms growing numb from the cold, I hooked both hands over the float and continued to kick, head first and lying on my back. Low voices floated toward me across the water and light bounced off the walls of the cave.

I'd have to find a place to hide. I doubted I could even lift myself out of the water at this point.

As the light grew I pushed myself to kick harder but still they gained on me. The icy cold had seeped into my body and I found it increasingly difficult to move. A few more minutes and they'd round the corner. The light would find its way to me and I'd be dead in the water.

Literally.

This was the way it was going to end? Dying of hypothermia or a bullet to the head in a cave in Mexico, hunted by my ex-lover's thugs? Seriously?

Fuck that.

With supreme effort, I willed my legs to kick faster, ignoring the deepening numbness. Taking a full breath proved difficult but I kept moving, ignoring the voice in my head telling me my pursuers could hear me.

Without warning the current accelerated and my strokes became easier. I'd reached the channel divide. The float picked up speed as every kick propelled me faster and further along. Soon, the sound of gurgling current replaced the splashing of the men behind me and once again I found myself in complete darkness.

Exhausted, I clung to the float, wishing I'd asked the guide more about the river. How deep was it? Were there rocks or other obstacles I might run into? How long until I reached a place where I could get out?

And more importantly, did the channel remain open, like it was now, or did it narrow in places where I'd have to swim underwater?

Claustrophobia loomed large and I struggled to climb onto the dive float, hoping to at least pull a portion of me out of the water. I managed to make it part of the way as the current rock-and-rolled. The flashlight almost took a header off the float and into the water before I managed to grab it.

I hit the on button and shined it around me, trying to get a sense of my surroundings. The flashlight illuminated a limestone tube rushing by with smooth sides. The swift current precluded my pulling off somewhere even if I would have found a place. Anxiety turned to unmitigated panic when I realized I had no control over direction or speed and no way to stop other than trying to slow down by scraping along the side. The thought of deep abrasions and broken bones from being a human drag anchor stopped me from trying.

To keep myself from freaking out, I flicked off the light to eliminate the visual and slid further into the water. If the cave narrowed too much, the leading section of the float would get stuck first and hopefully keep my head from getting smashed in. Although then my lower body would be at risk of smacking into a submerged rock or something equally hard.

I sped along in the current and envisioned hurtling toward oblivion. Holding on tight to the float and the plastic bag with my pack inside I fought to stay in the center of the tube. Too late, I slammed against the rock wall and scraped along the side, my arm too numb to feel anything. I lost my grip but regained it a split-second later.

That must have been a turn. What's going to happen next? How can I minimize the danger?

When would this rollercoaster ride be over?

My fingers felt like lead sausages and I was afraid I wouldn't be able to hang on long enough to see this wild flume through. The float and I were slicing through the water now, unable to stop. My arms tiring, I dropped farther behind, carving a trough through the water with my chin. If I'd had the strength, I'd have switched to feet-first, a much safer position, but it wasn't going to happen. Arms extended with my fingers gripping the sides, it was all I could do to hang on. The speed continued to increase, inching the float from my grasp and then...

Nothing.

The float slid from my hands as the bottom dropped out from under me, weightless for a few breathless seconds—and then falling, plummeting into the blackness. Dread shot up my spine as I tensed for the landing and held my breath.

Moments later, I plunged beneath the water's surface. I struggled to ascend but the power of the water pummeled me, forcing my body beneath the surface. Numb from the cold and beyond exhausted, I stopped resisting and hung suspended in the cold, dark depths.

Panic reared its head as my lungs screamed for air. Disoriented, I flailed my arms and tried to swim away from the waterfall and rise to the surface.

I emerged with a gasp, sputtering and gulping in air. Still encased in darkness and fueled by adrenaline, I struck out swimming in search of the float and plastic bag with my pack.

Relieved by the lack of current, I headed left. The sound of lapping water told me either a rock or the side of the cave was nearby. As I inched my way toward the noise my hand hit something hard that gave. My fingers curled over the flashlight. I fumbled with the switch and turned it on. The beam had grown weak but lit up my surroundings well enough.

A ledge ran along the side of the cave about six inches above the water. Those six inches could have been a mile as far as I was concerned. The adrenaline had vanished, leaving me weak and numb. The effort it would take to climb from the water looked insurmountable. I strafed the cave with the light and saw a second ledge on the other side, leading to the top one, forming a step. My pack bobbed nearby. All I had to do was swim across and climb up.

I would've had the same reaction if I'd been gazing at a sheer rock wall.

It wasn't going to happen.

You're so close, Kate. Don't give up now. Swim.

Not a fan of death by hypothermia I left the flashlight on and pushed off from the wall, one-handing toward my pack, sinking lower in the water with each stroke. The struggle to keep my head above water matched that of my effort to draw closer to the pack and the ledge. Finally, my left hand found the rock and I dragged myself up and over the lower ledge, flopping over onto my back.

I rested for a moment, listening to my ragged breathing and feeling my heart pound in my chest. Once I'd gotten my breath under control, I sat up and reached for the plastic bag holding my backpack. After several tries, I finally succeeded in untying the knot. I unzipped the pack and pulled out the towel, my t-shirt, the shirt I'd stolen, my jeans and boots.

After a brisk rub-down, I dried my hair and then wrapped the towel like a turban around my head. Wet, cold, and barely able to feel my lower extremities, I rolled onto my hands and knees and pushed myself upright to pull on my jeans. It took far longer than normal to dress and putting on my socks and boots ended up being a major undertaking, but I managed. I remembered the Chiclets and after several tries opened the box and popped a couple in my mouth. Anything to keep my teeth from chattering.

I held the weakening light in front of me and staggered along the upper ledge, careful not to deviate and fall back into the water.

I'd walked for several minutes when I came to another channel that split off to my right. Either I'd have to try and jump across or continue along the other way to the right.

I turned right.

I'd lost track of how long I'd been stumbling along when I felt a warm gust of air from somewhere in front of me. *Wishful thinking, Kate. Just keep going.*

The further I went the warmer it became, until the tunnel jagged to the left and I rounded a corner. Ahead of me a faint glow beckoned. I blinked to be sure. The light remained. Hope rose in my chest and I continued toward the source, my body responding to the possibility of warmth.

The temperature rose and soon I gained the company of some curious flying insects: a dragonfly, two bees, the occasional moth. These were followed by several bats whizzing around my head. A tiny buzzing erupted near my ear. I'd never been so happy to hear a mosquito in my life.

The tunnel widened and I found myself in a wide cave. The river, still a trickle, had largely been replaced by rocks and sand.

I clambered out of the cave's mouth and into the fading light of day. The afternoon heat permeated my body and I stood with my head back and eyes closed as I soaked it in.

A couple of minutes later, I remembered to turn off the flashlight, and then let my pack fall to the ground. I opened my eyes and took a look around. Lush jungle surrounded me.

As the bats continued their dive bombing, I picked up my pack and walked along the rocky ground, not knowing where to go but grateful to be out of the caves and somewhere warm…

…and away from the men who hunted me.

21

I DIDN'T STRAY FAR. WITH only dense jungle as far as I could see in the short walk I took, I realized I was too tired to continue. The afternoon sun had set, and the shadows were lengthening. I wanted to be somewhere near shelter since it looked like I would have to stay there for the night.

Back at the mouth of the cave, I placed my pack high in the rocks above the entrance and climbed up next to it, tucking myself out of sight behind a large boulder and pulling out the gun to keep nearby. Night had fallen and I didn't trust myself walking around with only the weak beam from the flashlight. Luckily, my body temperature had recovered to the point that I didn't shake involuntarily. I shook out the plastic bag my backpack had been in and slid my feet inside, wrapping the top around my calves for warmth. At least now I had a chance of surviving the lower temperatures the evening would bring.

I nodded off for a time, but jolted awake at the crackle of dry grass and twigs snapping in the underbrush. Instantly alert, I grabbed the gun and aimed it at the noise, peering around the rock to stare into the darkness. Though the moon still hung low on the horizon and much of the terrain remained in shadow, I could just make out a dark shape by a bush several yards from the cave. I tensed and tracked it with the gun, waiting for my unknown visitor to wander nearer so I could get a good look at what I was about to shoot.

As it drew closer, the outline of an animal materialized. I held my breath and continued to wait, hoping it would leave after getting a drink from the shallow pool inside the cave. It stopped as if waiting for something. I scanned the darkness behind it and another, taller shape appeared. As the two shadows drew nearer, I realized the taller shadow was human.

I debated shouting a warning, but thought twice and stopped myself before I did. Not only would I give away my location, but if it was one of Salazar's men, I'd be toast. Yes, I was situated above them, hidden in a crevice, but moving away from my position quickly wasn't an option unless I jumped and that could result in an injury.

And a little thing like being shot to death.

The two dark forms advanced toward me. Dry-mouthed and hands sweating, I kept the gun trained on their approach. The shapes morphed as they revealed more detail the closer they got. The man wore a pair of night-vision goggles and carried a pack on his back. He stepped from the bushes, accompanied by a large dog. I fought my rising hopes that it might be someone from camp.

That would be too much like wishful thinking.

I lowered the gun and waited for both figures to walk closer. A spasm gripped my leg. My feet knocked a rock loose and I watched in horror as it bounced to the ground below. The man's head snapped up and he reached behind him, sliding a rifle around to the front. The dog stilled. The man turned and scanned above the cave. I shrank back, out of his line of sight, still unsure if he was friendly.

"Kate?" he said in a low voice, taking a step forward and then stopping. "It's Quinn."

Quinn?

Breathing again, I sat up. "What are you doing out here?" I asked as I pulled the plastic bag off my feet. "God, I'm glad to see you." I put the bag and the gun inside the backpack and zipped it closed, then climbed down, sliding the last few feet to the ground. Artemis ran to greet me and I bent down, letting her lick my face.

"We've been looking for you since we got word from Ernesto. Are you all right?" he said, sliding his NVGs off.

"I'm fine. How did you find me?" It's not like the place was on a map.

Quinn shrugged out of his backpack and knelt down, rummaging inside.

"Ernesto told us he'd mentioned the river system to you. After combing through town and not finding you, One Shot and I went to Wild Cenote, hoping you'd taken Ernesto's suggestion and were somewhere nearby. I talked to one of the guides there who remembered you. He told us about the two men taking the kayak from the entrance at gunpoint and heading into the caves, and we knew somebody was after you."

"But how did you figure out I'd be here? There's got to be dozens of places where the rivers terminate."

Quinn stood up and handed me an energy bar. Gratefully, I accepted it and tore off the wrapper, polishing it off in two bites except for a small piece I offered to Artemis. She snuffled at it and then inhaled the piece, licking my hand for more.

"I got lucky. Lalo and One Shot are covering two of the larger outlets. There were three more on the list to check tonight before we went back for additional manpower."

"They shot Charlie." I said. Quinn nodded, his face grim.

"Yeah. When he didn't come back right away, I sent my guys out to find him, even before Ernesto called." He stared past me into the dark. "I wish I would've been there."

Deep, gut-wrenching guilt worked its way up through my stomach and into my chest. It must have shown on my face.

"It's not your fault, Kate. Charlie knew the risks," Quinn said, his voice brusque. "There's a good possibility the ambush might not have been meant for you. There's been chatter about a new cartel in the area. It's possible they meant us."

"Which means it's going to be more dangerous for you guys."

"Yeah. Like I said, we're aware of the risks. Frankly, I'm surprised they didn't catch on sooner."

He picked up his pack and slung it over his shoulder.

"How's Pascal doing?"

"He wanted to be part of the search party. I told him no." Quinn raised his hand and glanced at his watch. "We should go."

We trekked through the jungle along an invisible path only Quinn and Artemis could see. Quinn had glow-in-the-dark tape on the back side of his pack which made following him much easier. The pack bounced like an unblinking firefly in front of me.

About half an hour later we came to one of the camp's trucks parked along a faint path. He grabbed the mike attached to the CB radio.

"Six to base, over."

The radio crackled. "This is base, over."

"Precious Cargo secure. I say again, Precious Cargo secure. How copy, over."

"Copy Precious Cargo secure, over."

Quinn signed off and slid into the driver's seat. I climbed in the other side with Artemis and shut the door.

"Thank you, Quinn," I said, my voice quiet. "I don't know how to repay this."

Quinn turned. "Sure you do, Kate." He waited a moment, watching my reaction. "We could use you, if you're willing."

I started to protest but he held up his hand.

"Hear me out. Pascal and I had a conversation after you left with Charlie. He suggested I'd missed an opportunity with you. I had to agree with him."

"What do you mean?"

"We have a mutual objective. We both want to wipe Salazar off the face of the earth."

"And?"

"And I think I know a way to do that, if you're up for it. It involves some risk."

He turned the key in the ignition and the truck sprang to life. Realizing how cold I was, I reached my hands toward the warm air vents. Quinn noticed and turned the heater on high. "Besides," he said, "where else are you going to go?"

He was right, at least about not having anywhere to go. Salazar's people weren't going to stop coming after me. We pulled onto the dirt road while I fought with myself. Then an idea occurred to me.

"Is there a way to broadcast that you guys found my corpse tonight? They'd stop coming after me if they thought I was dead."

Quinn appeared to consider my request. "Possibly." We came to a crossroads and he turned left. "I'll make a deal with you. If you agree to do what I'm about to ask you to do and it works the way I think it will, then afterwards if you don't want to continue for whatever reason, we'll find a way to fake your death and make sure everyone knows."

"What's in it for you? You're taking a chance on me being able to bring something to the table. I don't have anything you guys need. I can shoot a weapon, but you've got plenty of guys to do that."

"According to Pascal there's a reason we found you at the cenote the first time. If it weren't for you, he probably wouldn't be here. That might be the extent of it, I don't know." He stared out the windshield as he drove. "What I do know is when you offered to act as bait in exchange for his life, you showed courage. I respect courage. And, you have an insider's knowledge about Salazar. Those reasons alone are enough to put you on the team."

Not sure what to say, I turned to look out the window at the road flowing by. I was sick of Salazar and Anaya and all the killing. And the running. Would joining a group of men whose sole purpose was to eliminate the cartels be any better? The memory of having a clear shot at Salazar in the SUV and my inability to pull the trigger came roaring back. What if, down the line, I was confronted with the same scenario? If the opportunity arose, would I be able to kill someone? If not, what if my inaction led to someone on the team getting killed? Was that what Quinn was asking me to do?

Did I want to live that life?

What kind of life lies ahead of you now, Kate? My stubborn refusal to see the truth was annoying. Maybe the time had come to work within my reality. If that meant I had to learn to kill someone or whatever it was Quinn was suggesting, then maybe I needed to learn. Soldiers at war had to be ready to defend their country by all means necessary. How would this be any different? These men were defending their country from the cartels. True, they didn't have the public blessings of the government, but I doubted many in the government wanted them to succeed.

I thought of Lalo and how he'd gone home for a wedding against the cartel's orders and realized too late that his family would pay the price. Now he was determined to help bring them down, whatever it took. Would Cole's death just be a footnote in the annals of southwest history? *Arizona Sheriff Found Dead of Gunshot Wounds at Rest Area.* What happened to all the rage I felt at his murder? Would I give up that easily? Cole deserved more.

I took a deep breath and turned to Quinn. "I'm in."

22

WE ARRIVED BACK AT CAMP about an hour later. Quinn had me wear a blindfold, 'for my protection'. That may have been part of the reason, but I knew he was far more interested in protecting the camp in case I was captured by the wrong people.

Some of the men were playing Texas Hold 'Em in the mess tent while others cleaned their guns or huddled together in hushed conversation. Still others preferred their own company and had retired early to their tent or hut. I didn't see Blondie anywhere. When I mentioned it to Quinn, he walked over to talk with one of the men playing cards.

"Their ETA is fifteen mikes," he said when he walked back to join me. "When you're ready, I'd like to debrief you, alone." Quinn's demeanor may have been calm and steady, but I detected a driving intensity in his eyes I hadn't noticed before.

"I'm ready now, if you are."

"Sure."

I followed Quinn outside and back to his tent, Aries and Artemis close behind. He pulled the flap aside for me to enter, then walked in behind me.

"Have a seat." He indicated a chair by the table and sat across from me. The dogs curled up on their respective beds.

"Thanks again for coming to look for me. I appreciate it." I clasped my hands on the table. "I'm so sorry about Charlie," I added in a quiet voice.

He nodded and cleared his throat. "When Lalo came back with the news about Charlie, I assumed you'd been taken."

"It's getting real old, Quinn. I'm tired. I don't know how to do this anymore."

"Yeah. About that." The look on his face told me I wouldn't like what came next.

His eyes cut through me. I felt like a bug about to be pinned to a bug board.

"Are you willing to give up your old life, never see anyone you used to know?" he asked. "Learn how to out-gun, outwit and out-kill the cartels? Because that's what we do. We're not a kinder, gentler, politically correct kind of organization. We expect and achieve results."

I took a deep breath before answering.

"I've gone over and over this in my mind and I keep coming back to the same conclusion: I don't have any place else to go." I watched the two German Shepherds asleep in their beds, content with their role in Quinn's life. "I've lost everything that meant anything because of Salazar. Eventually, the hatred I feel for him is going to get me in the kind of trouble that I won't be able to escape.

"Pascal says your organization can harness that hatred and show me how to use it while at the same time help your cause. I'd like to see if he's right." I leaned toward him, placing my palms on the table. "I'm very aware that if I leave again, I'll be looking over my shoulder for the rest of my life however long that might be. The way things are going, I doubt I'll see my next birthday."

Quinn studied me long and hard. He nodded as though he'd made up his mind about something and said, "What we discuss in here is to remain strictly confidential. You're to tell no one. Agreed?"

"Agreed."

"I want you to infiltrate Morales' compound."

The shock must have shown on my face.

"Hear me out, Kate." He leaned forward, elbows on his knees. "You've got something Morales needs: information on Salazar. What he does, how he plans—the same intel you gave me. He doesn't know where you've been these past few days, since I highly doubt he's contacted Salazar or Diaz directly. At least, not yet. Not while Salazar's on the offensive."

"What do you mean, 'not yet'?"

"There's the distinct possibility Morales may reach out to Diaz to join forces if they believe there's another cartel making a play for the area. I need to be sure that doesn't happen."

"And you want me to feed Morales false information about Salazar?"

"It doesn't even have to be false information, but yes, that's what I'm suggesting."

Stunned, I tried to imagine myself going to Morales with information. All I could see was my untimely torture and death. My palms sweating, I got out of my chair and paced the room.

"When I said I'd be willing to help, I didn't expect this."

"I won't throw you to the wolves, Kate."

I turned on him, my heart rate sky rocketing. "But that's the way it sounds, Quinn."

"If you'll have a seat, I'll explain."

After a few deep breaths, I sat down, arms crossed. "You were about to tell me how I'm not going to end up as crocodile food in a lake somewhere in the Yucatán?"

"It's going to be dangerous. I won't kid you. But we will take every precaution to keep you safe."

"I've heard that line before, Quinn. Believe me, it does nothing to alleviate my concerns." When it came to Salazar, there was no 'safe'. "How do you intend to set up a meeting with Morales? There's no way he'll bite if he thinks another cartel is trying to set up shop here. Wouldn't the timing alone be suspicious?"

"Ernesto, my friend from the hotel, is connected to Morales by blood. Suffice it to say, Morales will at least listen if the information comes from him."

"What, you mean he's his cousin or something? How do you know you can trust him? Blood almost always trumps friendship in the cartel world."

"You don't need to know. What matters is that a trusted source presents Morales with the possibility of gaining inside information on his enemy. He will have heard about the shootout in town by now. We're sure the men who came after you belonged to Salazar, or they wouldn't have gone to such lengths to capture you." Quinn sat back in his chair, a wry smile on his face. "It's the perfect cover story. You narrowly escaped with your life and have now decided to turn the tables on your old lover, Roberto, in the hope that his enemies will destroy him. Hell hath no fury, right?"

"Say I agree to do what you ask. How do I get whatever information I find out to you without him getting suspicious? I may not know him personally, but I know how cartel bosses work. It's not like he'll give me the run of his compound."

"Not at first. Stay with me here. Best-case scenario: you feed him just enough information to make him believe you're a valuable asset in his fight against *El Castillo*. I'll help you with that." Quinn tapped a manila folder on the table in front of him. "You slowly gain his trust and he gives you more leeway. Once you've achieved that, you can ask to be escorted into town. I'll give you three drop sights in different areas where you can leave coded messages which I'll pick up at irregular intervals. If I need to get a message to you, I'll do the same."

"And the worst-case scenario?"

Quinn shook his head. "Don't worry about that. I've got it covered."

"Don't worry? How the hell am I not supposed to worry about things going to shit?" I jumped to my feet and resumed pacing. "I'll give you a worst-case scenario. Yucatán Kate's going to be Yucatán dead."

Quinn crossed his arms over his chest. "Your call, Kate. I could give you a gun and throw you out there with the rest of the men, but I think you've got a hell of a lot more potential than that. This could work. You are the one person who holds the key and can make the difference. As long as you do everything I tell you to, you will be safe."

The word *could* is what threw me. I decided to play along. "You said coded message. I can tell you right now, my memory isn't great if I'm stressed out. I'd say infiltrating a drug cartel is the ultimate definition of stressful. How am I supposed to be able to remember a code?"

Quinn pulled out a piece of paper with a drawing of a flower on it. "What do you see?"

"A flower."

"Look closer. Especially the smaller petals in the interior and the leaves along the stem."

I stared at the crudely drawn flower for several minutes before I realized that the shape of the leaves and petals formed words. I glanced at Quinn.

"There are words hidden in the leaves."

"Exactly. As long as the message you write is contained within those two elements of the drawing, I'll be able to read it. Anyone else who sees this will think it's just a drawing, as long as you keep it from being obvious."

"I think I can handle that." I drew in a deep breath. What else could I do? I had to trust Quinn knew what he was doing. I'd seen how he tried to keep his men safe. I had to believe he'd do the same for me. I stopped pacing and turned to face him.

"What happens afterward, assuming I survive?"

"If we both agree, then you stay on with us and we work together to eradicate these motherfuckers. Deal?" He reached across the table.

I'd probably be more than ready to leave Mexico by then, but at the least I'd have helped repay a debt I feel I owed Quinn. And, if I got lucky, Salazar would be dead and one less problem. I slid my palm in his and we shook.

"Deal."

When I returned to the mess tent, Blondie and Lalo had returned and were playing cards with the poker party.

I grabbed a cup of coffee and had a seat a few chairs down from the raucous group. Blondie folded and came around to my side of the table and sat down.

"Glad to see you, Kate. You look a little worse for wear."

I smoothed my hair back and smiled. "Yeah, going over a waterfall has a tendency to mess with your wardrobe."

"No shit?" Blondie sat back in his chair, eyebrows raised. "You are one lucky *gringa*. Word is the two men after you were Salazar's favorite trackers. You know what losing you means to them, right?"

"Wild guess. They have to find another job?" I asked, knowing full well Salazar was one click shy of crazy town and would probably have them decapitated or something equally horrific, just to show he wasn't getting soft.

Or sane.

Blondie snorted. "Yeah. I don't think they'll be around long enough to collect unemployment."

Two down, hundreds, no, *thousands* to go. What Quinn's guys were attempting hit me hard and I had to fight feelings of panic fueled by the enormity of the situation and what I was about to do. How did they get up every day and not think about the futility of their mission? Perseverance might be one thing, but this was going above and beyond. *What am I getting myself into?*

"What's next for Yucatán Kate?" Blondie asked.

I shrugged, remembering Quinn's warning to play it close and not tell anyone. "Quinn said it's okay for me to stay here until things calm down. He mentioned something about me monitoring radio transmissions while you guys are out fighting the good fight."

"Did he mention anything about getting you some physical training?"

"Yeah. I start tomorrow." Quinn thought it would be a good idea for me to learn some techniques to supplement my brief Krav Maga training before I infiltrated Morales' camp. I think it was his way of mollifying any fears I had of my going into the lion's den without direct backup. The only thing that would assuage my fears at the thought of infiltrating Morales' kingdom would be a ballistic missile targeting both his and Salazar's compounds.

That, and a plane ticket to Tahiti.

"Good idea." Blondie peered at me, frowning. "You look a bit freaked out."

"Must be because I'm afraid I won't be able to hack it in this heat." Or, maybe it was because I was scared shitless Morales would find me out, torture me, and hack my head off with a dull machete.

Yeah. Probably that.

He grinned. "Piece of cake, Kate. Piece of cake."

The next morning almost killed me.

We started promptly at six, before the heat of the day sucked the energy from everyone in the group. My training partner, Hector, was a tall muscleman from Mexico City. He'd begun training the week before, as did the other five recruits. I marveled at how he didn't let the humidity and rising temperatures bother him like the rest of the guys. When I asked him how he did it, he shrugged and told me he had good genes.

The introduction to our instructor, Buck made me seriously rethink the whole training scenario. The calisthenics weren't bad, compared to the obstacle course and two-mile run with a thirty-pound pack in ninety-degree heat. We'd get the sixty-pound ones in two days. Memories of being chased through Mexico with a backpack filled with Salazar's money came back to taunt me and I redoubled my efforts at meeting and surpassing the challenge. It did keep my anxiety level at a low boil, which I guess was Quinn's point in enrolling me in hell.

We broke for lunch at noon, then were back at it until three-thirty. As a reward for not dying during training, we were allowed an hour of free time before dinner. It occurred to me that if I'd wanted to be in the military, I'd have joined already.

Over the next few days, we learned to fight using techniques from Jujitsu, Tae Kwon Do, and Judo. The challenge helped me ignore the heat and my increasing fatigue. What little training I had came in handy when it was time to spar with Hector. He was no slouch, though, and I found myself on the ground more than once. When I asked him why he was there and not back home in Mexico City during one of our twenty-minute lunch breaks, he stared into the distance, seemingly lost in his memories.

"Seven months ago, my wife and I were in Cancun on our honeymoon. We'd just finished a romantic dinner on the beach and were walking back in the moonlight to our waterfront hotel. Two SUVs drove by on the street, going fast. A few minutes later, they returned. One of the windows rolled down and I saw a gun."

Hector hesitated as he picked at a piece of tomato on his sandwich. Then he cleared his throat. "The bullet shattered the right side of Claudia's head, destroying her face." He took a deep breath before he continued, his face coloring. "They told me she didn't suffer. They also told me that it was probably some drunk local. They refused to confirm my accusations that it was a cartel member. That kind of thing *never* happens in Cancun." He crumpled his napkin into a tight ball. "*Pendejos.*"

When he turned toward me, his eyes radiated a pain so raw I caught my breath. "She was only twenty-three. We'd just moved into a new house—" Hector stopped, blinking back tears.

I didn't say anything. What good would it do? Words were a hollow offering to a person reliving a nightmare. In my experience, the most respectful response to another's suffering was to stay quiet and listen to their grief.

He wiped his eyes with the back of his hand. I offered him my napkin, which he took.

"I met one of Q's men in a bar in Cancun a day before I left. I'd had a few drinks and told him my story. He suggested I meet with Q. At the time I wasn't in any condition to stay in Cancun, much less fight and I told him that. He assured me that was normal but gave me his number in case I ever changed my mind." He stared at the ground, remembering. "I flew Claudia's body home, attended her funeral, tried to resume my old life. But I couldn't. The senselessness of her death ate at me until I couldn't control the anger, couldn't live with myself. That's when I called."

I wondered how many more there were like Hector—innocent bystanders brutalized by the cartels in the vicious war being conducted across Mexico. I also wondered if Quinn's band of fighters were just the beginning. How long would the folks living in this country allow unfettered evil to thrive? A chill raced along my spine as I thought about the possibilities. It was time for a revolution, time for survivors to rise up and take back their country.

All it would take was a match on the dry tinder of revenge.

Mexico was ripe for change.

23

AT THE END OF THE week Quinn called me into his tent for a meeting. The shadows of late afternoon had just begun to lengthen into early evening, lessening the sun's searing heat. Not exactly looking forward to this meeting, I wondered if my time to go into Morales' camp had arrived.

"You wanted to see me?" I asked, taking a seat at the table. Aries padded over so I could scratch him behind the ears. Artemis followed seconds later and nosed him out of the way.

"I did," Quinn said, watching his dogs. "Buck tells me you're doing well. That you pick things up quickly and are able to translate new procedures and strategies into practical, realistic goals. In his words, you're kicking ass."

I smiled in spite of myself. "That's good to hear. It's hard work, but I like it. For the first time since I escaped from Salazar I feel like I'm doing something constructive with my life."

"I have to tell you, I didn't think you'd last a day, not with Buck on your ass." Something close to a smile tugged at his mouth but then was gone. "I'm glad to say I was wrong."

"Thanks, Quinn. That means a lot." I continued to scratch Artemis behind the ears, switching to Aries when his muzzle pushed her out of the way. "Before we get into why you asked me here, I'd like to ask you a personal question, if it's all right."

"Such as?"

I detected a slight cooling of his attitude toward me, but I pressed on. "How did you come to be here in the Yucatán? I mean, obviously you've had experience in the military or something similar. I've watched how you run this place and it's close to what I know of standard operating procedure. Why not work with the DEA or the CIA to help the Mexican government fight the cartels? It's got to be more difficult without those agency's resources."

"Not as difficult as playing by the rules."

"Okay, then why Mexico? There are a million other deserving causes in the world where your abilities would be in demand, and for a good price. It doesn't look like you're making a lot of coin," I said, and glanced pointedly at his austere accommodations.

"Believe it or not, sometimes it's not about the money."

I felt like one of his shepherds with a bone and I didn't want to let it go. The Rottweiler scowl moved across his face, but I ignored the warning.

"Look," I said. "You know my motivation. I want Salazar to pay. I take full responsibility for the colossally stupid mistake I made of being the girlfriend of a cartel boss. But I've paid dearly for being naïve and it doesn't look like Salazar's ever going to let it go. I'm tired of looking over my shoulder, wondering if today might be my last."

"But you haven't been entirely truthful, have you?"

"What do you mean?"

"What about the money?"

Crap. I had hoped to keep that little tidbit in the background. I wondered who told him. It was probably common knowledge in certain circles. Sighing, I looked him in the eye. "By money I assume you're referring to the cash I stole from Salazar?"

Quinn nodded. "Talk about a bad idea."

"Well, yeah. Of course it was. I don't like to dwell on my mistakes. I lost it all before I even made it back to the States." Except for the large stash I buried at Lana's place all those years ago. Technically, since I buried it near the base of a tree in her side yard I didn't consider that portion lost, although I had no idea if it was still there. Someday, after this was all over and Salazar and Anaya were nothing but a bad dream, I planned to go back to see what happened to both Lana and the money. If she got lucky and found it, at least the cash went to a good cause. I could see her pulling the plastic bags out of the hole I dug, filthy with age and dirt, and finding all that money still intact.

"Maybe, but it doesn't change the fact that you weren't completely up front about your past."

"Everybody's got secrets, Quinn."

Aries whined and nudged my hand. Artemis laid her head on my leg and looked up at me, her soulful eyes begging for attention. I ducked my head and focused on the two dogs, waiting to see if Quinn would give me anything further.

"Okay. You want to know why I'm here?" He slid his chair toward the table. "Because my contribution is effective. There's a movement in this country that's been gaining momentum. It started with a core group of men who got the idea that they could fight the cartels. Problem was, they didn't have any idea how to strategize, how to organize, how to fight smart." Quinn paused before continuing.

"A joint task force between the CIA and DEA fostered the first group, gave them training and weapons, helped build them into a fighting unit. Then another group cropped up, and another. Soon, there were several small pockets of fighters being trained and armed, ready to go at the cartels, fight them on their own terms."

"That's great, right? People are fighting back."

"Sounds good, doesn't it? The CIA informed the Mexican government who then decided to take things into their own hands. In essence they deputized the men and let them loose on the cartels with their blessings."

I knew where this was headed. "But now that the government knows about them, cartel moles have infiltrated these groups and they're getting creamed."

"Bingo."

"You used to work for the CIA?"

Quinn snorted. "Not exactly. You could say I was aligned with a different kind of organization."

I knew all about the cartel infiltrating government agencies. My ex-bodyguard, Eduardo, had been murdered before he made it into the witness protection program because somebody somewhere got the information to Salazar or Anaya that he'd helped me escape. And, the safe house where I'd been staying before testifying at Salazar's trial had been blown to bits. Luis and I barely escaped with our lives. Both instances were traced to a mole in either the Mexican government or the DEA field office. Not knowing which agency might be involved, I refused to go into the protection program. In my mind, it would be the same as painting a big red bull's eye on my back and telling Salazar exactly where to find me.

"That's the reason you don't work closely with the government," I said.

"Would you?"

I studied him for a moment, sensing there was more to the story. Lalo and Victor's motives flashed through my mind, and finally it clicked. "Something else happened. Something you can't forgive." I almost missed the telltale twitch in his eye. "That's it, isn't it?"

He answered with stony silence.

"Fine. You don't want to talk about it. I get that. Why relive the past, right? Except that means I'm operating on assumed information about you, and relying on assumptions isn't a great way to stay alive."

He remained quiet. I could almost hear his brain whirring away, accepting and then discarding possible responses.

"Everyone has to rely on assumptions to some extent. But, you're right. At least you were honest with me when I confronted you about the money you'd stolen. In return, I'll be up front with you about why I'm here." He paused, evidently collecting his thoughts. "I'd recently retired from twenty years in the organization I mentioned earlier. My wife, Maria, and I had a small home outside of Merida. I wanted to settle down and start over, leave my shit-storm of a life behind me. On occasion, I'd be called out to consult, for lack of a better word.

"After one of those consulting trips I came back to find blood on the kitchen floor and Maria gone. Four hours later I received a phone call indicating she'd been kidnapped by members of a well-known drug cartel. Someone had given my name to them in return for their life, linking me to a recent raid on their leader's headquarters which resulted in his arrest."

Up to this point, he'd recited the story without emotion, as though it had happened to someone else.

"But you didn't have anything to do with the raid since you were retired, right?"

He let out a long sigh. "Groundwork I'd done a few years before led to my organization finding the location, but I wasn't involved in the raid, no."

"What happened to Maria?" I asked, even though I knew the ending.

"What usually happens in those kinds of situations. Maria was killed before I could get to her."

"I'm sorry, Quinn." I knew what it was like to lose innocent lives because of past actions. Maybe that was why he was able to tell me. Or, it could have been bullshit, giving me something to file away in my brain, allowing me to make connections that weren't really there, but I didn't think so.

He cleared his throat and shifted in his seat. Emotion wasn't something that made a regular appearance with a man like Quinn, and it obviously made him uncomfortable.

"Now that I've given you what you wanted, I'd like to get to why I asked you here."

"Of course." I felt a small flame of anxiety ignite in my solar plexus.

"The email you sent from Tabai reached your guy in the DEA."

"You've heard from Luis?"

"He contacted me a few days ago requesting my permission to send someone to talk to you."

"Who?" My mind whirled. With the chaos of the last few days I'd forgotten about the email.

"He's waiting for you in your hut. I brought him in the back way so there wouldn't be any questions from the men. I'll take him out the same way when you're done."

"How much does this person know?"

"Nothing, other than our mission is to eliminate the cartels by whatever means necessary. That's all the DEA knows, at this point. We don't share our plans and they don't share theirs, unless there's the possibility of an overlap. I didn't tell either Luis or this guy anything about you infiltrating Morales' group. I suggest you don't either."

My mind raced as I walked to my hut. I understood why Luis didn't come here himself. He'd been promoted to supervisor the year before and was happy to stay in the relative safety of the U.S. But who did he send?

I wasn't going to deny it, if Luis' guy was here to get me out of Mexico, the temptation to take him up on his offer loomed large. But if I accepted their help, then I'd be going back to the way things had been. Running. Looking over my shoulder. Not being able to form close relationships.

Same old, same old.

I walked the last few yards to the door of my hut and opened it, the internal battle raging between the two Kates. My guest sat in the corner of the hut on the lone chair Pascal had given me to use, his face in shadow. He stood when I entered and walked toward me.

I froze when I realized who it was.

24

S AM AKIAQ HADN'T CHANGED MUCH, except for the subtle crow's feet at the corner of his dark eyes. Like when I first met him, he wore his black hair pulled into a ponytail. He still had the appearance of a runner; long and lean with powerful legs.

I checked my impulse to go to him. It had been over six years since we'd seen each other or spoken, and I didn't know how well it would play. Once I'd caught my breath, I smiled.

"Sam."

"Kate." Never one for long soliloquys, Sam usually conserved his words. When we first met I'd been hard-pressed to get more than one or two-word answers out of him. It was only later, after we'd been intimate, that he opened up and I'd gotten to know the real Sam. Now, his tranquil expression acted like a balm on my restless, beat-up soul.

Not knowing how to begin, I stayed uncharacteristically quiet. Sensing my mood, he walked over to me and enveloped me in his arms, murmuring in my ear that it was good to see me again.

My arms rose of their own volition to return the hug. He still wore the same, masculine cedar-scented aftershave. A wave of memories surfaced and I melted into him.

It didn't take long for the tears to come. Unable to control myself from releasing years of guilt and pain over being responsible for him being shot and left for dead on the side of a highway in Alaska, I wept quietly, pissed off that I didn't have a tissue, not to mention feeling like an idiot for breaking down as soon as I saw him.

So not what I'd envisioned.

He let me finish, holding me against him in a gentle hug until the last sob. I broke away first, stepping back to wipe my cheeks with my hand. He reached in his pocket and pulled out a handkerchief.

"Thanks," I said, accepting it and drying my eyes. "Sorry. Not the way I expected this moment to go."

"Why wouldn't you see me when Luis first contacted you in Arizona?"

The tears came close to spilling over again when I saw the hurt in Sam's eyes.

"There is—was—someone else. I didn't want to complicate things." I folded the handkerchief, keeping it in my hand in case the waterworks started again. "The same woman who shot you, shot and killed him when he tried to protect me."

"You mean Cole Anderson?"

"Luis told you?"

Sam nodded, a guarded look on his face. "You haven't heard?"

My hand stilled. "Heard what?"

"Cole survived. He may have lost the hearing in one ear, but he's alive. They're keeping him in a medical coma until the swelling in his brain goes down."

My knees liquefied and I reached for something solid as the world shifted. The whole breathing thing wasn't working too well at the moment. Hyperventilation appeared imminent.

Sam took my arm and guided me across the room, then lowered me into the chair.

"But I saw the article…" Why would Angie go to the trouble of showing me a doctored news release?

"The DEA planted the article in the paper—in case whoever shot him wanted to finish the job."

"Is he all right otherwise? There's no brain damage?"

"From what Luis told me, he'd been coherent before they induced the coma." Sam grew quiet. "He couldn't remember what happened."

My heart skipped when I saw the look on Sam's face. "You're not telling me something."

Sam took a deep breath and let it out. "Cole didn't remember you."

"He didn't—"

"The doctors said his spotty memory is due to trauma from the bullet wound." Sam fixed me with his gaze. "He's lucky to have survived, Kate."

I closed my eyes, trying to absorb the news. Relief filled me now that I knew Cole was among the living. I ignored the fact that he didn't remember me or our last year together. Those memories would be with me, always. Like our disastrous trip to the Caribbean when we'd almost died at the hands of Vincent Anaya. Or, a year ago last spring, when we both thought Sterling had died in a mine collapse. Cole believed my story when I didn't think anyone would. And, let's not forget crazy banker Dave, Simon Boudreaux and Wild Horse Ridge…

Okay, so those memories weren't exactly happy, but there were good times in between that we spent together, just the two of us and his two girls. My resolve hardened at the thought of Abby and Lauren. They deserved stability. Not a woman constantly on the business end of a catastrophe.

"What happened to the trucker with the shotgun?"

"He made it. The article mentioned his death for the same reason."

"Thank goodness." I took Cole's memory loss and both of the men's survival as a sign telling me I'd made the right decision. I couldn't go back and try to pick up where Cole and I left off, much as I wanted to. He'd be better off without me. I could, however, try to help Quinn's guys obliterate the monsters who thought so little of human life and hopefully save other innocent lives in the process.

Then there was Sam. Confusion clouded my mind and I stood up, edgy as hell and feeling my flight reaction kick in. I paced between the hammock and the door and tried to work off the nervous energy. Sam folded his arms across his chest and leaned against a roof support.

"Why did Luis send you?" I asked as I continued pacing, not trusting myself to look at him. "I emailed Luis for help. I didn't expect him to send you."

"I asked him to. He knows our history. Getting his permission wasn't easy. I had to prove I'd be the best choice. He's protective of you, Kate."

I stopped pacing. "Luis has been good to me. I'd have been dead long ago if it weren't for him. And you." I held his gaze, hoping he'd understand how much he meant to me, but knew it would never be enough.

"I'm here to bring you back. Luis had a new identity made for you." He reached into his back pocket and produced a shiny new passport. He flipped to the first page and turned it toward me. "Your new name is Kathryn Reid and you live in Seattle, Washington."

He handed me the passport and I stared at the new me. Luis had used an old picture, but I hadn't changed much, except for the hair color. The dark blue booklet held the keys to the kingdom. I could go anywhere. As long as I left both Mexico and the U.S., I'd probably be safe, at least for a while.

But then the same shit would happen all over again. Eventually, someone from my past would find me. Depending on the price on my head, I'd be on the run again. I'd have to rip up the threads of my life and start over somewhere else. I couldn't live that way.

I wouldn't live that way.

"Tell Luis thank you and that I'll pay him back for this."

"You can tell him yourself. Two tickets to Phoenix are waiting at the Cancun airport. There's a connection to Seattle the day after tomorrow."

"Sam, I—"

He bridged the distance between us, stopping just short of full-body contact, and reached out to run his hand along my cheek, waiting for permission. Unable to help myself, I turned my head to kiss his fingers, wanting to feel more of him, my emotions raw. He slid his hand around the back of my neck and pulled me toward him, covering my lips with his own. After a moment's hesitation, I returned his kiss with the pent-up emotion of a drowning woman in search of air.

Cole's face floated through my mind, triggering a soul-ripping serving of guilt. I stopped and backed away.

"I've missed you," Sam murmured.

I closed my eyes and a confusing array of images wound their way into my mind: Angie with a gun to Cole's head; Pascal lying on the ground next to Quinn's burning truck; Sam in his officer's uniform, his blood saturating the snow around him.

"I can't."

"Can't what?" He placed his hand on my arm. "Kate. Relax. Talk to me."

"We can't." I tried to turn away, but he tightened his grip. "What we had was a brief, wonderful affair." I shook my head when he tried to interrupt. "Hear me out, Sam. You almost died because of it. Because of me. I won't let that happen again. I can't go back with you." At the look on his face, I rushed to finish.

"Please understand. I have to stay. I have a reason to be here, a role to play. If it works the way I think—no, hope—it will, then maybe I'll have a future and we can see how things go. But not until then."

Sam didn't say anything as he watched me. His ability for silence and thoughtful reflection hadn't diminished since I'd last seen him. Someone who never rushed to fill an empty space in the conversation, Sam preferred to allow room for the idea to grow, evolving into an organic, singular meeting of minds.

On the other hand, I usually grew nervous if a pause went on too long and always figured out a way to fill it.

"Say something, Sam."

Still quiet, Sam let go of me, his arm dropping to his side.

"What Quinn wants you to do is dangerous, Kate."

"Quinn said he didn't tell you anything."

"He didn't have to. The fear is written on your face."

I crossed my arms. I'd have to work on that. If Morales sensed my anxiety, things could turn ugly in a hurry.

"It's the only way, Sam."

He sighed and moved toward me. I tensed, trying to keep myself from being drawn into his orbit. He placed a card in my hand and closed my fingers over it. I glanced down to read it: *Sam Akiaq, Private Investigator, Seattle, Washington.* The card also listed a post office box, email, and website.

Surprised, I looked up. Although he smiled, sadness etched his face.

"You're in Seattle?"

He nodded.

"Is that why Luis listed it on my passport?"

Sam didn't answer. I stepped closer and touched his cheek.

"Sam. If—when this is all over..." I let the sentence hang in the air, afraid to finish the thought.

"I may not wait."

I dropped my hand. "I know. I would never ask that."

He moved past me. When he reached the door, Sam turned and gave me a long, searching look. "Seattle's beautiful this time of year."

And then he was gone.

25

L ATER THAT EVENING, QUINN STOPPED by my hut. He stood in the doorway, arms crossed, the look on his face unreadable.

"I see you're still here."

"Barely."

"Good," Quinn said. "It looks like Diaz is ramping up to make his play. We've gotten word reinforcements are coming."

"What's Morales doing in response?"

"One Shot says he isn't doing anything, which worries me. He thinks they're going to join Diaz to take out the phantom cartel."

"How? Do they know where we are?"

"Not to my knowledge, no."

"Are you telling me it's time to go?"

"Morales took the bait and agreed to a meet. I'll drop you off outside of Xoc in the morning."

In the morning. I took a deep breath, trying to squelch my fear along with the feeling I should've left with Sam.

Quinn peered at me, brows drawn together. "You okay?"

Shit. I gave him a quick smile. "Sure. Ready to go." I had to work on my facial expressions. Panic burned in my gut.

My time had run out.

After Quinn left, I slid out the folder he'd given me on Morales and went over it one more time, committing to memory what little information I found in the pages before me. The picture clipped to the outside showed a middle-aged man with thinning hair and glasses. The fact that he'd made it to mid-life told me he was a careful man.

Hugo Morales, 47, was born and raised in Valladolid, Mexico, in the heart of the Yucatán. His father had been a merchant. His mother worked at home. Both had been killed in a car accident when he was 27. Morales began his career as an enforcer for a local drug lord at a young age, and worked his way up to head his own cartel, mainly by killing the competition.

He married Rosa Fernandez Pena, a local beauty contest winner, and had two sons, one of whom died in a violent gun battle with authorities at the age of seventeen. Known as 'The Sultan', it was rumored Morales preferred adolescent girls for his sexual conquests, keeping a group of them available, like a harem. In my opinion, that alone would be enough reason to wipe him off the face of the earth.

He ran his enterprise with ruthless efficiency, and gave generously to the Catholic Church. With a long history of quietly moving large amounts of methamphetamine and cocaine across the border, until now he'd operated with relative impunity, allowing his brethren in Sonora and Sinaloa to hog the spotlight.

The lucrative enterprise had come to the attention of the larger cartels for his hidden routes into the U.S. Now, with the Federal police and Mexican Navy shutting down many of *El Castillo's* time-tested supply routes into the U.S., Leonardo Diaz had come to town to take control away from Morales.

I closed the folder and put it away, the information eerily familiar. Although ten years younger Salazar had worked his way up to head his cartel in much the same way. Ruthless and efficient, successful cartels ran circles around legitimate businesses, in large part because they operated outside the law and used fear and intimidation to get their way. Quinn's group and others like it just might have the right idea, I thought, even though the idea of using violence to end violence had a certain irony.

Eyes burning with fatigue and exhausted from the emotional rollercoaster I'd been on, I collapsed into the hammock and fell asleep, confused thoughts of Cole and Sam swimming through my brain.

Morning arrived much too soon. I forced myself out of bed and headed over to the mess tent to grab some coffee. Pascal sat at one of the tables by himself, eating breakfast. His bruises had faded to a dull greenish-yellow and the swelling had gone down on the bad eye.

"Mind if I join you?"

"Please." He pulled out the chair next to him.

"Your bruises are healing nicely," I said, setting my cup down on the table as I took a seat.

"Physical injury is far easier to heal than its spiritual twin." He took a bite of scrambled eggs and washed it down with coffee. "Emotional damage takes longer and is more difficult to heal. Many times it leaves an invisible scar." He held my gaze for emphasis. "How did your visit go last night?"

"Too short." I should have realized Pascal would be able to hear what Sam and I had talked about. His hut was right next to mine, obviously not an oversight on Quinn's part.

Pascal's expression softened. "Don't worry, Kate. I didn't tell Q. We all have to deal with our pasts at some point. I'm just glad you decided to stay."

His reply reminded me of where I was headed that morning and my mood crash-landed into my stomach. It must have shown on my face, because Pascal covered my hand with his.

"You're going to do fine, Kate."

"How much do you know?" I'd avoided speaking to anyone about the plan to infiltrate Morales' camp.

"I know you're leaving this morning." He scanned the mess tent to make sure no one was within earshot and leaned in closer. "You won't be alone, Kate. Don't go into this thinking Q's hanging you out to dry. It's not like that."

"But how do you know? Quinn doesn't give up information easily. It's difficult to know what I'm going to be dealing with in there."

Pascal leaned back in his chair. "I think his whole idea is not to overwhelm you with information. Then your responses to anything Morales throws your way are genuine. He gave you the file on him right?"

"Yeah. I know all about his freaky tendencies, if that's what you mean." Was there no one in this business who didn't have some kind of weird shit going on with their little psyches?

"It'll go a long way toward understanding who you're dealing with."

"How do you know Quinn?"

Pascal set his cup on the table, eyebrow raised at the abrupt change in subject. "He told you about Maria?"

"He did."

"She was my sister."

"I'm sorry." So Pascal was Quinn's brother-in-law. It made perfect sense why a secretive man like Quinn would trust someone from a completely different culture than his like he did Pascal. He was family. "What about Blondie?" I asked. "And where is he, by the way?"

"Off site. After he told us he thought Morales and Diaz were possibly moving toward a united front, Q asked him to pick up a few things we're going to need."

"Are you planning something?"

"You don't need to know, Kate."

"Good point. Sorry."

Quinn appeared in the doorway and gave me a nod, then disappeared. I turned to Pascal and gave him a hug, careful to avoid the bruises.

"I have to go. Take care of yourself, Pascal. I mean it."

He hugged me back and smiled. "I will. You do the same. See you when you get back."

"Sure."

If I got back.

Quinn took his time driving to Xoc. The meet with Morales would take place at a small roadside restaurant on the outskirts of town.

Barely a block long, Xoc itself consisted of a shop selling colorful hammocks, a tiny *panaderia* that doubled as the local convenience store, and the cinder-block restaurant where I was to meet Morales. On a feeder road and framed by jungle, a couple of block homes nestled comfortably alongside a few traditional Maya huts. Chickens and dogs outnumbered inhabitants by far.

Quinn stopped the truck near the last curve before town and I got out. I felt naked without a gun, but Quinn insisted I go in unarmed. It made sense, but I still missed having a weapon.

He turned the vehicle around and I watched as he drove away, the enormity of what I was about to do finally sinking in. I considered my surroundings, knowing I could disappear into the jungle and take my chances on the run.

A little late for that, Kate. If you were going to back out, you should have taken Sam's offer to get you out of Mexico.

I hated when I was right.

With a deep sigh, I headed toward Xoc and my meeting with Morales.

26

THREE BLACK SUVS WERE LINED up outside the squat cement building, acting as a vehicular barrier. Men in sunglasses with machine guns stood sentry next to two of the vehicles.

Still early, the street looked deserted except for a skinny, fawn-colored mutt nosing at a can of overflowing garbage. Ignoring my abject fear, I walked to the door of the restaurant, aware that my legs weren't as steady as they'd been a few minutes ago. Two men in short-sleeved shirts and black jeans carrying machine guns emerged and blocked my entry. They could have been twins, except one had a goatee.

"I'm here to see Hugo Morales. He's expecting me."

The bodyguard with the goatee slid his gun over his shoulder and patted me down. Not finding a weapon, he gave a nod to whoever lurked inside the café.

A voice from within said something unintelligible and the two thugs parted, allowing me to enter.

The unexceptional whitewashed interior of the restaurant stood in direct contrast to the lone figure seated at the end of the room near one of four tables. Clean-shaven and wearing a bright red polo shirt and expensive jeans, the man appeared to be in his mid-twenties. Sporting an ostentatious gold watch, thick gold rings on several fingers, and expensive ray-skin cowboy boots, the man before me could have been Hugo Morales—twenty-five years ago. He appraised me with a cool, calculating gaze, one arm draped across the back of the chair, his legs stretched in front of him.

"You're not Hugo Morales," I said in Spanish.

Just so we were clear.

"I am his son, Ben Morales. Anything you need to tell him, you can tell me."

I folded my arms across my chest to disguise the tremor in my hand. "What I have to say is for Señor Morales only."

The tips of Ben's ears flushed red, the first indication I'd pissed him off. He shot out of his chair and slammed his hand on the table. The salt shaker danced close to the table edge.

"*What* did you just say to me, bitch?" His voice echoed through the low-ceilinged room.

Mouth dry, I clenched my jaw, keeping my gaze steady.

"I meant no disrespect, but my words are for your father's ears only." If I didn't convince Morales' son to take me to him, the operation would be over before it had begun.

And I'd probably be dead.

The room grew still, as though the building held its breath. The two thugs near the door moved behind me. I turned my head, acknowledging their presence. Then I refocused on Ben and stared him down like I would an angry dog, ignoring the sweat trickling down my back.

A smile formed on his lips as a deep-throated chuckle escaped him, turning into an outright guffaw. "My father told me you were crazy to come to him with information about his enemy, Roberto Salazar. Now I know this to be true." He circled his finger around his ear and crossed his eyes.

I waited until the laughter of the three men subsided before I answered. "I *loathe* Roberto Salazar." I spit the words out, letting them fall between us like spent fireworks. "I will do anything to destroy him."

Ben Morales narrowed his eyes as he sized me up. The two bodyguards, who I'd nicknamed Mutt and Jeff, remained motionless behind me. I took it as a good sign.

"How do I know you are not working for Roberto Salazar or Leonardo Diaz?" He sat back in his chair with one leg sprawled to the side. "And how do I know what you have to say is worth my father's time?"

Showtime. "I lived with Roberto Salazar and have recently been his guest at the hacienda." I watched him, trying to gauge his reaction. The deadpan expression on his face would come in handy at a poker tournament. "I know him. I know his quirks, his way of thinking, of planning attacks. I also know where his office lies within the hacienda, where the security cameras are, and where he keeps his prisoners." I added the last comment taking a wild guess that Salazar had captured one or more of Morales' men in the last raid. Ben's eyebrows shot up.

Bingo.

A mask fell back across his face and he shrugged.

"If what you are saying is true, then you have some value." His gaze slid down my body and back.

I took a deep breath as I suppressed a shudder. Now, for the *pièce de résistance*.

"His hatred for me burns as hot as my own does for him. He will agree to many things he ordinarily would not if he thinks he can somehow get to me. Vengeance is a powerful motivator, as I'm sure you well know."

He appeared to mull this over as I remained still, my life a matter of small consequence in Ben Morales' world. The red and white clock on the wall boasting a Coca Cola advertisement ticked off the seconds. Somewhere, a rooster crowed. The cooler across the room clunked as it cycled through.

He waved his hand toward me, a bored look on his face.

"Take her to my father."

Mutt and Jeff stepped clear and I turned and walked out the door. I exhaled as relief washed through me.

I was in.

27

T HAT THEY DIDN'T BOTHER TO blindfold me told me I was travelling on a one-way ticket to Morales-land.

Mutt drove, with Jeff and his goatee in the passenger seat and me in the back. Approximately half an hour later, we pulled off the road near a nondescript traditional Maya hut flanked on both sides by heavy undergrowth and a smattering of palm trees. Nothing broke the monotony of thick vegetation in either direction as far as I could see. Another of the vehicles that had been parked next to the restaurant pulled in behind us and waited.

Jeff mumbled something into the radio. A few moments later a section of greenery began to move as a camouflaged gate swung open to reveal a gravel road cutting a deep swath through the jungle. We drove through the entrance and bounced slowly along the length of it, hitting every pothole imaginable. I twisted in my seat to look out the rear window and watched as two heavily armed gunmen closed and locked the gate behind the second SUV.

Fifteen minutes later we broke through dense cover, arriving at a clearing. Mutt parked the truck and he and Jeff got out, motioning for me to do the same.

Given the extensive amount of shade surrounding us, the temperature had plunged to a manageable level. I took a deep breath and tried to relax. The jungle humus smelled thick and dank. Crawling with sound, insects buzzed past me while brilliantly colored birds screeched overhead in the canopy.

The two gunmen motioned for me to follow them through a copse of trees, most of which had been shot through with bullet holes, and along a winding path. Security cameras spaced evenly apart dotted the limbs above us.

Soon we came to another gate. Made of metal it stood approximately four feet high. Mutt depressed a button on his key fob and the gate swung open. As we passed, he brushed the corner and leapt backward with a yelp. Jeff laughed and shook his head.

"Cabrone."

Apparently the gate was electrified. Good to know.

A rusty, corrugated steel wall perforated by another slew of bullet holes with a crude door in the center stood a few yards past the electric gate. Mutt knocked three times and followed it up with a short tap. The hinges protested as the door creaked opened and we walked through.

I caught my breath at the vista before me. I'd expected a war zone. What I saw were stunning landscaped grounds with an enormous limestone fountain surrounded by a riot of colorful plants ranging from bird of paradise to plumeria to Royal Poinciana. Multiple banana, mango, and papaya trees punctuated the space. An ancient corbelled arch heavy with pitaya vines preceded the front steps of a large stone building built to resemble a Maya palace.

Salazar's men hadn't made it this far into the compound, apparently.

Situated on a sloping block base, numerous shallow stairs led upward to the first level. Warrior masks decorated the fascia of the bottom section on both sides, as well as the walls of the second level. Supported by two columns, an expansive opening sat back from the steps. Above the entrance, three fierce, curved-nosed masks grimaced over the heads of visitors, with a frieze cut into the stone beside them. The upper façade mimicked the slope of the base and was decorated with intricate stone mosaics and alternating geometric designs.

I followed the gunmen up the stone steps and through the dark entrance into the cool interior. As my eyes adjusted, colorful carpets with geometric designs came into focus. Several potted palms lined the walls. Obviously meant to act as an additional line of defense, the unfurnished room flowed into a short hallway leading toward a steel door.

Mutt walked up to the key pad and entered a combination. The lock clicked and we pushed through.

The room we entered had been furnished with sturdy teak furniture adorned with cushions in a subdued pallet. The lack of windows and muted silence gave the vast room a vault-like atmosphere. A set of tall double doors adorned most of one wall. Absurdly, I flashed on Dorothy and her cohorts cowering in the great hall before they gained an audience with the Wizard of Oz.

We definitely weren't in Kansas, Toto.

Tapestries lined the other walls, interspersed with more Maya masks and art, each with its own spotlight. The scale of the surroundings didn't surprise me after having read about Hugo Morales in the file Quinn gave me. Personally, I would've pegged him as more the conquering-hero type, prone to Napoleonic tastes.

"Wait here," Mutt said. He crossed the room to the double doors and knocked, then stepped back. A tiny red light over his head indicated the presence of a security camera. A buzz sounded and the door clicked. Mutt held it open and I walked through. Both the guards followed me in.

The room was a continuation of the one we'd just left; soaring ceilings, limestone walls covered in tapestries and Maya masks, no windows.

Hugo Morales sat behind a substantial desk, his thinning hair combed to one side, a pair of thick reading glasses perched on his nose, shirt sleeves rolled to his elbows. A single lamp illuminated his face. Not a particularly imposing man, his pallid complexion and the way he held himself suggested too many years of rich, fatty meals followed by too much booze and cigars. He looked up as we entered and set down the file he was reading. We stopped about halfway to the desk.

"Kate Jones?" he asked, an air of privilege and power surrounding him like a thick coat of varnish.

I nodded.

"Come closer," he grunted and crooked his finger, motioning me forward.

I stepped toward him, stopping a couple of feet from the desk.

"My son tells me you might have something I can use." He peered over his glasses at me, sizing me up.

"You're either very brave or very stupid to come here. I haven't decided which."

I remained silent.

"Maybe a little of both, eh?" He smiled, his full lips spreading thickly across his face.

A shiver spiked along my back. I concentrated on breathing.

"Sit down." Morales waved at one of the two chairs near the front of the desk.

I sat. My eyes were drawn to a figurine to his left of a female skeleton holding a scythe in one hand and an owl in the other. About two feet high and dressed in gold lamé with lace robes, she wore a crown covered in strands of multi-colored Mardi Gras beads. At her feet were several small candles and a wreath of fake flowers. Morales followed my gaze.

"You know this figure?"

"*Señora de la Noche*. Lady of the night."

He nodded, apparently pleased I knew. "*Santa Muerte*. Protector of all who work in darkness."

"I've never seen her with an owl. I assume it represents wisdom?"

"Wisdom, yes, but it also symbolizes a messenger." His gaze intensified and I averted my eyes.

"I'm used to seeing images of the other guy the cartels pray to," I said.

Morales snorted. "You mean *Jesús Malverde*. That is because you have been consorting with common thieves. *Señora de la Noche* is a jealous saint. She must be the only one to whom we ask for protection." He leaned back in his chair and clasped his hands behind his head.

"So tell me, Kate Jones. What kind of information do you have that I could possibly want?"

"Like I told your son, I know your enemy, Roberto Salazar. I lived with him for three years. I know his quirks, how he plans. I also know important things about the hacienda where he's staying: where his office lies, where he keeps prisoners."

"And how do you know this?"

"I was recently his prisoner."

Morales leaned forward. "How is it you are free? What I know of Salazar, he would not allow someone he deemed valuable to escape. Especially not someone he hates as much as you profess."

"For that, I can thank you. The hacienda came under fire the day after I arrived. From what I understand, the attack was due to your forces. It created enough of a diversion to allow me to escape." I paused, letting the information sink in. "I have come to pay you back for your unintentional assistance."

Morales grinned. "And eliminate a powerful enemy in the process, eh?"

I smiled back, meeting his gaze head-on. "Yes, of course. But he is also a powerful enemy of yours. This would be a win-win situation."

He considered me for a moment, letting me sweat.

Come on, Hugo. It's buy-in time. If he didn't go for my story, I'd have to think of something more compelling to get him to keep me around.

"Hmm. A win-win. That is true. Or, it would be, if I needed the information you say you possess." Morales fingered the hem of *Santa Muerte's* robe, a thoughtful look on his face. His gaze locked onto mine. "In reprisal for our attack, Salazar returned the favor. But we were ready for him. We acquired a hostage who has even better information than you.

My heart dropped at his words. I inhaled and exhaled slowly, trying to squelch the anxiety rising in my chest.

"If Salazar's hatred for you is as potent as you say, then using you as bait in combination with our other captive will work out even better than I envisioned."

"Who did you capture? I can tell you if he'll be more interested in me or them. Or if he'll tell you anything."

Morales chuckled. "I'm sure you can. Either way, if Salazar is not sufficiently motivated by my offer of making you available to him, then I can sweeten the deal by adding our other prisoner."

"All of Salazar's men are intensely loyal," I said. "They're well-trained to give false information. I doubt you'll gain anything usable."

"Oh, I think we will. This one has been known to switch allegiances as long as there is a substantial reward involved." Hugo Morales nodded at Mutt and Jeff. "Take her downstairs."

They each grabbed an arm and walked me toward the door. I twisted to glance back at Morales.

"Seriously? I came here with an offer of help and this is how you treat me?" Panic bloomed inside of me as I strained at Mutt and Jeff's grip, trying to break free. Plan A wasn't working and I wouldn't be able to implement the Plan B Quinn and I had thought of doing in case A didn't pan out. Plans C and D didn't apply to this situation. That left Plan E and I hadn't paid attention. "You could use some work on your social skills, Hugo."

"Wait." Morales ordered.

Mutt and Jeff stopped. I watched, hopeful, as Morales came around his desk, reached into his pocket and brought out his phone. He held it up, squinting at the back and took my picture. The phone disappeared into his front pants pocket.

"Evidence for Salazar."
Then he turned and walked away.

206

28

THE DOOR TO MY CELL clanged shut, followed by a key scraping in the lock as Mutt and Jeff left me alone in the cold, dank room. I rubbed my arms to keep warm as I took a quick inventory of my surroundings.

Thick block walls with a rusty metal door. Check.

Three floor-level openings too small to crawl through, possibly for air circulation, but more probably for cleaning purposes. Check.

One five-gallon plastic pail, no handle, the latest in luxury bathroom décor. Check.

Filthy blanket bunched up on the cold, hard floor. Check.

No water, no food, no toilet paper. Check, check, check.

The only light came through the small openings at the base of the rear wall and a larger, barred one at the top. Cold, damp and dark. Morales sure knew how to treat a girl.

Unsure what to do, I dropped to a crouch, not wanting to sit on the cold floor and lose precious body heat too early in my stay. To keep myself from panicking, I ran through the meeting with Morales, wondering how I could have done things differently. Quinn said he had my back in case Morales didn't take the bait. It now appeared that I was to be the bait.

Good job, Kate. Now what?

Pascal told me Quinn wouldn't hang me out to dry. I had to believe him or my reason to panic had just grown exponentially.

Did Quinn have someone working for Morales? If so, why would he need me to gather information from inside? Unless his guy wasn't too far up in Morales' food chain. If I knew anything, it was how paranoid the leader of a drug cartel could become. They trusted no one, especially those lower in rank.

Mistrust came with the job—the cost of doing business in a violent, power-hungry culture where the struggle for dominance superseded loyalty, friendship, even sanity. Whenever anyone mentioned how ruthless the players on Wall Street were, I laughed. They didn't have a clue about ruthless.

Cruelty was rewarded. Madmen who would ordinarily be considered serial killers in polite society continually rocketed to prominence for their creative techniques of meting out punishment and death. Making money using any means possible was the cartels' jihad against powerlessness and obscurity. Take away their money and influence and all that remained were bullies and thugs on the playground of life.

Not that the thought was any comfort to me at this point.

Wired from the stress of meeting Morales and my panic rising from not knowing what he had planned for me, I paced the eight-by-five room until I couldn't anymore. Occasionally a scraping sound would filter into the cell through one of the openings near the floor. I'd crouch near the holes and listen, even tried to say something, quietly, in case someone was on the other side. I never got a reply.

The blanket looked dirtier than the floor, but it was all I had. I shook it out in case I had company, and then folded it over a few times to make it thicker. I sat on top of it with my legs crossed and propped my upper body against the wall.

The shadows lengthened and darkness fell. Outside, a chorus of frogs began their nightly symphony, peppered by the occasional screech of howler monkeys. With nothing visual to occupy my mind, memories of Cole drifted back to haunt me: the dimple in his cheek when he smiled; the image of his cowlick in the morning before he showered and how I loved to run my hands through it, trying to tamp it down; the way he'd bite his lower lip when he was concentrating.

Don't think about Cole. Keep your mind on the present.

Sam's face appeared and I leaned my head back, wondering how he could still want to be with me after all these years, knowing that if I got out of Mexico alive without killing Salazar, I had to stay away. To go to him would be to play roulette with his life. Despair crashed through me at the memory of not leaving with him when I had the chance.

Don't kick yourself, Kate. You did what you thought was right.

As it was, the short time I had with Sam would probably be the last positive human contact I'd experience if I couldn't escape. Worst-case scenario: ending up back under Salazar's thumb. If he didn't kill me first, I'd have to endure the brutal, mind-numbing life of a trafficked slave. If he called Morales' bluff and passed up the chance to get his revenge, then Morales would have no further use for me and I'd be dead.

Either way, it wasn't good retirement planning.

I thought about my family in Minnesota, to whom I hadn't spoken in years for fear they'd become targets. My sisters, judgmental of me and my choices as they had been in the past, were still family, as were my parents. I'd changed so much over the years I doubted we'd have anything in common, but it was comforting to think of them.

Night finally reached its long, dark fingers into my room. Exhausted and emotionally spent, I curled into a ball on the small square of blanket and closed my eyes, waiting in vain for sleep.

Early the next day, someone slid a small bottle of water and an open can of tuna fish under the door for breakfast. After that, the day stretched on with no visitors.

Too much time to think wasn't good, especially with an overactive imagination, so I distracted myself by trying to remember the lyrics to my favorite songs. I'd already gone through several albums and was now on my top ten John Hiatt songs when another bottle of water rolled under the door.

"What, no surf and turf? I'm disappointed," I said to whoever was on the other side.

"Consider it spa food, *puta,*" came the answer. "You got the fish because he wants you alive. For now."

The day wore on and I watched the shadows on the wall morph into odd shapes as the light faded through the opening near the floor for the second time. I considered marking the wall to keep track of my stay, but realized I probably wouldn't be around long enough to lose days. I heard nothing except the occasional slam of a distant door or footsteps past my cell, making for too many lonely hours of thinking about how Morales intended to kill me.

When would he make his move? Did he intend to trade me for one of the men Diaz captured? Salazar wouldn't go down that road again. Not after losing two of his men the last time. Although, I doubted Morales knew about Quinn's ruse to trade me for Pascal, so he might.

With nothing better to do, I hunkered down and tried to meditate like Sam had taught me back in Alaska. It worked for about ten minutes before I drifted off.

I jolted awake to the sound of screaming.

Instantly alert, I strained to hear which direction it came from. Disoriented, I wondered how long I'd been out.

Another scream echoed through the room. I scrambled to the far side of the cell and leaned my head against the cold block. Unintelligible words interspersed with groans filtered through the cutouts at the base of the wall. Two distinct voices became apparent. The main one sounded patient, almost bored. The other had a more erratic quality I recognized from my days of living with Salazar—uneven modulation punctuated by moans.

Torture.

Ignoring the filth, I lay on my side on the floor, my ear to the opening in the wall and continued to listen, the words beginning to form a coherent whole.

"I want to see Morales—" A sharp crack cut the prisoner's words short. "Aughh…unh—"

My stomach twisted with his groans. He'd spoken in Spanish, but my ear caught a slight American accent.

"You son of a bitch, just wait until I get my hands on you—" Another crack split the air and he screamed.

"You're done, Sterling."

John Sterling? I caught my breath. That explained Morales' blasé attitude toward my offer of information. Of course he wouldn't need my help if he had one of Salazar's right-hand men. Sterling knew a lot more about Salazar's recent operations than I ever would. Panic rose in my chest. Quinn and I hadn't thought of a plan to deal with this scenario.

I was on my own.

"Fuck you." His words came out wet and semi-indistinct, like he'd been smacked across the mouth a few times. The memory of his cruel grin when I saw him at the hacienda popped into my mind. I allowed myself a brief feeling of satisfaction at his capture, but got off the happy-train early, knowing I could be next.

"You're the one who's fucked."

There was a brief pause in the conversation followed by a scraping sound as though a piece of furniture was being dragged across the floor.

Sterling's tormentor continued to mock him. "Why? Because after tonight, there won't be any fucking *El Castillo.* Diaz and Salazar are going to be crushed and then who's gonna save your sorry white ass, *pendejo?* Especially since you're DEA. The boys are gonna like having their way with you, eh?"

"*Was* DEA, asshole. You still have to deal with the new kids on the block," Sterling said, his breath coming in short bursts. "I hear they're swimming in guns and money. Joining forces with *El Castillo* is the only way to fight them off."

"Bullshit. Morales' got them covered too, man. You have no idea who you been dealing with when it comes to Mr. M. Besides, that ain't no cartel, bitch. Guys are a group of fucking farmers with pitchforks. Only one we gotta worry 'bout is a Special Forces *cabrone* named Quinn."

At the mention of Quinn and his men, my pulse kicked into high gear. How did Morales' guy know they weren't cartel? And how the hell did he know Quinn was Special Forces?

Sterling answered, but I missed what he said. I willed my thudding heart to slow so I could hear more.

"Nah, man. Morales sent a message to Diaz that he wanted to join up to fight this other *cartel* and Diaz took the bait. Then he made sure that Quinn guy found out. Did it under the radar so they wouldn't think they were bein' set up."

"That'll be a shit storm. What if your boss gets caught in the crossfire?" Sterling said.

The other guy chuckled. "Mr. M's already taken care of that. Me and the rest of the crew will be waitin' to pick 'em off whenever they show up. He won't even be there."

"Good plan, except Diaz won't bring Salazar. He's not stupid. If Salazar finds out Morales set him up, you can say adios, amigo and hello, dead."

"Your buddy Roberto? He's coming to the party, too. Mr. M let him know not only do we got you, which I seriously don't think they give a shit about, but we also got his bitch. There's nothing easier than playing a man who's got a thirst for revenge."

Sterling's chuckle lacked mirth. "I assume you're talking about the American woman who fucked him over. He's not stupid enough to put himself in danger, even for her."

"That's where you're wrong. Salazar's got a hard on for that *pinche gringa*, and not in a good way." His laugh ricocheted off the walls. "It's gonna be a good night. The blood's gonna flow."

A scraping sound followed by footsteps echoed across the room.

"I'll give you one more chance to tell me where Diaz and Salazar are keeping the guns. If you don't, you know how this works, yes?"

"*Chinga tú madre.*" Sterling's epithet came out clipped.

"I'm shocked you'd bring my mother into this, *cabrone.*" The man's laughter had the irritating cadence of a jackhammer. "Hold his head back while I wrap the towel around it." His request was my first indication there might be another person standing nearby.

The sound of splashing resonated through the room. I waited, knowing what came next, my stomach twisting. Torture is a hard thing to listen to, no matter who's on the receiving end, and waterboarding is no exception. Thank Abu Ghraib for the technique getting widespread usage. The cartels loved anything that made a person panic before they killed them. The more the victim struggled, the better.

The splashing continued. Soon, choking and coughing erupted, followed by loud thumping. I imagined Sterling straining against his restraints, panicked by the feeling of drowning.

"I told you to hold his head, man." Morales' man hissed.

"I'm trying," came the reply. The thumping and choking continued. Numbly, I wondered if they knew how long they could keep it up without killing him. Morales' men didn't strike me as the kind of guys who took pride in doing enhanced interrogation right. Try to get information out of him dead, I thought.

"Take it off."

The splashing stopped.

I turned away and pushed up to a sitting position, not wanting to hear any more.

Panic shoved its way to the front of the line when I realized I would probably be next, especially if Sterling died before they got any information. I climbed to my feet and paced the room, trying to work out a way to escape. Once the interrogators left, I could try to get a guard to open the door in the hope that I'd be able to escape. The only thing I could come up with was to scream. The main problem being that screaming could bring more than one guard. Not the best idea, since I only had a blanket and a five-gallon bucket to work with.

If I stood behind the door with the blanket and threw it over the head of the first guard to disorient him, would I have enough time or room to bring him down before anyone else showed up? Or would I have to contend with two at once? My confidence in my ability to disable two armed guards in such small quarters wasn't high, but what else could I do? If I stayed and did nothing I'd be dead or worse. If I managed to escape, I'd not only avoid Morales' torture and Salazar's hell but I'd also be able to warn Quinn's men before they walked into Morales' trap.

I waited for several minutes after I heard the other cell's door slam shut, and made sure I only Sterling remained next door before I picked up the folded blanket and bucket and crossed the room to the door. With a deep inhale I banged the bucket hard against the door and screamed for all I was worth.

It didn't take long before I heard footsteps. They sounded like one set, not two. With a quick prayer that I hadn't summoned Sterling's torturer I stepped behind the door, shook out the blanket and screamed some more.

"What the fuck are you yelling about, bitch?"

It sounded like Mutt. Another voice joined his and my optimism faded. *More than one. Not good.*

"No, man, I got this. You go on ahead. I'll catch up with you," Mutt mumbled.

The key scraped in the lock and the door opened. I waited until he'd stepped into the room before I threw the blanket over his head and at the same time launched myself at him in a body-slam.

"What the fuck?" he yelled and staggered forward, clawing at the blanket.

I pushed off him and pivoted while he was still disoriented, then threw a roundhouse kick with my right leg. He groaned and snapped his upper body back as my shin connected with his kidney. I wound up for another kick before he pulled the blanket free, but aborted when his partner, Jeff raced into the room, gun drawn.

With barely a glance in my direction he raised a gun with a suppressor, walked up to Mutt and shot him twice in the back of the head. Mutt dropped to the floor, his blood spreading in a wide circle, soaking the blanket. Jeff spun to face me and grabbed my arm.

"I'm with Q. Let's go," he said, and we raced out of the cell.

29

WE RAN THROUGH A DARK passageway before coming to a flight of stairs. Jeff brought his hand up. I stilled as he checked above and behind us and then motioned for me to follow him.

The two of us climbed the stairs and then stopped again at the top of the landing, a steel door blocking our way. He unlocked the door with one of several keys hanging around his neck, and eased the door open slowly, gun drawn. After checking both directions, we proceeded into the next room.

Staying low, we sprinted through the room to the other side. When we reached the next hallway, he paused to assess our surroundings. The place was deserted. No one had shown up to stop us and I was a little freaked out.

"Where is everybody?" I whispered.

"Morales sent most of his guys to the meet. A few stayed behind."

"To defend the compound if things went to shit."

Jeff nodded.

"You've got to warn Quinn. The meet's a setup. Morales is going to try to wipe out Diaz and Quinn at the same time."

"My first priority is to get you out of here and safe. Q's orders. Once I've accomplished that, I'll contact Q."

Jeff pointed across the room to another door. We covered the distance quickly and slipped through. It was a side exit leading to the lower level of Morales' Maya temple. The front of the temple glowed brightly, like New York City on a Friday night, as did the landscaped grounds and fountain. Thankfully, our side of the building was encased in darkness.

I followed him down the steps to ground level. We avoided the main entrance and the two gunmen leaning against the arch, having a smoke. Jeff pointed to a grove of banana trees to our left. We crept alongside the gardens until we were well hidden from view. Jeff motioned for me to stop.

"We're going to have to transition to the main gate on foot," he said, his voice low. "Stealing a vehicle will attract too much attention. We shouldn't have any problem until we get there. Morales has two gunmen covering the main gate. There are three others hidden at various positions along the road, but I've got that handled."

"What about the metal fence and the electric gate?"

"I know a way around them both. We'll cut through the jungle, then get back on the road once we've cleared them." He glanced at me. "Ready?"

I nodded.

He took off through the jungle at a brisk pace and I followed. He must have memorized the route, because it wasn't long before we angled right and found the road again. Once we were back on the level and with the way clear, we broke into an easy run.

As we rounded a curve in the road, Jeff slowed and waved me behind a tree before walking several yards further. The full moon illuminated a dark figure as it emerged from the jungle to join him. Quiet laughter accompanied the flare of a lighter. A moment later, Jeff stepped to the side and the figure crumpled to the ground. He bent over to grab him under the arms and dragged him off the road.

Jeff sprinted back to join me, wiping his hands on his fatigues.

"One down," he quipped.

We continued along the road, stopping twice more while Jeff took care of the next two guards.

Once we'd made it past the third gunman and rounded a second corner, the main gate came into view. We stopped just before the end of the tree line, a discrete distance from the two guards. Jeff rolled up his pant leg to reveal an ankle holster with a gun. He slid it free and handed me his 9mm Sig Sauer.

"Take this in case we get separated. My plan is to eliminate both guards. If something goes wrong, create a diversion. If something goes really wrong, shoot them. It's got a full magazine and there's a bullet in the chamber." He reached into his pants pocket and pulled out a second. "This one's full, too."

"Thanks," I said, pocketing the extra ammunition. "Hey—what's your name?" It didn't feel right referring to him as Jeff anymore.

"Jesús."

"That's appropriate," I said with a smile. He smiled back and was gone.

I stood behind a pair of low growing palms and peered through the leaves at the two guards standing next to the gate, speaking in hushed tones. They both looked up and smiled as Jesús walked over to them with a greeting and asked to bum a cigarette. The guard to his left slid his machinegun onto his shoulder and dug in a pocket. Metal glinted in the moonlight as Jesús stepped into him. The gunman sank to his knees with a quiet groan. The second guard yelled and fumbled with his gun. Jesús swiveled, drew his weapon and shot him twice. He fell forward, landing with a thud.

Jesús turned and motioned for me to join him. I stepped from behind the palms and was about to cross the road when another man appeared. I froze, unsure if he'd seen me.

Jesús noticed the look on my face and spun around. The other man fired first. The report from Jesús' gun echoed a split-second later.

The other man groaned and dropped to one knee, still holding his gun. Jesús staggered back a step, his hand to his chest. I moved quickly, crossing to where the other gunman struggled to stand, his weapon now level with Jesús' chest. I gripped the Sig Sauer with both hands and squeezed the trigger.

The gunman faltered before collapsing backward. I ran to him and kicked the weapon from his hand. I needn't have bothered. His eyes stared upward, unseeing.

Jesús groaned, his knees buckling. I left the dead gunman and ran to help him.

"How bad?" I asked.

He moved his hand, revealing a massive amount of blood saturating his shirt. His breathing was ragged and an ominous hissing sound emanated from the wound. I helped him over to the guard shack so he could sit down while I searched for a first aid kit. I found several gauze bandages and a roll of duct tape.

First aid, cartel style.

I wadded up the gauze and ripped a length of tape free from the roll, which I used to keep the gauze in place over the wound. He leaned forward and I patched where I thought the bullet exited as best as I could with the remaining gauze. Then I secured both bandages by winding more duct tape around his torso.

"I've got to get you out of here," I said.

Jesús shook his head. Sweat streamed down his face. "No. You need to leave, now. I'll tell them Quinn's men shot us and left us for dead, and you got away." He leaned his head back with a grimace. "It's up to you to warn Quinn. I'll never make it."

"Where are they?"

"Five kilometers west of here at the Ixchel ruins, north side. There's a small wooden sign on the road. Keep your eyes open. It's easy to miss. The meeting site is about one and a half kilometers in."

"Why there? Isn't it a tourist attraction or something?"

"Morales owns the land. He kicked out the archaeologists before they were through with the excavation. No one uses it except him." He waved me away, wincing from the effort. "Go, now. The control for the gate is in the hut. Red button. Leave it open."

"I can't just walk away. You risked your life to save me."

He glanced at his chest and then at me. "You've done all you can," he said wheezing. "You need to save yourself, or this was a pointless exercise. If you don't leave now, they'll kill us both."

He was right. I forced myself to walk into the hut, found the control panel and pressed the button. The gate swung open.

"Thank you, Jesús," I whispered as I placed a bottle of water I'd found inside the hut in his hand. Torn between leaving him and going to warn Quinn, I slipped through the gate.

30

THE MOON ILLUMINATED ENOUGH OF the road to see where I was going. Five kilometers was a long way to travel with time running out for Quinn and his men. I turned west and broke into a run.

There wasn't any traffic on that section of rural road, so when the headlights of a vehicle slid into view I immediately dropped into the shallow ditch, out of sight. The SUV that passed looked familiar. I realized it matched the one Quinn had used to drop me off outside of town two days earlier, and I rocketed out of my hiding place, waving my arms and yelling for them to stop.

The taillights brightened as the driver slammed on the brakes. Its backup lights blinked on and the SUV reversed toward me.

I breathed a sigh of relief and ran to meet it. As I drew even with the driver's side the window powered down. Blondie sat in the driver's seat.

"God, am I glad to see you," I said, still breathless from running.

"What the hell are you doing out here?"

"Long story. We have to warn Quinn about the meeting with Morales. It's a trap."

"I'm on my way there. Get in."

I'd made it halfway around the front of the SUV headed for the passenger side when it struck me that he'd been driving *away* from the ruins. He'd just said he was on his way there. Wary, I walked to the side of the truck and opened the door but didn't get inside.

"You're saving me a long walk. Twelve kilometers is one hell of a trek."

"No doubt. Hurry up. You can tell me what you know on the way."

The Ixchel ruins were less than five kilometers from where we were, not twelve, and in the opposite direction. I looked down as if I'd dropped something.

"Shit. Hold on a minute," I said, and took a couple of steps back while watching him out of the corner of my eye.

Blondie's smile never wavered as his hand moved toward his shoulder holster.

I dove for the rear wheel well and slid the gun from my waistband. With my back to the tire, I listened for Blondie's next move. The driver's door squeaked open, the crunch of boots on gravel echoing through the still air.

Heart slamming in my ears, I gauged the distance from the truck to the jungle to be about fifteen yards. I couldn't decide whether I should run or try to kill him. My hesitation made my choice for me. Blondie's footsteps were too close.

"What are you doing, Kate? Stop playing games. We've got to go."

I sprinted around the open passenger door to the front of the SUV, then turned and leaned against the hood, aiming through the narrow opening between the door and the truck.

One thing in my favor: he didn't know I had a gun.

Blondie walked around the side of the SUV, his right hand obscured by shadow. As soon as I had a clear shot I fired, hitting him in the right shoulder.

I'd sort it out later if I was wrong.

He staggered back, gripping his shoulder. "What the fuck…?"

The object in his now-useless hand glinted in the moonlight. I rounded the passenger door, giving him and the truck a wide berth.

"Drop it," I said, aiming at his head. Hyper-focused from an adrenaline spike and heart galloping wildly in my chest, I thought my head would explode from the pressure. Palms sweating, I repositioned my grip on the gun.

"What are you doing, Kate?"

"You were headed the wrong direction."

His eyes narrowed imperceptibly as his left hand snaked toward the gun.

I fired.

The bullet ripped through his skull, splattering brain and blood and bits of bone against the truck window. His gun clattered to the pavement as he slid to the ground, smearing a trail of blood down the side of the SUV.

Bile rose in my throat and I fought to keep from retching. I turned away from the gore and slammed the passenger door shut, then ran around to the driver's side and climbed in. The keys dangled from the ignition.

I took several deep breaths to calm myself and waited for the nausea to subside. Blondie's betrayal hit me hard. No one was who they appeared to be in this horrifying fight for survival. I didn't know who to trust.

Quinn. I had to get to Quinn.

With shaking hands, I turned the key and the engine roared to life. I slipped it into gear and hooked a U-turn, spitting rocks. Flooring the accelerator, I sped toward the ruins.

31

TEN MINUTES LATER, I LOCATED the tiny sign for Ixchel. I turned onto the narrow road and followed it another kilometer before I parked deep in the brush and got out. I continued along the road, stopping every few yards to listen. The absence of gunfire meant Morales hadn't begun his assault.

A row of parked SUVs came into view and I slowed my pace, giving them a wide berth in case either Diaz or Morales' men had left a driver with their vehicles.

Behind the SUVs stretched a vine-covered wall, about three-feet high. I followed it to the end and then cut into the site, staying low and keeping to the shadows before coming to a partially excavated ruin. Not knowing where Morales had his men stationed and assuming Quinn and his guys were somewhere nearby, I did the best I could to keep out of sight and out of their line of fire.

I hugged the ruin and moved forward before coming to a narrow break leading to another building. Chichen Itza had a similar structure called *El Caracol*, or The

Observatory, although the round tower on the platform here appeared to be much smaller. Bright light from the inner square, or plaza, of the ruined Maya city illuminated steep stairs built into the side of the structure. I crept closer to the source of the light.

Brightly lit torches stood equidistant to each other, surrounding a rectangular table upon which rested a large bottle of tequila and several glasses. At least seven ancient buildings in varying sizes and states of disintegration and excavation loomed over the square, giving the place a *Temple of Doom* feel. The tallest structure stood at the far end of the plaza with a large square base, tapering to the top like a pyramid. The ruin would have been used as a temple for religious ritual, including decapitating enemies and tossing them off the top level down the steep stairs to bounce and roll into a rapt crowd.

A comforting thought.

Men with machine guns stood at various points on opposite sides of the plaza. From what I could see, the gunmen on the far side bore tattoos on the same side of their necks, marking them as Salazar's men. I assumed the ones closest to me were Morales' thugs.

Six chairs had been placed at the table, three to a side. A man, uncannily similar in size and coloring to Morales, but definitely not him, stood a few feet away from the table, speaking with two other men I didn't recognize.

A younger, dark-haired man wearing glasses stood with his arms crossed, alone on the opposite side of the table from the Morales look-alike. Salazar and Diaz were nowhere to be seen.

The pretend Morales turned and addressed the younger man.

"Where is your father?" He glanced at his wristwatch. "They're late."

The man with the glasses shrugged. "They'll be here when they get here. My father is not a man to be rushed."

The imposter frowned and murmured something to his companions.

At that moment, a hand clamped over my mouth while another gripped my arm. The scream died in my throat and I froze, afraid to draw attention to myself and afraid to struggle, not sure if they had a gun. The person holding me relaxed their grip and I turned my head.

Barely recognizable behind heavy camouflage paint, Quinn released his hand from my mouth, finger to his lips. I exhaled in relief as he drew me further into the shadows.

"It's a trap," I whispered when we were out of earshot of the plaza. "Morales knows you aren't cartel. He's going to kill everyone here."

Quinn nodded, digesting the information. "That means someone—" He stopped.

"It was Blondie, Quinn. He's dead."

His jaw twitched, but he didn't say anything.

"Did you hear what I said?" I asked. He was taking this too well. No one could be that cold.

His eyes held mine. "Yes. I heard you."

"And?" His apparent lack of concern bothered me. Weren't they friends? Is this how Quinn reacted to a betrayal? Then it hit me. "You knew?"

"After the Morales raid. I suspected, yes."

He paused for a moment before he tapped his ear with his finger. When he noticed my frown he turned his head to reveal a tiny radio transmitter hidden in his ear.

That was how he'd been able to track me so quickly. Knowing Quinn, he had men stationed at the front and both sides of the site, all wirelessly connected, probably using the cartel's own cell towers.

"They know. Go to Plan C. Watch your backs." He tapped the transmitter again and turned his attention to me. "Did anyone see you leave?"

"Not unless you count the dead guards. Jesús helped me escape."

"Why didn't he come instead of you?"

"He's been shot," I said.

"Dead?"

"Not when I left, no."

Quinn grew quiet. I imagined him retooling his strategy, adding and subtracting scenarios to his plan and, I assumed, figuring out how to get his men back to camp unharmed.

"I want you somewhere safe when the shit hits the fan," he said.

"Why not abort? You're not seriously thinking of going ahead with this?"

"We may never get all the players in one place again. I want to take advantage of the situation. We'll worry about Morales later."

"Then risking my life to come here and warn you had no effect at all."

"It did. The plan's changed. We'll be better prepared." He did a quick scan of our surroundings. "Follow me." Quinn left, his shadow ghosting along the back of the ruins. I followed.

He stopped when we reached the rear of the pyramid.

"Stay out of sight until I come for you. See the area over there in shadow?" He pointed to a walled section, the interior encased in darkness near the foot of the pyramid.

"Yeah."

"Wait there until I come for you." He glanced at the bulge in my t-shirt where the butt of the gun protruded. "You have ammo?"

I nodded.

"When I approach I will use the word *Beyoncé* so you'll know it's me."

"Good choice."

"Be careful." Then he was gone.

"You too," I said to the air.

I headed for the enclosure, but changed my mind at the idea of not knowing what was going on around me. Although I'd be hidden from sight I'd also be blind. The more I knew the better I'd be able to protect myself and offer help if needed.

I crept along the side of the pyramid until I had a good view of the plaza, careful to remain out of sight.

It looked like everyone had arrived. The principal players sat across from each other at the table, three to each side. Salazar leaned forward, listening to the man seated across from him. An older gentleman with graying hair wearing a goatee, probably Leonardo Diaz, was seated next to Salazar. Diaz's son sat to his left. Gunmen stood behind them.

Morales' men were lined up across the table from Salazar and Diaz. They too had armed guards standing at attention behind them. The pretend Morales gestured as he spoke. Salazar's eyes kept cutting left and right, as though nervous. Diaz appeared bored, like he had more important places to be. The shape of the plaza and the way the ancient buildings were situated created a bowl effect and their voices carried on the still evening air.

"So you see, gentlemen, everything has been written down in this document before us and signed by myself and my two lieutenants. All that is needed are your signatures and the agreement will become law for both sides," the pretend Morales said.

Salazar rose from his chair, a dark scowl on his face. At first glance it looked like he'd packed on more weight, but then I realized he wore a bullet-proof vest.

"Where is the woman?" he asked, his arms crossed. "She's part of the deal and I don't see her." Salazar made a show of looking behind him and to each side. Then he turned back to the other man, eyebrows raised. "You promised to deliver her to me. I will not sign until you have held up your end of the bargain."

Morales' decoy began to protest, but Diaz raised his hand and he grew silent.

"Roberto is right. Certainly, the delivery of the woman is a small piece of our arrangement. But how are we to judge the solidity of the agreement when even this insignificant request is not attended to with respect?"

"You have seen by the photograph that we have her." Pretend Morales pointed to a document on the table in front of them.

Salazar shook his head. "I repeat: You will not get my signature until I see the American *puta*."

The imposter sighed and stood up. It must have been a signal, because Morales' men went for their guns. Salazar reached for his as Diaz's son leapt to his feet. Diaz himself didn't have a chance. Gunfire erupted from both sides hitting him numerous times in the chest and head. Salazar dove under the table as his bodyguards returned fire. More gunmen surged from the shadows and stormed the plaza.

Heart in my throat, I raced along the side of the ruin, headed for the enclosed area. Sudden movement to the right caught my eye and I froze. A man I didn't recognize with an AK-47 ran past the place where I'd intended to hide, his attention on the chaos in the plaza. I held my breath and stood motionless until he passed.

My panic rising, I scanned the steep side of the pyramid and caught my breath. *Shit.* Easily seventy feet high, waiting out the battle above the fray would be better than remaining on the ground, but I ran the risk of being exposed for part of the climb.

The thugs in the plaza would be focused on the gun battle raging there, and I didn't have much to choose from for places to hide.

My mind made up, I climbed onto the first step and then the second. The distance from one stair to the next rose half-again higher than modern construction and made the climb more difficult.

Something rustled in the jungle behind me and I pivoted in place, hand reaching for my gun. I stared into the darkness searching, heart pounding in my ears, but nothing moved.

Stop being such a pussy, Kate. You can do this.

I turned back to the pyramid, determined to make it to the top. Eyes trained on each stair in front of me I climbed, hand over hand, and didn't look down.

Out of breath by the time I'd reached the last step, I owed as much to the adrenaline coursing through my body as to the strenuous climb. The lighting from below didn't reach the top of the pyramid—I'd be safe enough for now as long as no one from below had seen my ascent.

A rectangular structure took up a third of the pyramid's platform. I crept around the block walls to the front until I came to an open doorway leading to a small room. To my relief, neither Morales nor Diaz had decided to use the place as a lookout. Tactically, it wouldn't have worked as well as the other ruins surrounding the site.

The low spreading branches of an ancient tree partially obstructed the view of the plaza.

A narrow ray of moonlight spilled through the doorway, illuminating a bench in the middle of the room. As I walked inside, I tripped over the threshold but caught myself before falling. Both it and the lintel had been carved to depict a wide-open mouth with a row of sharp teeth above and below the doorway, its canines intact. I crossed to the bench and ran my hand along the smooth stone. One end had been carved into the shape of a feline head with two pointed ears, likely a jaguar. A pair of dark gleaming stones took the place of eyes. The other end resembled a tail.

The steady stream of machine gun fire told me the cartels weren't finished. Too nervous to sit, I got up and paced the small room, walking to the doorway and listening to the two groups as they tried to obliterate each other. I wondered if Quinn's guys had engaged yet, hoping like hell they hadn't. At least now they knew Morales' plan.

I left the room and walked to the edge of the platform. The sheer height of the temple had been misleading when seen from below. The view from the top looking down held no such deception. I'd been off by about ten yards, the drop being closer to one hundred feet. Vertigo gripped me and I took a step back.

Pebbles scattered behind me. I half-turned, expecting to see Quinn or one of his men but stopped short when something hard pressed against my temple.

"Don't move."

I froze at the sound of Salazar's voice. Dread crawled through me like maggots on a corpse.

"Now, why would Morales let you go? Unless you two were working together." He shoved the barrel of the gun harder against my head. "When I saw you climb the pyramid I realized everything had been a ruse to destroy Diaz and *El Castillo*. I'd had my doubts about the meeting, but Leonardo insisted they were reasonable people." He sighed. "There are no longer rules in this business. I understand now why Anaya decided to leave." He gripped my arm and turned me to face him.

I contracted my stomach muscles and leaned forward slightly as I turned, hoping my shirt would hide the Sig. His eyes narrowed and he stepped back. His right arm hung limp, a dark stain on his sleeve.

"Set the gun on the ground and kick it to me," he commanded.

My mind raced for a way to use the Sig first without getting killed as I grasped the gun and slowly slid it free. He tracked me as I leaned over and placed it on the ground.

"Don't try it, Kate. You'll be dead before you take your next breath."

I straightened and after a brief hesitation kicked it to him. *Keep him talking.* "I thought you wanted payback. I doubt shooting me will be satisfying enough."

"Anaya's idea had a certain symmetry to it, I'll grant him that. As we have seen, you're much too devious. I think you would eventually find a way to escape. As a result, my plan for you has changed." He stared at me, his expression unreadable. "Many nights I envisioned this moment. In my fantasy you beg me for mercy as you lay dying. I loved you, gave you everything, yet you repaid my kindness with betrayal." He motioned toward the ground with his gun. "On your knees. Beg my forgiveness and crawl to me."

"No." The word rose from somewhere deep inside me and hung in the air a moment before detonating between us. At that moment I could truly say I'd rather be dead.

Salazar's face darkened. Breathing heavily, he took a step closer, gun shaking, his rage palpable. "On your knees, *puta*." The words exited his mouth like bullets from an assault rifle.

My knees shook as I fought my fear, but I stood my ground. I tried swallowing but could only clear my throat. Cold, hard clarity pervaded my mind. If I had to die, the one thing I could control was how. I would no longer be victimized by my past.

"Never," I said. "Your time will come. I don't know how or when, but I hope your death is as cruel and pitiful as you are."

Eyes bulging, Salazar advanced another step, spewing obscenities like a broken sewer pipe. I'd seen him blinded by rage like this only once before when he'd been bested in a shooting match by an underling. Back then, he'd made the crucial mistake of losing control. His accuracy suffered and allowed the underling to escape with his life.

He closed the distance between us and I thrust my hand up, knocking the gun sideways as it fired. Ears ringing from the gun's report, I lunged forward and slammed my hand into his windpipe. He staggered back as he dropped his weapon and clawed at his throat. I dove for the gun, then backed away and circled wide.

Aim for the head, Kate.

His gaze flickered from me to the gun in my hand as he fought for breath. He backed away, searching for the Sig I'd kicked toward him earlier. It lay behind him, near the edge of the pyramid.

"Don't move."

"You can't kill me," he rasped. "Remember the field?"

He must have been aware of my failed attempt to shoot him when he drove past me at the agave field. *Don't let him get to you. You're a different person than you were.*

Was he right? I'd been able to kill Blondie, but my life had been threatened. Now that I'd gained the upper hand and he was unarmed, I hesitated.

As though reading my mind he said, "You wouldn't kill an unarmed man."

"I guess we'll find out, won't we?" The words didn't sound as threatening as I wanted them to. "By the way, I heard Sterling rolled over on you pretty fast," I said, trying to distract him as I moved in an arc to get closer to the Sig. "So much for loyalty, eh, Roberto?"

Salazar grimaced as he tracked me. "Torture can be unreliable." He watched me for a reaction, but I'd gone way past letting him get to me regarding something that happened eleven years ago. My fear remained rooted to current events.

"Especially when your idea of persuasion involves decapitation, right? Kind of hard to have a conversation when your head's not attached." Memories of Eduardo, the man who helped me escape from Salazar years before, came rushing back. Another person who'd lost their life because of me.

Because of Salazar.

"Ah. I see you are still upset about Eduardo," he said, his voice a hoarse whisper.

I hadn't used enough force when I hit him.

"Eduardo didn't deserve to die. He helped me because he knew you would kill me if he didn't."

Salazar took a step toward me but stopped as I repositioned my grip on the gun. He narrowed his eyes

"Tell you what." He fought to take a breath. "I suggest a truce. Let bygones be bygones. Put the gun down and you'll never see me again."

I would have laughed if it hadn't been for the whole scared-as-shit part of this conversation. "As good as never seeing you again sounds, that would be like trusting a rattlesnake not to bite. How stupid do you think I am?"

Kill him now, Kate.

"I have no weapon." He raised his left arm and turned to the side.

Nervous, I widened my stance and gripped the gun with both hands, afraid I'd freeze again. "Face forward." I'd never killed an unarmed person before.

It's Salazar. You can't really consider him a person.

With little warning, he swung around, reaching behind his back with his left hand. A gun gleamed in the moonlight.

I fired twice. One bullet went wide, the other hit him just below the vest.

Like air escaping from a balloon he exhaled, eyes widening in surprise. Hand pressed against the bloody wound he staggered backward, stopping just short of the edge.

Without hesitation I advanced toward him, memories of Sam and Cole and Oggie and Eduardo feeding my courage, and fired once more. The bullet carved a perfect hole above his right eye. His head snapped back and he stumbled. This time, his foot hit air.

And then he was gone.

32

I BLINKED SEVERAL TIMES, STILL holding the gun in the same position as when I fired, unable to process what had just happened. As my brain finally caught up, I crossed to the spot where Salazar stood just moments before and peered over the edge.

He'd landed face-up, one hundred feet below me, his arms and legs turned outward like a broken action figure, his neck bent at an awkward angle. Dazed, I put one hand out and sank to the ground, afraid my knees would liquefy.

Disbelief decided to have a party with the possibility that I might have been hallucinating and I slid near the edge to have another look.

Still there.

For the second time I sat in a daze, gripping his gun, and stared at nothing. Sporadic gunfire in the plaza below somehow worked its way into my conscious mind and I snapped back to reality. I scrambled to my feet, grabbed the Sig lying on the ground and ran to the stairs at the back of the pyramid.

Still steep.

I took a deep breath and trained my gaze on the step below me rather than taking in the entire stairway, and made it to the bottom of the pyramid without falling. I had to see for myself that the bastard was dead. Not verifying if someone lived or died could come back to bite you.

I wouldn't make the same mistake twice.

He'd gone off the far side of the pyramid so none of the gunmen in the plaza would have seen him fall, which meant they also wouldn't notice me checking. I rounded the corner and walked over to the body.

He looked dead, all right. I reached down and felt his carotid.

No pulse. Yep, dead.

I straightened. The gunfire erupting in the plaza behind me faded into the background. I knew in an abstract way that I should be concerned, maybe find a place to hide, but someone had hit the pause button and time decided to stand still.

How could Roberto Salazar be dead? He'd been a part of my life for so long, I'd never allowed myself to entertain the thought that he might actually be gone someday. When you plan your life around someone else, whether it's because you live with them or because they want to kill you, the result is the same when they no longer exist: *you have to adjust.*

So many lives had been lost because of him. And, because of the stupid mistake I'd made all those years ago. It surprised me that I didn't feel some kind of emotion at his demise: joy, pain, closure, something. In death he resembled any other man—not the coldblooded monster I'd been running from for over ten years.

Confused by my reaction, I turned away. An unfamiliar aspect of myself had taken the reins and gunned him down. I didn't know if I wanted to see her again.

Although, it was comforting to know she was there.

At a loss, I left the body where it lay and made my way to the other side of the pyramid, unsure what to do. Disorientation tended to be an unhelpful state of mind when surrounded by cartel members shooting the hell out of each other. A twig snapped and I looked up, startled to see Quinn walk toward me.

"What happened? Lalo said you climbed the pyramid."

"Salazar's dead," I replied, my voice matter-of-fact.

Quinn glanced over my shoulder, then back to me. "Where?"

I nodded in the body's direction. "On the other side."

"Stay here," he said and disappeared into the shadows.

Snap out of it, Kate. You're not free from danger yet. My mind skated to the unfamiliar Kate who shot and killed Salazar with no emotion, searching my memory for an explanation.

I didn't have one.

A few minutes later Quinn came back, his hand to his ear.

"Affirmative. He's dead. Out." He lowered his hand and glanced at me. "Those bullets yours?"

"Except the one in his arm."

Quinn studied me for a moment before releasing the magazine from his gun and replacing it with another from the side pocket of his fatigues.

"Now what?" I asked, doing the same.

"Diaz and Salazar may both be dead, but these guys will continue to fight until there's nobody left. Especially since it looks like Diaz's son made it out alive."

"Are you going to stick around and help things along?"

He nodded. "We'll continue to pick them off."

I must have looked like shit, because he squinted at me and asked, "Are you all right?"

"Never better." I gave him a quick smile. A slight tremor in my hands signaled the adrenaline was about to wear off.

He didn't look convinced, but evidently decided to let it go. "Good job tonight, Kate," he said, and cleared his throat. "The thing with One Shot, I mean."

"Thanks." Losing a friend, even if they weren't who you thought they were, is difficult. For a man like Quinn who rarely made them, I supposed it would be even harder.

He pointed toward a barely discernible trail in the undergrowth to our left. "I'll lead. Have your gun handy. Wait for a count of five, then follow me."

With a quick scan of our surroundings, Quinn moved out of the shadows and into the open, heading for the trail.

"One, two, three—" Four died in my throat when I noticed movement to Quinn's right. A man with a gun emerged from the shadows. I'd barely raised the Sig to take aim before Quinn spun around and dropped him with his pistol.

I made sure he hadn't brought company before I ran to join Quinn. He crouched next to the body and turned it over to get to the gunman's weapon. My hands shook as I lowered my pistol and looked down, relieved when I realized I didn't know the deceased.

Quinn and I turned at a faint squelch of radio static coming from further down the trail. He tapped his ear transmitter.

"Lalo. What's going on?" he asked, his voice terse. His expression grew dark as he slid the dead man's gun into his belly band. After a couple of seconds he glanced at me. "We need to leave, now."

We took off at a run opposite the trail, reaching the shadowed safety of the observatory as an army of men burst through the jungle, weapons drawn, headed for the plaza. They hadn't seen us.

"Morales' second wave," Quinn muttered, his jaw clenched. "Come with me."

We slipped through the shadows, past the SUVs and into the jungle. I froze as another person materialized to our left, but Quinn shook his head and I lowered my gun.

"He's one of ours," he said.

The other man drew near and I realized it was Hector. Quinn motioned for him to come closer.

"Hector, I need you to take Kate back to camp. According to Lalo, there's a clear route from here to the highway if you stay away from the main drive. Morales blocked the road leading out, so you'll need to cut through jungle. Go to the first rendezvous point."

"Roger that," Hector answered.

Quinn tapped his ear mike. "Lalo? We need to regroup and close the net. Go to Plan F."

Hector moved into the shadows. I turned to follow, glancing behind me.

Quinn had already disappeared.

Late the following morning, I headed for Quinn's tent. Pascal had been monitoring the firefight from camp on the radio and told me everyone had made it back several hours before. My relief at the news of Quinn's and the other men's safety matched the relief I felt at Salazar's death.

The flap was open and Quinn and the two shepherds were inside. I hesitated at the door, waiting for an invitation. He looked up from what he was doing and motioned for me to enter.

"Have a seat."

"Thanks." I sat across from him. Aries and Artemis padded over to me for pets. "Pascal says everyone got back all right."

Quinn nodded. "Yep. All accounted for. By early reports, we took out a big chunk of Morales' soldiers, but Morales himself is still alive and I'm sure will regroup. Diaz is dead, along with your buddy and the men they brought with them. I'm sure it won't be long before Diaz's son avenges his father. They always do, one way or another." He sighed. "We'll be ready for them."

"You've got a lot of work ahead. I don't envy you."

"Sounds like you've made up your mind," Quinn said, studying me.

I lowered my gaze as I stroked each dog behind the ears. "I haven't. Not yet. I need time to think away from here, away from your men. From you," I added, keeping my eyes on Aries.

"I understand."

I looked up and caught a glimpse of raw emotion deep in his eyes before the mask returned. I gave the dogs one last pet each and stood to leave.

"Thank you, Quinn. For everything."

"Keep in touch, Kate. Let us know what you decide."

"I will."

33

THE SULTRY OCEAN BREEZE HELD the promise of a tropical storm. Although not as warm on the coast as it had been inland, the intense heat still worked its way under my skin, flattening my energy with the unrelenting damp. I sipped my margarita in the shade of a palapa and played with the paper wrapper from my straw, coiling it around my finger, then uncoiling it, wondering what my next move should be.

I smiled as Pascal returned from the bar with a couple of fruit plates and another *cerveza* for himself. He placed everything on the table and took the seat across from me.

"Thanks," I said, spearing a slice of mango with my fork. I leaned back in my chair, feeling relaxed for the first time in longer than I cared to remember. I'd treated myself to a couple of days at a resort on the Riviera Maya in order to rest and give myself time to sort through my options, compliments of Quinn and his men. "I take it Quinn's not coming?"

Pascal took a long pull of his beer and shook his head. "He said to tell you whatever you decide to know he'll always have your back. He also said to tell you he kept his promise."

"Promise?"

"The rumor of your death."

I smiled. A little misinformation would go a long way toward my safety, especially with Angie and Vincent Anaya still at large. "Tell him thank you for me."

Pascal's calm gaze flickered. "I take it you aren't coming back."

I traced little circles on the table with my finger. "I can't. Much as I appreciate the offer, I have to figure out who I am now that Salazar's gone. For eleven years I planned my life around the possibility he might be lurking in the shadows, waiting for the right time to strike. Since he's no longer a consideration, I want—need—to adjust to my new reality. I don't want that reality to revolve around death. I've had enough."

"Are you going back to Arizona?"

"I don't know." My mood plummeted at the thought of never seeing Cole again. How could I go back to him or his girls after what happened? Not only did I endanger Cole and his kids' lives, but since I'd been in Mexico I'd done a complete one-hundred-and-eighty degree turn—transforming from victim to victor—even though the victory left me hollow and without direction. I was no longer the old Kate. I didn't have a clue what the new Kate wanted out of life and it wouldn't be fair to him if I went back and tried to start over, especially since he didn't remember me. I took another sip of my drink, trying to squelch the memories flooding back.

Pascal studied me with interest. "I think you have many miles to go before you will be able to rest. Have the spirits gone?"

"I thought you might tell me."

Pascal closed his eyes and took a deep breath, letting it out in a long sigh. I waited patiently as he did his thing and scarfed a piece of pineapple off my plate. I wondered if the curse or whatever bad juju had been following me had finally decided to pack up its things and torment someone else. I traced the outlines of the jaguar figurine, now hanging from a silver chain around my neck. I hoped so.

A couple of sips of margarita later Pascal opened his eyes.

"Well? Are they gone?"

He shrugged. "Does it matter?"

I leaned forward. "Hell yes, it matters. Are you trying to tell me they're not? They have to be. Salazar's dead." The old shaman in Sonora had said I would lose everything before the bad spirits were finished. Hadn't I done that? Hadn't I lost everything several times over?

"The spirits have indicated Salazar is not the only one associated with your misfortune. But," Pascal glanced at the jaguar necklace. "You have help. No longer are you on your own in this fight."

I leaned back in my chair. He must have been referring to Vincent Anaya. I assumed Anaya would lose interest in me once he'd been informed of Salazar's death. Another thought occurred to me and my heart dropped to my stomach.

"Do you mean there are more than those associated with Anaya?" I asked. Where the hell did I pick up *more* of these stupid things? It's not like I'd gone looking for a sale on bad spirits.

Pascal's gaze intensified. "The hunted becomes the hunter, gaining allies and enemies as she moves through life." His expression softened and he placed his hand over mine. "Don't feel bad, Kate. Not everyone is chosen to follow this path. If I were you, I'd be honored."

Now there was a depressing thought. "Honored because I'm a magnet for crap? Not likely, Pascal." I gulped down the rest of my margarita and signaled the waiter for another.

It was going to take a lot more than a couple of margaritas to make me feel better. At the very least it would take a disappearing act. Maybe I could outrun the suckers.

"Have you heard anything about Jesús?" I hoped he'd made it. When I left him at Morales' guard shack, it hadn't looked good.

Pascal's expression grew serious. "Not yet. Quinn is working with another informant from Morales' camp, so we should know something soon. It appears Morales' use of his own men to act as bait didn't go over well."

"I can imagine. You'll let me know, won't you?"

"Of course."

The beginnings of a plan began to form in the back of my mind. I was going to need money—and lots of it—if I intended to disappear with any real chance of success. Sonora wasn't too awful this time of year, at least not yet. Hot I could handle. It's the humidity that killed me.

Pascal smiled. "Your face tells me you know where you're going."

I sighed and held up my glass in a toast.

I'd have to work on that.

ABOUT THE AUTHOR

 **DV Berkom** is the USA Today bestselling author of two action-packed thriller series featuring strong female leads **Leine Basso** and **Kate Jones**. Her love of creating resilient, kick-ass women characters stems from a lifelong addiction to reading spy novels, mysteries, and thrillers, and longing to find the female equivalent within those pages.

After years of skipping off to locations that could have been movie sets, she wrote her first novel and was hooked. *Bad Spirits,* the first Kate Jones thriller, was published as an online serial in 2010 and was immediately popular with adventure fans. *Dead of Winter, Death Rites*, and *Touring for Death* soon followed before she began the far grittier Leine Basso crime thriller series in early 2012 with *Serial Date.*

D.V. currently lives in the Pacific Northwest with her husband, Mark, and several imaginary characters who like to tell her what to do. Her most recent books include *Shadow of the Jaguar, Dakota Burn, Absolution, Dark Return, The Last Deception, A Killing Truth,* **Cargo, The Body Market,** *Vigilante Dead, A One Way Ticket to Dead,* and *Yucatán Dead.*

For more information, please visit her website at www.dvberkom.com.

NOTE FROM THE AUTHOR:
Thank you for reading YUCATÁN DEAD. If you would like to find out more about Kate or my other novels, please see the links below:
Facebook: www.facebook.com/DvBerkomAuthor
Twitter: twitter.com/dvberkom
Website: www.dvberkom.com
Pinterest: pinterest.com/dvberkom/
***Sign up for my free newsletter and be the first to find out about new releases: **http://bit.ly/DVB_RL**

Other books by D.V. Berkom
Kate Jones Thriller Series:
Kate Jones Thriller Series Vol. 1
(Bad Spirits, Dead of Winter, Death Rites, Touring for Death.)
Cruising for Death
A One Way Ticket to Dead
Vigilante Dead

Leine Basso Crime Thriller Series
A Killing Truth
Serial Date
Bad Traffick
The Body Market
Cargo
The Last Deception
Dark Return
Absolution
Dakota Burn
Shadow of the Jaguar

Keep reading for an excerpt from the next book in the explosive Kate Jones Thriller series, **A One Way Ticket to Dead:**

A ONE WAY TICKET

TO DEAD

A POWERFUL ENEMY. A FIGHT FOR SURVIVAL.
A SHOCKING BETRAYAL.

DV BERKOM

1

I NEVER DREAMED I'd come back.

I shouldn't have.

Even though I told myself things were safer compared to when I'd passed through all those years ago, deep down I knew I was only kidding myself.

The deepening shadows brought scant relief from the blistering heat, although the lower the sun dipped on the horizon the more bearable it became. The sun set early in this part of the world. I took a deep drink from my water bottle and wiped the sweat from my face with the back of my hand.

And waited.

I'd changed my hair for the umpteenth time and wore brown-tinted contacts so I'd blend, but there's only so much a girl can do to change her appearance short of surgery. Thanks to Quinn and his lies, the men who had tried to kill me thought I was dead. For now. The ruse wouldn't last long, not if someone from the old days got curious about the new American woman in town.

No sense lingering longer than I had to. Find the stash if it was still there, then get the hell out of Mexico.

The tiny house on the even smaller lot looked like the owner had lost interest and decided to let nature take its course. Dirt-green vines strangled the walls as if they were trying to squeeze the last drop of moisture from the filthy stucco. The cracked and faded flower pots flanking the walkway grew dirt in profusion, their long-dead occupants a distant memory. Two lime trees in the side yard still shaded my target. The ground looked like it hadn't been disturbed in all the time I'd been gone.

If my luck held.

I'd spent the day and evening before casing the place, watching for signs of life. The house appeared abandoned. How much longer could I stay without arousing suspicion? More time than absolutely necessary in Los Otros made me nervous, and I itched to get the deed done.

My stomach growled as I walked back to the rental. With a loan from Luis, my contact in the Drug Enforcement Administration, I'd chosen an unassuming Nissan Versa with plenty of dings and scratches. I told him I needed to find someone before going back to the States now that Roberto Salazar was dead. At first Luis had argued, asking why I'd even consider staying in Mexico, but finally relented when I told him I owed my life to this person. Nothing he said would change my mind.

Memories of the old man who'd saved me from being gunned down in the street eleven years before flooded my mind. *Oggie.* Vincent Anaya's right-hand guy, Frank Lanzarotti, put a bullet in him as we left Oggie's house. I'd never forgiven him and felt grim satisfaction when

Frank had been shot. This final trip through cartel-country wasn't only about the money.

I got in the car and turned on the air while I ate the now-cold tamale I'd bought earlier. I could have gone back into town and gotten something else, but wanted to keep my visibility to a minimum. Old friends would not be a welcome diversion and I'd already risked discovery by staying the previous evening at a nearby hotel.

Hours later, after I'd moved the car twice and taken a fitful nap, I parked in the dirt-track alley behind the house and cut the lights. From behind, the abandoned house took on a miserable, thoroughly depressive mien. I could almost make out the dark windows and back door, all three of which appeared as though they hadn't been seen to in years. The backyard where Lana served me dinner so many lives ago was grown over with tenacious vegetation, the kind that could survive drought-ridden, remorseless summers.

What had finally prompted Lana to leave? I tried to imagine her happy, dragging her sadness and the fallout from the choices she'd made to wherever the wave of her life deposited her. All that came to mind were bottles of cheap tequila on a beat-up nightstand and dark, lonely sojourns with men who didn't care.

Bad choices put me in this backyard of a tiny, run-down two-bedroom *casa* at the end of an unpaved street in a one-horse Mexican town. I hoped this wasn't another of those.

Bad choices, I mean.

I popped the trunk and walked around to grab the pickaxe and shovel I'd purchased the day before, along with a large backpack. My idea was to work as quickly as possible until I'd unearthed the stash of gallon-sized plastic bags, backfill the hole and leave. I glanced through the rear window at the glowing clock on the dash: a quarter past three. The post office wouldn't be open for hours. I'd have a long wait.

I walked along the back of the house to the side yard, picking my way past rampant prickly pear and creosote and paused in the shadows to listen. The wind slid past me, circling my bare legs, churning the dirt at my feet into a dust devil that swirled and crested, and then disintegrated into the night. The breathy *hoo* of an owl nearby assured me I wouldn't work alone.

The three other homes on the street remained dark, signifying no one on the block suffered from insomnia, at least not tonight. The houses were far enough apart and on the opposite side of the unlit street from where I'd be working so it was reasonable to assume my efforts would go unnoticed. One of the three boasted a noisy swamp cooler that clanked in protest at the stifling night air, helping to further disguise my activities.

I proceeded to the lime trees and leaned the shovel against the house. The new pickaxe broke through the caliche easier than I remembered and soon the earth resembled a miniature plowed field. Afraid I'd damage the plastic bags or wake up light-sleeping neighbors I reined in my enthusiasm a few inches deep and switched to the spade.

Though not as noisy, the shovel took much longer to dig the remaining depth of the hole. About an hour later, when I still hadn't hit what I was looking for, worry crept in like a feral cat scrounging for food. *What if it's not here? What if Lana somehow found it, dug it up, and is now living large somewhere in South America?*

Well, then I'd have to figure out something else. If it was gone, I'd be shit out of luck. I straightened and took a deep breath, collecting my thoughts. Panicked and wired from dodging death that night so long ago, I thought I'd be back to retrieve the stash long before now. A faulty memory could be the reason I hadn't found it yet.

Or Lana was dancing the tango in Argentina.

Discarding the tango possibility, I stepped past the freshly dug hole to survey the yard. Closing my eyes, I thought back to that night, the memories resurrecting long-buried emotions. So many years of running, of looking over my shoulder, never being able to live a normal life.

So many friends lost.

Fallout from a bad choice made long ago. Payback, I supposed, for being stupid and young and attracted to shiny things. My fingers curled around the onyx jaguar figurine I wore around my neck. Now that Salazar was dead, I hoped my life could get more or less back to normal.

Then again, what the hell was normal?

I opened my eyes and took in the lime trees, the house, the surrounding vegetation. The yard had looked different back then. Well-tended. Then it hit me.

Unchecked catclaw choked the tree trunks, creating an optical illusion. I'd misjudged the distance of the stash from the base of the tree and had dug too far out. Once again working the pickaxe, I hacked away with new purpose at the base of the overgrown shrub until I cleared a space where I gauged the target should be.

Rinse, repeat. Switch to the shovel.

Focused on digging, I didn't realize I had company until it was too late.

"Hey," a voice demanded in slurred Spanish. "What're you doing?" The rank smell of cheap tequila accompanied the words. Slowly, I turned.

His features semi-distinct in the darkness, the man swayed on his feet, his thick torso and muscled arms reminiscent of a man who worked long hours lifting heavy things. I gave him a half-smile and tightened my grip on the shovel.

"My friend Lana asked me to stop by her house and pick something up for her. I noticed the vines were choking the tree." I glanced over my shoulder at the offending catclaw. "She'd be very upset if one of her trees died, so I thought I'd clear some of it away before I left." Not a great story, but the man was obviously drunk, so I didn't think I'd have to be too convincing.

With a puzzled expression, he swiveled unsteadily on his feet, glancing first down one side of the street, and then back the other way before returning his bleary gaze to me and the shovel. His expression morphed from perplexed to concerned, transitioning to a leer.

"You're a liar," he slurred as he lurched toward me. "No one lives here." He took another step closer. "You do somethin' nice for me, an' this'll jus' be our lil' secret, yes?" he stage-whispered, reaching for his fly. I hoisted the shovel over my head. I couldn't afford to wake the neighbors.

"One more step and you're going to have one hell of a headache come morning," I said, my voice low.

"Huh?" He gaped at the shovel in my hands, incomprehension clouding his face. Frowning, he wiped his hands down the front of his shirt, his confusion obvious. He closed his eyes for a moment but lost his balance and stumbled to one side, barely catching himself before taking a header onto the street.

"*Aye carumba*," he muttered, shaking his head. Obviously unhappy with the way things were turning out, he waved me away, mumbling incoherently to himself as he zigzagged a path down the street.

I lowered the shovel with a sigh. I'd have to work faster, in case he came to his senses and raised an alarm.

Forty-five minutes later the muted clang of metal against dirt changed to a dull thud. I cut in around the spot with the edge of the shovel and then scooped out the rest by hand, revealing a dirt-encrusted bundle. My heart beat faster as I slid the tip of the shovel underneath the plastic bag and pushed down on the handle, leveraging the first package out of its resting place.

Eight gallon-sized bags later, I stopped to take a breath. I leaned the shovel against the tree and knelt down. The outer bags had become stiff from the dry and the dirt and the heat, but remained intact. I grabbed one and opened it, removing the inner bag, which was surprisingly flexible. I flashed on how long it would take for plastic to degrade when it wasn't subjected to light, like in a landfill. Our civilization would be long gone before that ever happened. For now, I had immense gratitude for the durability of plastic.

I slid open the plastic zipper holding the bag closed and reached inside for a stack of bills. Money in hand, I flipped through the hundreds with my fingers, fanning my face.

Still there. Still intact.

Yes.

Once all eight bags were safely inside the backpack, I zipped it closed and stood, kicking some of the dirt back into the hole to make it look less obvious. Since the house had evidently been abandoned and my visitor had been quite drunk, I doubted anyone would take notice, at least long enough for me to disappear. I picked up my tools and the hefty pack and returned to the car, my heart light. With Salazar dead, even if the home had been on a cartel watch list, it wouldn't be now. They were tenacious, yes, but that would be too obsessive, even for cartel thugs. Besides, they thought I was dead.

I threw everything in the trunk and climbed into the driver's seat. One more errand and I'd be long gone.

Goodbye, Mexico. Hello, freedom.

END EXCERPT